D1760580

KEEP YOU NEAR

Robin Roughley

LV 5035852 9

Liverpool Libraries

Copyright © 2017 Robin Roughley

The right of Robin Roughley to be identified as the Author of the Work has been asserted by him in accordance Copyright, Designs and Patents Act 1988.

First published in 2017 by Bloodhound Books

Apart from any use permitted under UK copyright law, this publication may only be reproduced, stored, or transmitted, in any form, or by any means, with prior permission in writing of the publisher or, in the case of reprographic production, in accordance with the terms of licences issued by the Copyright Licensing Agency.

All characters in this publication are fictitious and any resemblance to real persons, living or dead, is purely coincidental.

www.bloodhoundbooks.com

PROLOGUE

The boy was tall for his age, though not quite tall enough. He sat naked and shivering on the bone-hard wooden bench, the soles of his scarred feet hovered two inches from the pitted oak floorboards. The back of his whipped legs throbbed with pain as the heavy stack of leather-bound books, balanced across his thighs, bore down. Despite the mounting pain, he didn't move – the terror wouldn't allow it. He had no idea how long he had sat, unmoving, watching as the shadows lengthened and the timeworn, grimy room darkened. Glancing left, he peered into the gloom; he could just make out the lumpy shapes of old furniture covered by grey dustsheets. An ancient hat stand, home to a multitude of mummified flies trapped in the fragile covering of cobwebs, stood sentinel in the corner. High above, the occasional gentle coo of pigeons, settling on old wooden beams, drifted out into the trembling air.

He felt a trickle of blood seep down the back of his right leg, feverishly hot against his goose-bumped flesh. Despite eyes screwed shut, the tears still slid free and he gritted his teeth, hating this manifestation of fear.

Tentatively, he placed his hands flat on the bench, palms sweating, as he attempted to ease his weight from the plank of wood but his quivering muscles refused to bear the load. The books started to slide and he grabbed them before they slipped to the floor, his heart hammering, the pain making him gasp.

Beyond the high, fly-blown window, the last of the light flared and died; the boy lowered his head in despair as the shadows closed in around him.

Time stretched out, he tried to block out the agony, tried to think of something to break the cycle but all he could visualise was the girl, the smile playing around her lips. Staring at him with sly amusement in her eyes as she nudged the bone china plate from the kitchen table, slowly, inch by hypnotic inch.

The boy had watched – eyes wide in terror – as it fell to the flagged floor and shattered; before he could move she had been running for the door, scream rising, curly hair bouncing, she dashed out into the garden in floods of fake tears.

He had been on his hands and knees desperately trying to gather up the shards when the shadowed figure had stalked past the kitchen window and into the room.

Now he sat and shivered as the pain increased, a splodge of pigeon shit landed on his right foot and he watched it dribble to the tip of his big toe before dripping to the floor. A milky globule amongst the patterning of fresh blood – his blood.

When he heard heavy footfalls on the stairs, the boy snapped his head up, watching the shadow move back and forth, caught by the sliver of light at the foot of the door.

As the key rattled in the lock, he fought back the urge to scream, knowing it would be a hopeless reflex action, one guaranteed to bring further punishment, feeding his tormentor's malevolent spirit.

Inexorably, the door creaked open and light flooded into the room, forcing the boy to screw his eyes closed against the onslaught.

Once closed, the dread of opening them again ate away at his quivering defences.

Footsteps, slow and measured, thudded over floorboards twisted with age.

The boy tried to block out the noise but his senses seemed attuned to every sound and smell, the stale air that drifted into the room, the birds above trilling in alarm and – finally – the hot, sour breath on his sweating face.

Every second that slipped into infinity warped his young mind. He felt trapped in a terrible limbo, both frightened and yet desperate to see what was in front of him.

Cracking open one eye, he hitched in a sharp breath when he saw the familiar figure looming over him.

'*Have you seen the error of your ways?*' The voice was low and deep, little more than a rumble that seemed to set off a vibration of terror in the still air.

The boy tried desperately to formulate an answer but the terror had taken his voice, leaving him mute with fear.

'*Answer me, boy!*'

'*I...*' he managed to croak.

'*Whippersnapper!*' the man roared.

Half a second later, the side of his face exploded in pain as the shadow lashed out, the back of his huge, calloused hand smashed into his cheek; the boy clattered from the blood-stained bench, the books fell with a heavy thump sending up small eddies of dust.

Pain roared through mind and body, countless hours sitting unmoving with the weight of the books bearing down had left his muscles locked tight.

When he tried to draw his legs up, the agony erupted until he could bear it no longer. He lay, naked and shuddering, the scream trapped behind gritted teeth, the side of his head flaring red-hot, his ears ringing with pain.

Only when the door slammed shut and the darkness swallowed him did the boy give in to the despair.

Just before he slipped into the abyss, he was convinced he heard the sound of laughter, the voice high-pitched and full of merriment.

1

Eight-year-old Jenny Bell winced as the dying sun lanced through the trees on the right, sending out bright spears of laser light. Narrowing her eyes, the light coalesced into miniscule supernovas as she trudged along the deserted street, goody bag swinging from her right hand, a wedge of birthday cake clasped in her left.

Jenny stopped for a moment and eyed the cake with pink icing; her tummy felt full and yet she still took a bite before setting off again. She'd been at her best friend's house all afternoon, playing on the bouncy castle and dancing until she felt hot and bothered. Jenny had lost count of the amount of jelly and cake she had eaten at the party and now she felt so sleepy that all she wanted to do was get home and flop down on her comfy bed.

Her best friend, Kimberly, had loved the present that Jenny had bought with her own pocket money, a fizzy bath bomb from a shop in town and a pair of pretty earrings.

Jenny wiped the sweat from her brow with a hand sticky from the icing and jam. The cake clogged her mouth, she couldn't swallow, so, dropping the remains of the cake into the bag, she lifted out a small bottle, grimacing as she took a glug of the warm bubblegum-flavoured drink.

Burping lightly, she looked around, blushing in embarrassment.

Her dad had dropped her off at Kimberley's house before driving off to work. He had told her to be home by six p.m. and Jenny had promised that she would, but now she was starting to realise that she must have stayed longer at the party than she thought. Kimberley's mum had offered to take her home but Jenny had said she was fine, after all it was only a short walk home.

The sun gave a final flash of light and then vanished completely.

Suddenly, the air was tinged a strange, eerie, pink colour and Jenny felt the first fluttering of unease tremble through her body.

The street had that typical late-Sunday feel, cars were parked on driveways, a tabby cat sat on a wall, watching her with alien green eyes, yet there was no sign of anyone on the street, no children kicking a ball about, no adults walking their dog after a heavy Sunday dinner.

She set off walking again, suddenly keen to be home, the hem of her party dress flicking back and forth as her sparkly dolly shoes hurried her along the street.

The sweat she had wiped from her face was back, her hair felt straggly and damp and she started to pant even before breaking into an awkward jog. She thought of her brother, he was two years older than her and Jenny didn't like him one bit. He was always being mean and he loved to call her nasty names at every opportunity. Part of her mind cringed at the thought of arriving home with a bag full of cake and sweets, her face glowing red, her body tacky with sweat. She just knew that he would smirk and call her fatty, and she wasn't in the mood for nasty name calling.

A trickle of sweat seeped into her right eye and she winced at the sting, stopping to dab at her eye with the sleeve of her blue dress, her young face screwed up in discomfort. Jenny blinked as all the good memories of the day fell away, she felt sick, the jelly and cake sat heavy in her stomach. She started to run again, convinced she could feel all the food swilling around in her tummy. In the distance, she could see traffic on the main road flowing back and forth, one or two of the cars had their lights on and Jenny felt the fear grow as the light started to fade at an alarming rate.

When her phone rang, she staggered to a stop, her right hand rummaging in the pocket of her dress, a pocket crammed with toffee wrappers and bits of scrunched up tissue.

Pulling out the phone, she panicked when she saw her dad's name flash on the small screen. She knew he would be ringing to make sure she had arrived home safely, and Jenny also knew that he wouldn't be happy to find she was still on the street.

She hopped from one foot to another in indecision, the fear of having her dad shouting down the phone made her bottom lip quiver, though she knew she had no choice.

Taking a deep breath, she tapped at the screen, the apology forming on her lips when a hand clamped across her mouth and she felt herself lifted from the ground, her eyes suddenly wide with terror as fingers gripped her face, the scream locked in her throat.

The goodie bag and phone fell from her hand and hit the floor, seconds later Jenny Bell had vanished as if she had never even existed. In the distance, the cat watched the drama unfold, fur rising it spat in distress before jumping from the wall and dashing into the trees, as if it knew that something monstrous was stalking the deserted street.

2

Two weeks later

DS Marnie Hammond kept one eye on the television attached to the wall while she waited in the queue at the coffee shop. The screen showed an image of DCI David Reese answering questions about the missing Jenny Bell to the baying media throng outside Kirk head police station. Marnie sighed as she stepped to the counter and ordered her drink before turning back to the screen. Reese's face was etched with fatigue, his eyes held a look of despair, the same despair that Marnie recognised every time she looked in the mirror. Collecting her drink, she pocketed the change and weaved her way through the busy coffee shop, heading out into the wind and rain of a typical northern day. Despite the weather, the pavement was heaving with shoppers; shoulders were bumped and people scowled as the rain increased. Glancing up at the leaden sky, Marnie took a sip from the cup before navigating her way to the kerb. A truck rumbled by, coughing fumes into the squally air, the big wheels rolling through the standing water in the gutter.

'*Matty, wait!*' the voice blasted out of the crowd of shoppers, high pitched and panic-stricken.

Marnie looked right and saw the little kid dash forwards, his face split with a wide grin, his eyes seemingly oblivious to the stream of traffic that swept by on the busy road.

One or two people glanced at the running boy, his laughter unravelling into the wet air; at the last second Marnie lunged right and grabbed the hood of his jacket.

The boy's arms shot into the air, the jacket tightening around his neck, his feet skidding to a stop on the edge of the kerb.

Marnie kept hold, boy in one hand coffee cup in the other as a young woman burst free of the shoppers.

'*Oh, thank God,*' she grabbed the boy and scooped him up into her arms, her face flushed and fear filled. 'What have I told you about holding Mummy's hand?' she demanded in a trembling voice.

The boy giggled as if it was no big deal.

The woman turned to Marnie. 'Thank you so much,' she gasped, her face flooded with relief.

'Looks as if you have your hands full,' Marnie replied, returning the smile.

Wiping a stray strand of hair from her eyes, the young mother nodded. 'Would you believe, I'm just on my way to buy him some reins?'

Marnie sniffed, catching the scent of warm coffee. 'Probably for the best,' she said, as the rain intensified.

The woman looked up, letting the rain fall onto her burning face. 'Thanks again,' she said turning, within seconds she had vanished into the never-ending stream of shoppers.

Marnie checked the road before crossing and beeping the alarm on her car. Sliding behind the wheel, she closed the door with a clunk, sat back and took a sip of coffee.

Closing her eyes for a moment, she pictured eight-year-old Jenny Bell – taken from a street on the other side of town after walking home from a friend's birthday party. The phone and goodie bag, with a slice of half-eaten cake and bottle of pop inside, had been the only things left behind, pinpointing the exact location she had been taken. Neighbours had been questioned; Jenny's smiling face had appeared on television screens and the front of national newspapers. Fliers had been posted around the town and social media was awash with people trying to help, and yet they were still none the wiser as to what had befallen the girl.

There had been fifteen children at the birthday party and all the parents had been scrutinised at length, their movements checked and verified. The sex offenders' register had been studied and so far, every scumbag had been questioned bar one. She thought of Christopher Hambling, thirty-six with a thin, weasel-like face, the kind of face that when you saw it on the front of a newspaper screamed the word 'paedophile'. Hambling had been released from HMP Liverpool five weeks earlier and shipped over to a high-rise council flat in the middle of Kirk head. Unfortunately, when the police had raided the place there had been no sign of Hambling. Marnie had stood on the balcony with David Reese looking out over the town. To her right, she had watched children playing in the schoolyard, to the left the local swimming baths, the huge plate glass windows offering an uninterrupted view of the pool.

'Who the hell thought it was a good idea to give a paedophile a grandstand view of a local infant school and the sodding baths?' Reese had snarled in disbelief.

Marnie had felt the anger shift inside as she watched the children below, their faint shouts and screams floating up into the air as they raced around the playground.

To make matters worse, it had been a full week before they had even known about Hambling, some computer error had kept him off radar and by the time they arrived at the grotty flat he was long gone. Marnie had studied the man's file and the more she had read, the more uneasy she had become. Hambling had served twelve months for approaching a six-year-old girl in Liverpool city centre. The child had been shopping with her mother, and when she had turned around it had been to find Hambling hurrying away with her daughter held in his arms.

The police had been called and Hambling had protested his innocence, saying that the girl had been wandering, lost and upset, so he had picked her up and started to look for the mother. The trouble was, Hambling had been in trouble with the police before, in fact his record showed he had spent more time in jail than out of it. Now, he was missing – along with Jenny Bell – and the clock was ticking.

Marnie opened her eyes, the view through the windscreen made nebulous by the rain; she watched huddled figures walking along the pavement, those with umbrellas looking smug as they strode unscathed through the downpour.

Flicking on the wipers, she placed the cup in the holder, fastened her seatbelt and pulled away from the kerb, turning left onto Market Street. The street was lined with an assortment of outlets, the ubiquitous charity shops and kebab houses were all present and correct, one or two had large red 'sale' signs plastered over the windows as they tried to tempt the customer to part with their cash.

Pulling up at the pedestrian crossing, she watched an elderly couple cross the road, the man hurrying his wife along as the lights blinked back to green. Marnie waited until they were safely on the other side, then the couple turned as one, the little old lady waved, her wrinkled face beaming.

Marnie raised a friendly hand and pulled away from the lights.

Sudden movement, a figure sprinted past the front of the car, scruffy jeans and black sweatshirt, the hood pulled over his head, muddy, off-white trainers splashing through puddles.

'*Moron!*' she gasped, slamming on the brakes.

The runner swerved around her car and dashed across the road, feet flying he sprinted along the pavement, weaving around the shoppers like a slalom skier on a downhill run.

'*Stop him!*'

Marnie whipped her head left, the man in front of the newsagents had his right hand clasped to the side of his bloodied head, his left jabbing out across the street at the fleeing figure. Shoppers paused to look at the injured man who continued to gesticulate wildly, one or two gave him a wide berth as if they suspected some sort of madness in the air, something contagious.

Flicking on the siren, she planted her foot on the gas and the car shot forward, the runner threw a quick glance over his shoulder. When he saw the black car – lights flashing – closing him down, he sprinted blindly across the busy junction; horns blared, a taxi lurched to a stop, missing him by inches as he bolted to the other side.

Marnie slowly weaved through the traffic, then set off again in time to see the figure thrust his way through a block of bushes on the right… and vanish.

Pulling to the kerb, she leapt out and gave chase; pushing through the bushes, she emerged into a field partly submerged beneath large pools of standing water. Without hesitation, she sprinted forward, arms and legs pumping, her eyes – narrowed against the rain – remained locked on the target.

The figure cut left towards the dark shadow of the woods, and Marnie redoubled her efforts. Suddenly, he slipped and clattered to the ground, sliding forward like a footballer celebrating a winning goal, a sheet of water spraying up as he skidded across the wet surface.

By the time he'd regained his feet, she had closed the gap to ten yards.

He threw a panicked look over his shoulder, his eyes springing wide as she ran full tilt towards him. She almost paused in surprise, her eyes widening in recognition. He turned and set off again, one hand clasped to his ribs. His clothes saturated, dragging him down as he tried to kick on a pace.

Reaching the covering of trees, he disappeared into the shadows, but Marnie was right behind, her ears were filled with the crack and snap of branches, as she closed the gap. When he stumbled, she threw herself forwards her arms encircled his waist, they hit the ground hard and the runner yelped in pain. Marnie kept him pinned under her knees as she eased back and clicked on the handcuffs. Rolling him onto his back, she looked down, water dripped from the end of her dangling ponytail.

'Jesus, Luke, what have you been up to now?'

The teenager blinked and winced up at her. 'Sergeant Hammond?' he whispered in recognition, the rain falling onto his pale, upturned face.

Marnie sat back on her haunches, wiping the sweat from her brow. 'You promised me you'd stop all this nonsense.'

She could see the guilt in his eyes as he cringed into the sodden ground.

'The last time we spoke you were getting ready to nick another car, I only let you off because you begged me for another chance.'

'I'm sorry,' he mumbled.

'So, what is it this time, cigarettes, booze?'

Luke turned his head away, as if he couldn't bear to see the disappointment on her face.

Marnie sighed heavily and looked up at the high, bleak branches clattering in the wind, the clouds above scuttling across the filthy sky.

The trees seemed to loom in around her, the rain increased, her mind stuttered, and she felt the familiar sense of unease crawl over her skin.

Suddenly, the air was filled with a terrifying scream and she shook her head in confusion.

Luke Croft screamed again, and Marnie snapped her head down, the sound of terror wrenching her back to the here and now. The teenager had his head tilted to the right, eyes wide, his face smeared with horror.

Marnie followed his gaze, when she saw the small, skeletal arm, partially covered by a mash of fallen leaves, she felt her stomach lurch. Her eyes took in the stark, white bones, the fingers – stripped of skin and flesh – were curled as if grasping at the sodden earth.

Luke paused to draw breath, then he was screaming again, his body thrashing, trying to put some distance between himself and the grisly remains.

Leaping to her feet, Marnie snatched the collar of his hoodie and heaved him away over the ground, his feet scrabbling for traction, leaving black scars in the drenched earth.

'*Luke, calm down!*' she ordered.

The boy's terrified eyes swivelled towards her, the horror written large on his anguished face. '*It's a fucking arm!*' he screeched, his voice loud and piercing in the blustery, wet air.

Marnie placed a finger to her lips, and Luke closed his mouth with a snap.

With a nod, she turned away; closing her eyes for a moment she took a quick gulp of wet air before moving forward.

White bone shone against dark earth; falling to her knees Marnie swallowed the fear, her hands hovered over the bones, her mind shivered. When she saw the small, plastic, daisy ring lodged onto the little finger, she felt a sudden tidal wave of relief and then the door in her mind swung slowly open.

Beyond the door was a blackness so dense it seemed to suck any light from her mind. Overhead, the clouds continued to be pushed by the cold, north wind.

3

DCI David Reese folded his arms and waited for the room to settle, rain lashed at the window of the incident room, the young trees beyond swayed back and forth in the wind. It had been almost twenty-four hours since the remains had been found, and the faces that stared back at him were despondent.

Walking around his desk, Reese sat down and popped the button on his dark-grey jacket before snatching his tie loose.

Throats were cleared, one or two people coughed as the twenty-strong team waited for him to continue.

'OK listen up, here's what we have so far; according to pathology, the severed arm belonged to a female aged between five and nine – a child,' he looked up, making sure that the news hit home. 'They also state that there was no tissue left on the remains.'

Over by the door Marnie sighed, she knew that without tissue on the bones then gathering DNA could prove problematic, narrowing their scope to just the mother of the child.

When Detective Constable Paul Clark raised a hand, Reese nodded. 'Yes, Paul?'

'Do we have any idea how long the remains had been there for?'

Reese flicked open the thin, blue file on his desk. 'Well, it's early days and the experts are still trying to pinpoint the exact time frame, but considering the condition of the limb, we could be talking years. Now, the ring she was wearing was mass produced in China – the kind of thing you would find on a market stall or given away in a lucky bag,' he looked up, scanning the faces.

Clark ran a finger along the collar of his shirt, nodding in understanding.

Reese flipped the file closed again. 'We've checked the database and there are three, long-term missing children in the county. Piper Donald, India Foster and Suzie Walls, all three were aged between seven and nine when they disappeared so they roughly fall into the right age bracket. Of course, we'll be rolling this out nationwide but that takes time, so for now we concentrate our efforts locally, we go back over the case files on the three missing girls and we check thoroughly.'

'How are we defining long-term?' DI Oaks asked, her narrow face set with its usual scowl, framed by greying hair cut into a short bob tucked neatly behind her ears.

'Difficult to say, Pam,' Reese replied. 'All three girls lived within a twenty-mile radius of one another, Piper Donald has been missing for almost eleven years, Foster and Walls eight and ten years respectively. Now, as soon as we're finished here I'll be heading over to the Donald's home to speak to the parents.'

'Do we know if she was wearing a ring when she vanished?' Oaks asked.

Reese shook his head in the negative. 'There was nothing in the file to suggest she was but that will be one of the things I'll be asking the parents.'

'The killer could have been the one who placed the ring on the dead girl's finger,' Marnie offered.

The DCI sighed as he scrubbed a hand across his five o'clock shadow. 'Anything's possible but as I said, we should know more once the bone guys sort out the time frame.'

Oaks leaned forward in her seat and rested her elbows on her knees. 'So, it could still be one of the missing three and the limb was dumped in the woods?'

'That's what we need to find out, obviously, we have DNA samples from the missing children and we should know shortly if any are a match for the remains.'

'But what about the rest of the body?' PC Bev Harvey asked, this week her long, dark hair was scraped back into a high ponytail, shining in the overhead strip light, her blue eyes watchful.

Reese looked towards Marnie. 'DS Hammond, what's the latest on the search?'

Heads turned in her direction but she kept her eyes firmly fixed on Reese.

'The woods are still being searched and the cadaver dogs have been called in,' she explained. 'Soil samples have been taken from the immediate area and sent off for analysis, if anything is found then we should know in the next few hours.'

Standing up, Reese planted his hands on the desk. 'Good. We also have to consider the possibility that it was someone passing through Kirk head. After all, the woods run close to the main road, so it wouldn't have taken long to park the car, walk into the trees, and dispose of the body part.'

A collective sigh filled the room, and Marnie moved her weight from one foot to the other imagining something monstrous spreading body parts over a wide area, like some horrific Santa dropping off grisly Christmas gifts.

Reese looked at DI Oaks, his tie dangling down, brushing the desk. 'Pam, I want you to get a team together, concentrate on India Foster and Suzie Walls, visit the parents, reassure them the cases are still open, and see if you can get anything new from them.'

'Will do,' Oaks replied in a no-nonsense voice.

'As for the rest of you, I want all files on the three missing girls pulling and checking. I know we're talking years' worth but I want to be up to speed ASAP, so no shortcuts, check and double-check, is that clear?'

A tired chorus of 'yes, sirs' filled the room.

Reese pursed his lips and sighed. 'I know we're stretched thin, and you guys are already running on empty but let's not forget Jenny Bell is still missing, so I want you to remain focused. I want the parents, who either arrived or dropped their child off at the party, to be questioned again; see if anyone slips up second time around.'

'What about Hambling?' Paul Clark asked.

At the mention of the name, Reese's face darkened with anger. 'The Merseyside force are checking all his old haunts and known associates, though to be honest, it appears Hambling was something of a loner. The fact is, if he did decide to head back to Liverpool then he would be an idiot but stranger things have happened, so for now we keep looking. The local news is doing an update tonight, his mug will be there for everyone to see so let's hope it jogs someone's memory.' Reese smiled though he looked anything but happy. 'We need to stay on top of this, and we need to be ready because sooner or later Hambling will come crawling out of the woodwork. And when he does I want the bastard caught, no ifs or buts – is that understood?'

Heads nodded in agreement, over near the water cooler Marnie felt the tension building in her head. Closing her eyes, she pictured the woods, the branches clattering together, Luke Croft cowering on the sodden ground, his hoodie and tracksuit bottoms saturated, his narrow face stark, lips quivering with cold and fear, then the horror of finding the bones, coupled with the immense sense of relief as she realised the remains didn't belong to...

'Right, let's go and have a word with the Donalds.'

Marnie's eyes sprang open; Reese was standing directly in front of her as the last of the stragglers left the room.

'You OK?' he asked.

Clearing her throat, she nodded. 'I'm fine.'

Reese held her gaze for a moment longer than necessary. 'Glad to hear it,' he said as he brushed past. Marnie hesitated before straightening her shoulders and following him down the long, drab corridor.

4

Calloused hands scrabbled through the jumble, dark eyes searching, probing. Lifting the bundle of yellowing letters from the trunk, the man squinted at the writing before tossing them over his shoulder with a grunt of annoyance.

Dragging a hand across his brow, he eased back on his haunches. Gossamer cobwebs smothered the ancient oak beams. Dust motes floated in the weak haze of the bulb that dangled from a length of perished flex. Teeth clamped in anger, he leaned forward and continued the search.

He knew they were in here somewhere, they had to be. The thought that he could have somehow misplaced the trinkets was too terrible to contemplate.

Gripping the lip of the trunk, his hands tightened with terrifying force. He remembered a time when he knew exactly where everything was. Every single thing in his life had been compartmentalised. Closing his eyes, he took a gulp of stale air and gathered his emotions, pushing them deep inside until he felt a flimsy semblance of calm descend.

Time fragmented the memory, like an unruly child running rampant through the mind, turning order into chaos, scattering the memories far and wide. He would lie in bed, staring into the darkness, trying to gather the memories back to him, arms raised, fingers grasping at the fetid air. Last night he had been sprawled on top of the mattress. The shadows in the room shifting, the noises in his mind building, the sly laughter morphing into pitiful cries for help, then the crash of the plate as it shattered on the flagged floor, followed by the hateful sniffles of the boy curled on the cold, wooden boards. The cacophony of sound growing in volume until he felt his mind solidify in a single block of terror-tinged confusion. That was the reason he was here in the attic. He needed to reconnect; needed to touch the objects to anchor himself to the past and bring the hidden memories forth. Looming over the trunk he lifted out more junk, a couple of heavy, leather-bound books were tossed to one side. Picking up the bible, he flicked it open and studied the ancient family tree, handwritten in perfect copperplate, then he sneered in disgust – hurling it into the shadows, the pages fluttering like a distressed bird taking to flight.

Sweat ran down his broad forehead, confusion scrabbling at his skull like a starving rat desperately trying to get at the soft grey meat beneath. With a snarl, he loomed over the trunk and carried on with the search, his movements becoming more frantic as desperation warped the fabric of his crumbling mind.

5

Reese pulled up outside a neat bungalow, a newish Volvo estate was parked on the drive behind a cream-coloured touring caravan. Yanking on the handbrake, he looked at the light shining from behind a thin pair of curtains.

'Right, let's get this sorted,' he said, climbing out into the wind and rain.

Marnie followed suit and they hurried up the drive, shoulders hunched against the elements; Marnie glanced at the starless night sky before pressing the bell, her face expressionless as the hall light pinged to life. Seconds later, the door opened to reveal a man dressed in sweatpants and a hooded top, he looked to be in his late forties, cheeks covered with stubble, eyes watchful, his short, brown hair thinning on top.

'Mr Donald?' Reese asked, stepping forward and holding out his warrant card.

The man glanced at it and took a hurried step back, his eyes suddenly sparking with nervous tension. 'What do you want?'

'I wonder if we could come in and have a word?' the DCI asked, slipping the wallet back into his pocket.

'It's about our Piper, isn't it?'

For a moment, Marnie was convinced the man was going to slam the door in their faces.

'I'm sorry but we just need to clarify one or two things,' Reese replied with empathy.

The man looked at them both, the fear in his eyes shifting to terror and then his shoulders slumped and he sighed, a sigh full of pain and bewilderment.

'I'm John Donald,' he stepped back and opened the door. 'Piper's father,' he explained, dragging a hand across his face.

Reese opened his mouth to speak but Donald spun on his heels and hurried down the short hallway.

Marnie looked at her boss, she could feel the tension building, then they both stepped nervously into the hallway.

By the time Marnie had closed the door, Donald had vanished into a room on the right.

Seconds later they walked into a small, tidy lounge, the television was on, some wildlife programme with a lion chasing a zebra across barren tundra. Donald was talking in hushed tones to a woman who sat on the sofa, a magazine in her hands; when she saw the two of them enter the room, Anne Donald leapt to her feet, her face racked with fear, the magazine dropping to the floor.

'You've found her, haven't you?' she whispered, her hands came together and then instantly sprang apart as if electrically charged.

Reese stepped forward, all too aware that there was no easy way to break the news.

'I'm afraid we've found some remains but at this stage it's impossible to tell if they belong to your daughter.'

Anne and John Donald clung to one another like terrified children faced with a monstrous truth.

'Where, I mean, how...?' John asked, his chest rising and falling as the colour drained from his face.

'We found the remains yesterday, and...'

'Yesterday?' Anne asked, as she continued to cling to her husband.

Reese felt a trickle of rainwater slide down his back. 'They were found in Carlton Woods, now, at the moment we...'

'What do you mean by "remains"?' Anne asked in despair.

John looked at his wife before turning to look at Reese, his eyes burning with the need to know the truth.

Marnie tried to imagine what they must be going through, though she didn't have to delve too deep into her mind to find the truth. She knew exactly how the Donalds were feeling. The door in her mind started to swing open and she slammed it shut before the nightmare memories took her.

'At the moment, the woods are being searched,' she said, moving to Reece's shoulder.

'Please, just tell us what you've found?' Anne pleaded, the tears sliding from her eyes.

Reese could feel the heat from the radiator pumping into the room, making the air stifling. 'We've found the skeletal remains of an arm and we believe it's that of a young female.'

Anne's legs buckled and she collapsed down on the sofa with a thump. Her husband remained standing, though he swayed slowly from side to side like a tree being uprooted in stormy weather.

"An arm"?' he whispered, in a voice quivering with emotion.

'I'm afraid so,' Reese replied with a sigh.

Marnie looked at a mantelpiece lined with images of Piper Donald, held in silver frames, they showed the child smiling, a wide, open smile full of innocence.

In one, she was on a beach set against a backdrop of curling waves and a vast blue sky. Piper had a small, red, plastic spade in her right hand, a melting ice cream in the other. Another showed her beaming for the camera, dressed in her infant school uniform, white shirt, red cardigan, emblazoned with the school badge, a yellow, smiley-faced sticker placed just beneath. The final one must have been taken at Christmas time, Piper was sporting a paper hat smothered in tinsel, an unwrapped present in her hands, the smile still in place only this time one of her front teeth was missing, giving her face a mischievous look.

'We realise this must be hard for you both, but we need to know if your daughter was wearing a ring when she disappeared?' Reese asked.

Anne had her head buried in her hands, when she looked up it was as if she had aged, brief seconds adding years of torment to her anguished face.

"A ring"?' she repeated.

Reese nodded.

Marnie waited with bated breath as husband and wife looked at one another, when John Donald turned to her she knew the truth.

'No, Piper wasn't wearing any kind of ring.'

'Are you absolutely sure, I mean, perhaps she had some in a toy box or you bought her…?'

'Piper had nothing like that, when she was a toddler we were always careful not to give her anything small enough to swallow,' Donald replied, swiping the tears from his eyes with the back of his hand.

Anne looked at the three of them in rapid succession, as if she couldn't quite grasp the flow of the conversation.

'The remains we found had a small, plastic, daisy ring on the little finger,' Marnie explained, sliding the zipper down on her jacket as the heat became intolerable.

John shook his head rapidly from side to side. 'I've already told you, Piper had no rings. She wasn't like that, she preferred to play with her brother's toys rather than dolls and trinkets.'

'Yes, yes, she did,' Anne was suddenly back on her feet. 'My Piper was a proper tomboy, she liked to kick the ball in the garden and she was always playing with our Tom's toy cars and soldiers.'

Marnie could see the sudden relief in Anne's eyes, the fear was still there though now it was tinged with a hint of hope.

'I bought her a couple of dolls for her fourth birthday but she never ever played with them, she showed no interest in pink ribbons and bows,' Anne explained, dragging up a tearful smile.

'On the day she went missing, you'd been to the park?' Reese asked.

Marnie felt her heart pick up speed, her palms slick with sweat.

John Donald sighed, sliding his arm across his wife's shoulder.

'One of Piper's school friends had a party in the park. Though to be honest, we almost didn't make it.'

'Why not?' Reese asked.

'Piper had an appointment at the dentist, when we got there the surgery was full, apparently one of the dentists had called in sick and they were behind. By the time we got out we were running late but Piper insisted she wanted to go and give her friend her birthday present,' his voice drifted to a halt and Marnie had no doubt that John Donald was back in the park, reliving the day that his daughter vanished.

Marnie looked at Anne and saw the same distant look in her eyes, the horror slowly seeping back to swamp the fleeting surge of hope.

'The park was busy that day,' John mumbled, his eyes locked on a world of inner torment. 'It was the first week of the school holiday and the sun was out. I mean, we never thought for a moment anything would happen.'

Anne sat back down, her tearstained face blank with shock.

'You know what it's like when you have a load of kids together, they all seem to blend into one?' John carried on, his bottom lip trembling. 'The place was full of families picnicking on the grass, and...'

'You don't remember anyone suspicious, anyone at all?' Reese asked.

John Donald blinked several times, like someone trying desperately to wake from a smothering nightmare.

'I've been through this a thousand times in my mind,' he paused, looking down at his wife. 'In fact, we both have and there was no one, no one who made you stop and think. After Piper vanished, the police questioned so many people but everyone said the same thing, they saw nothing out of the ordinary. It was just a normal, sunny day in the park. I mean, there were plenty of pictures taken that day and the police went through them half a dozen times but it all came to nothing.'

Marnie almost took a fearful backward step as she listened, hypnotised by the words.

'Right, well, I'm sorry, I realise this is very difficult for you both, though I'm sure you can appreciate we needed to check the facts,' Reese said by way of apology.

John nodded before sitting down by Anne's side.

'Of course, as soon as we know more, we'll be in touch,' Reese finished with a sigh.

'We'll see ourselves out,' Marnie said, turning and heading for the hallway.

As she left the room she glanced over her shoulder, John and Anne Donald remained seated, matching tears slowly sliding down their cheeks; Marnie turned away from the distressing image before heading back out into the wind and rain.

6

The man's eyes widened when he saw the waxy, brown, paper bag nestling inside the trunk, he grabbed it like a drowning man clinging to flotsam in stormy seas, pulse quickening he tore it open. When he saw the small skirt in his hands he buried his face in the material, breathing in deeply, searching for the scent of fear, the whiff of corruption.

Nothing. With a snarl, he glared at the red rose printed on the fabric, the vibrant colour had faded and he felt the moorings in his mind slip. Although her scent had long since vanished, he could still recall her eyes – innocent, bright blue and wide with terror.

Closing his eyes, he conjured the room, the hard bench, the roosting pigeons, the blood stained floor. He pictured the ghost memory of the boy shuddering, the back of his legs oozing red.

'*Weakling,*' he hissed.

The man leaned over the trunk, peering into the shadowed past. He could see the vague imprint of the girl huddled in the dusty corner, her hands covering her ears against the thud of heavy boots, fear shimmering in the air, pure and sublime, ready to fill him completely. Then the memory flashed and died and he groaned in anguish.

He held the skirt up and studied it; in the end, he had used up all her fear, drank her terror until he felt bloated with power. A glut of fear, the words burned brightly in his mind. His lips twisted in a snarl as he tried to cling to the memory.

Tossing the skirt to the floor, he reached down and lifted the small pink shoe from the box. He went through the same ritual, smelling the shoe, licking the leather with a tongue like sliced liver, in an attempt to conjure the memory. For a fleeting second a face swam forward from the shrouded depths of his black mind, a face framed with fair hair, a spray of freckles on her pale skin and then the image faded and he felt the fear bleed back into his mind. Somewhere in the stifling air he heard the sound of sobbing, he tilted his head in confusion and looked back towards the attic door.

'*Mummy!*' the voice trembled before fading to nothing.

Shaking his head in mounting fury, he dropped the shoe and continued the hunt. When his hand came across the wooden Russian doll, he felt the power surge through him as he held it up to the light.

'*Yes!*' he hissed, popping it open.

An identical doll lay within and he felt like clapping his hands, the thrill increased, his mind suddenly reconnecting with the past. He lifted the lid from the second doll to reveal the third, hands now shaking in excitement.

Clicking open the last of the dolls he sighed, reverently lifting out the small ringlet of hair, he let it curl around his finger. He tried to recall her name, his eyes screwed shut in desperation but his mind started to fragment.

The man rocked backwards and forwards in distress, his stuttering brain grasping for the memory, then his eyes sprang wide and he felt the flush of fury lance through his mind.

'*The one that got away,*' he whispered, his mind travelling back through the dark mists of time.

7

Reese pulled onto the station car park; easing into a parking bay he rested a hand on the wheel before turning to Marnie.

'So, what do you think?' he asked.

She watched the wipers swish back and forth, part of her mind was still locked in the house, watching the parents of Piper Donald reliving the nightmare they had tried so hard to forget. 'The fact that she wasn't wearing a ring on the day she vanished proves nothing, the killer could have placed it there after the event.'

Reese sighed heavily, 'I realise that.'

Marnie unclipped the seat belt, her lips set in a thin line. 'Perhaps Pam will have more luck with India Foster and Suzie Walls,' she offered.

'Somehow, I doubt it,' Reese replied, staring out at the rain.

When Marnie reached for the door handle, Reese placed a hand on her arm and she turned to look at him.

'Look, I know this is hard for you, but...'

'I'm fine,' her voice came out a little too harshly and then she sighed as Reese raised an eyebrow.

'I just want you to know that if you need to talk you can always come to me, you know that, don't you? It wouldn't go any further.'

Marnie nodded in understanding and climbed out, pulling the car keys from her pocket. The wind howled, sucking the warm air from the vehicle and whipping at her hair. Reese watched her stride across the car park and settle behind the wheel of her car, vanishing from view when she slammed the door closed.

Headlights sprang to life, illuminating the rain bouncing off the tarmac, she backed out of the space, tail lights flashing before she pulled onto the deserted road.

He pictured the bones in the woods and Piper Donald's parents living a life of never-ending anguish. Reese thought of his own daughter and shuddered as he tried to imagine what it must be like to lose your child, to never find peace. The thought made him break out in a cold sweat and suddenly he felt the need to go home, to check that she was still there, still safe.

With a shake of the head he eased back in the seat and drummed his fingers on the wheel. He'd worked with Marnie Hammond for two years and as far as he was concerned she was one of the best young officers he had come across, she was smart and fearless and knew how to get the job done with minimum fuss. He just hoped that this latest case wouldn't reopen old wounds.

Reese sighed, one more thing to add to his list of concerns. He checked his mirrors and set off, suddenly desperate to get home and kiss his daughter good night.

8

By the time she made it home, Marnie felt weak with fatigue. Shrugging out of her jacket she headed into the kitchen, and turned on the light before crossing to the sink. The house still held that new build smell – a mixture of paint and freshly cut timber. Stifling a yawn, she flicked the kettle on to boil, opened a drawer and pulled out a battered pack of cigarettes. Her face grave, she grabbed the matches and lit one, drawing the smoke deep and blowing it out on a sigh. When she caught sight of her reflection in the darkened kitchen window she frowned.

She hadn't had a cigarette for months but finding the bones of the young girl had shaken her to the core. Taking another pull, she turned on the cold water tap and doused the red ember, before tossing it into the bin.

Armed with a steaming mug of coffee she left the kitchen, turned off the light and, heading into the hall wearily climbed the stairs.

Five minutes later she slipped into a steaming hot bath and sighed as the heat seeped into her chilled bones.

Easing back, she closed her eyes and pictured the Donalds, wondering if they were still sitting, unmoved, on the sofa, locked in the never-ending nightmare. It had been over ten years since their precious daughter had been taken. Ten tortuous years of not knowing what had happened to her, clinging to the hope that she could still be alive and yet secretly, in the dark recesses of their minds, they knew the truth. When a child was taken it hardly ever ended happily, statistics had shown that if the victim wasn't discovered within the first forty-eight hours then chances were that child was dead. She pictured Jenny Bell hurrying home from the party, the goodie bag swinging from her hand. The parents had been questioned, their faces wrought with shock and terror, the father had dropped Jenny off before heading to work, the mother had been at home with the latest addition to the family, an eight-month-old boy named Dale. Jenny's older brother had sat with his parents listening but not quite grasping what was happening, when the mother had burst into tears the boy had run from the room, his own cheeks suddenly slick with tears. Now the parents were beginning their own tortuous journey into that netherworld of horror and heartache.

Steam filled the bathroom as Marnie sank further down in the water, ensnared in the warm embrace. An image of Hambling floated into her mind, his thin face marked with old acne scars, his sly eyes staring out at the world. She pictured him moving silently along the deserted street, his brow coated with sweat, his twisted mind howling in glee as he reached out his long arms and...

Marnie felt herself drift away, panic flared but her mind and body were too tired to react.

Behind closed lids, time rolled back and suddenly she was eleven-years-old again. Sitting on short cropped grass, the sun rapidly fading, the wind starting to gust. Her young sister was standing on the other side of the play area leaning against the wire fence, her face set in a sulk. The swings creaked back and forth, the increasing wind causing the roundabout to start lazily spinning.

Tilting her head to the mottled sky, Marnie watched the ominous clouds gathering like old bruises on parchment-thin skin.

They still had another forty-five minutes before Mum arrived to pick them up after work, and the way Abby was behaving it would feel like an age.

Their time in the park had started well enough; the sun shining as the two girls enjoyed fun on the swings and roundabout, but inevitably, the novelty had worn off and Abby had started to complain.

'I'm hungry, I'm thirsty,' she'd whined.

Eventually, Marnie had walked her over to the ice-cream van to stock up on fizzy drinks and ice-cream, and for a while, Abby had calmed down, the two girls laughing as they flew back and forth on the swings, trying to see who could touch the bright, blue sky.

After twenty minutes Abby had grown tired, and then she'd started to complain again in that whingeing voice that always grated on Marnie's nerves. She had done her best to keep Abby amused, but her heart hadn't really been in it. The truth was, she'd wanted to go shopping with her friends, but ever since Dad had left, her time was swallowed up having to babysit her eight-year-old sister.

Marnie plucked angrily at the grass as she realised that eventually her friends would stop asking her, and then she would be left with no one but her brat of a sister for company.

Sliding the chain from the collar of her T-shirt, she began to rub her thumb over the silver cross with the red garnet stone. She thought of her father, storming down the drive, a suitcase clasped in his right hand. Marnie had watched from her bedroom window, the cross held tight in her clenched fist, feeling nothing but relief when he climbed into the car and drove away without a backward glance.

It had been six months since he'd left, the house seemed quiet and peaceful, no longer ringing with her father's strident voice as he complained about anything and everything.

The flip side was that their mum had to work longer hours to pay the bills that seemed to drop through the letterbox with frightening regularity.

Marnie sighed and looked over towards her sister. Abby had moved to the right, edging towards the hole in the wire fence; her head still bowed, her right foot kicking at the dusty ground.

Suddenly the air grew darker, the bank of threatening clouds dousing the fire from the sun.

Turning, she looked out across the park, but the place was deserted as if the other children had somehow known that bad weather was on the way. When the thunder rumbled overhead, Marnie winced, the thump travelling down through her body, shaking her to the core and widening her eyes in fear.

Leaping to her feet she watched, mesmerised, as a spear of crackling light illuminated the tumultuous clouds, wind tore across the open parkland, tossing her hair back while the shadows from above moved slowly over the earth like an insidious, creeping oil slick.

Another roar of thunder and she cried out, her hands fluttering into the charged air, her heart racing. She looked across the play area, half expecting to see Abby running towards her, eyes wide, hair streaming out behind her, but the play area was empty.

Time stretched out, Marnie blinked in confusion, her eyes travelling left and right, searching for her sister.

"*Keep your eye on Abby, there are some bad people out there, Marnie.*"

Her mother's words drilled into her brain, and then she was running forward, her head snapping from side to side as the black shadows continued to cut off the dying light.

'*Abby!*' she screamed her sister's name, her hair writhing in the howling wind.

Dashing across the play area, she cut right until she came to the gap in the fence. Marnie hesitated, her eyes searching the tangle of bramble and bracken, the creeping sense of dread escalating and then she was scurrying through the bushes, her heart picking up speed when she failed to find her sister. Seconds later she burst free of the undergrowth, the thunder crashing again as she sprinted out into the field.

Marnie skidded to a halt, the fear rising to mind-shattering proportions – Abby was being carried away, slung lifeless, over the shoulder of a tall man dressed in black; his long stride taking him across open ground towards the ancient strip of woodland that led eventually to the car park beyond.

"*Bad people out there,*" her mother's face materialised in front of her panicked eyes. Marnie stood rooted to the ground in terror, and then she sprang forward.

'*Abby!*' she screamed again as the thunder roared.

The water in the bath cooled, Marnie's head twisted left and right, her legs thrashing, water spilling over onto the bathroom floor. Locked in the nightmare, she shivered in terror, her young face hardened with brittle determination; she bolted forward, her feet flying over the grass. The fear rampant but tempered with a burning anger, a "bad man" had Abby, and it was her job to get her back.

The heavens opened, torrential rain hammered down, and within seconds she was soaked: her hair plastered to her head, the sleeves of her blouse flapped over her hands, feet slipping and sliding on the wet grass. Gritting her teeth, she continued to run, her eyes mere slits against the onslaught, watching the nightmare play out. The man reached the trees, stopping for a moment to glance over his shoulder before vanishing into the woods.

'*No!*' she screamed, trying desperately to increase her speed.

Ten seconds later she reached the first of the trees, after the barrage of sound in the field, the rain bouncing off the canopy of leaves sounded strangely hushed. Marnie hesitated, swiping the rain from her eyes she leaned forward, trying to peer into the shifting shadows, her heart thudded to the crash of yet more thunder. Glancing over her shoulder she looked out into the rain-soaked field, the fear clawing at her senses, threatening to root her to the spot.

Grabbing a handful of wet hair, Marnie gave it a vicious tug that made her gasp in pain, and then she was moving again, her trainers squelched as she dashed forward along the cinder path; to her terrified mind it felt as if she were running over a blanket of small, crushed, animal bones.

On either side trees loomed, tall and threatening, their thick ancient trunks running with water, the only sound that of the pitter-patter of rain falling from the leaves. Rounding the corner, her senses reeled when she saw the empty path running arrow-straight into the gloom.

Marnie felt the tears slide from her disbelieving eyes, the bad man couldn't have got away so fast, it was impossible.

The snap of a branch to her left, she spun around, her wet hair whipping across her face, the fear blossoming… the monstrous figure exploded from the shadows.

Marnie tried to dodge the blow, but the fist slammed into the side of her face sending her crashing to the ground in a jumble of limbs, her left cheek mashed and lacerated against the rough, cinder ground.

'*Whippersnapper!*' the voice bellowed.

Marnie tried to move but couldn't, her ears rang with pain, her left cheek felt numb, the rain fell like diamond chips of freezing ice on her burning skin.

The shadow loomed, and she tried to swivel her eyes towards him but nothing seemed to work.

Rain continued to hiss around her, she could feel the attacker's eyes studying her, the weight of his gaze almost stopping her heart.

Marnie blinked the mix of rain and tears from her eyes, her vision swam and then refocused.

Abby lay less than six feet away in a patch of vibrant ferns, she was on her side, her eyes closed, a feather of wet, fair hair clung to her ashen cheek. Large hands reached down and plucked her from the earth – the way children will often remove a wild flower in full bloom, to be taken home, only to wither and die, torn from their roots.

Inside, Marnie screamed a sound so full of horror and heartbreak that it blasted all reasoning from her mind.

Abby's hair trailed down as he casually hoisted her over a shoulder and walked away into the downpour.

Inside, Marnie Hammond felt a small part of her die, the part that had belonged to Abby, the part that instinctively knew she would never see her sister again.

Marnie's eyes sprang open, for a couple of terrified seconds she was still locked in the nightmare, the thunder rumbled through her mind and then she lunged up, sending the water cascading to the floor. She gripped the sides of the bath, the scream locked in her throat, the water ice cold around her, chilling her bones and freezing her heart.

9

The boy sat against the gnarled trunk of the huge oak, the ground shadowed with dappled shafts of dying light. He winced as he stretched out his legs, the pain thrumming through his aching bones. His young face pale and drawn, dark circles clung beneath his weary, fear-filled eyes.

The garden stretched away from the huge rambling house, when he raised his gaze a flash of hatred passed across his face. Somewhere close by he could hear the cawing of crows roosting in the trees.

He tried to clear his mind but as always, the fear was never far away, that feeling of walking on eggshells, of waiting for the next time when the looming figure noticed him with dark eyes promising pain.

The boy cringed, slowly drawing his legs up and looping his arms around his knees.   •

When he saw the figure appear at one of the upstairs windows, he licked his lips nervously. He could see the pale blob of her face, her curly hair sprouting out in all directions.

The boy gripped his knees hard, his stomach muscles tightening at the sight of *her*.

When she turned and vanished he heaved a sigh of relief, dark clouds scuttled across the sky and suddenly it started to rain. High above, he heard the rain hitting the leaves before falling to the bare, dry ground beneath.

The boy watched tiny puffs of dust rising into the air as the rain increased, he sniffed, the air laced with that strange odour of dry earth hungrily soaking up the rain.

Suddenly the heavens opened, the house seen now through a curtain of grey.

The earth around his feet began to liquefy, tiny rivulets of brown water trickled down the slope, before joining others and picking up speed.

Swiping the rain from his brow, he squinted against the onslaught, his saturated clothes shrinking tight to his skin, setting off a trembling, his teeth chattering, eyes narrowed as the rain intensified.

Despite the conditions, he never even considered seeking shelter in the house.

Even if he had wanted to it wouldn't have been possible; looking down he felt the weight of his wretched life bearing down as the thick cord rope, that lashed him to the tree, soaked up the water.

The man snapped out of the stupor, his face twisted in a snarl of fury and hate. Gradually the hissing of the rain died and he blinked into the gloom of the attic. Then the sound of crying reached his ears, the pitiful wail drifted into the room, ending with a plea for Mummy. He shook his head and looked down at the ringlet of hair in the palm of his huge hand. The smile spread across his face as he closed his fist around the prize.

10
Two months later

Marnie closed the file with a sigh, placing it on top of the pile to her left.

'Well, that's the last one, and we've found nothing,' she said with a heartfelt sigh of disappointment.

Bev Harvey stifled a yawn, stretching her arms to the ceiling as Marnie wandered over to the water cooler.

'It was a long shot, boss, I mean, Piper Donald has been missing for over ten years and since the initial investigation no one has come forward with any new information.' Bev said, as she tided her desk.

Marnie filled a plastic cup from the cooler before turning. 'I spoke to Pam Oaks earlier and it's the same with Suzie Walls and India Foster, hundreds of statements taken at the time they vanished, all leading nowhere. Then we have Jenny Bell, I mean, how can she just have vanished from the face of the earth and no one see a thing?' She asked, before draining the cup and dropping it into the bin.

'Yeah, and where the hell is Hambling hiding?' Bev pondered, tightening the rubber band that kept her hair in place.

Marnie sighed, after Jenny Bell had vanished, the press had been all over the case like a rash, and yet now, ten weeks later, she had been pushed from the front pages by some idiot politician who had been caught with a prostitute while his wife and three kids sat at home playing happy families.

The team had been through every shred of evidence, followed every possible lead no matter how vague or tenuous but Jenny was still missing and Hambling remained at large. Kirk head wasn't a big town, though Marnie knew there were still plenty of places to hide, old mills that had long since closed down – the windows boarded up and sprayed with graffiti – that would offer a hiding place to someone on the run. She thought of the empty council houses on the outskirts of town, perhaps he was hiding in one of those or even the dense patches of woodland that circled Kirk head. The thought that he could be hiding locally and looking for his next victim ate away at Marnie's resolve, and she rubbed at her eyes in frustration.

'Do you think the girls could be linked in some way?' Bev asked.

Marnie chewed at her bottom lip, everything had been checked and then double-checked and as far as she could see there were no links to be made between the three missing girls and Jenny Bell.

The DNA results had come back negative and it was clear that whoever the arm in the woods belonged to, it wasn't one of the missing three. The soil samples hadn't led to anything substantial, within ten feet of the remains they had found three empty beer cans and a crisp bag wrapper along with a metal pin badge that had rotted away until only the rusted pin remained with flakes of metal attached. They had also discovered two foil condom wrappers and some torn pages from a pornographic magazine.

'I don't see how they could be connected, I know Reese is chasing up cold cases from other forces but so far he's had no luck,' Marnie replied, gazing out of the office window. The weather was starting to turn, the blustery rain giving way to bright sunshine, she could see a young couple walking opposite, the woman wearing shorts and a vest top, the man stripped to the waist as if he were strolling along in one-hundred-degree heat.

When she turned, Bev was on her feet, her desk tidy as she slipped her coat from the back of the chair.

'Have you got anything planned for the weekend?' Bev asked, shrugging the jacket on.

For a couple of seconds Marnie was taken aback by the question. 'Nothing at the moment,' she replied lamely. 'What about you?'

Bev smiled, pushing the chair back under the desk. 'Got a date with an old friend.'

Marnie raised an eyebrow. 'Oh yes, you kept that quiet, didn't you?'

A slight blush rose in Bev's cheeks, though the smile stayed in place. 'Believe it or not I used to go to school with the guy, I haven't seen him since the day we left but he popped up on Facebook and asked me out for a drink.'

'Just like that?' Marnie asked.

'Well no not exactly, though it turns out he's never been married and he admitted that he had a "thing" for me when we were at school.'

'So, what does he do for a living?'

'Funeral director.'

'Charming.'

'Come on, boss, someone has to do it.'

'Bet he turns up with flowers,' Marnie said straight faced.

Bev laughed, checking her watch. 'I'd better get going or I'll be late…'

'For your own funeral.'

'Sod off,' Bev grinned, heading for the door.

Marnie turned back to the window, watching the constant stream of traffic drive past the station. The weekend stretched out in front of her, another weekend sitting in an empty house waiting for the nightmares to come calling. Turning from the window, she ran a hand across her tired eyes.

For most people the weekend was something to be celebrated, something to look forward to, but to her it was simply forty-eight hours to kill until duty called.

With a heavy sigh, she picked up her coat from the chair and left the office, half a minute later she walked out into the sunshine and headed for the car park.

Opening the car door and stepping back, Marnie waited for the heat to escape before getting behind the wheel.

Clicking on the air-con she paused, one hand resting on the wheel; there were two options, either go home and watch crap television or head into town and get a coffee.

Mind made up Marnie pulled out into the traffic, destination Costa Coffee.

11

The view from the window revealed a large, unkempt lawn set on three levels, connected by flights of worn, stone steps; the ancient oak stood central on the third plateau, the branches bursting with young leaves flourishing in the sunshine. Open fields interspersed with thickets of woodland stretched away to the shimmering horizon.

Turning from the window, the man looked around the room with dead eyes, in one corner the grandfather clock ticked, the sound strangely muffled in the still air.

Dipping into his pocket he pulled out the ringlet of hair, his mind reaching back for the memory.

He could see the girl's image, the lens in his mind coated with greasy fingerprints, flickering like some ancient reel of celluloid, grainy with age, the tape heads removing the image of the girl a thin layer at a time.

Slowly, the smile turned into a sneer, he tried to hold onto the moment but the lens clouded over, the tape snapped and he knew the memory had been removed from his grasping mind.

'*Whippersnapper!*' his voiced boomed out and was absorbed by the thick stone walls, then thrown back at him, the word mocking him down the years.

At one time, he had a key for every door, no room in his mind was out of bounds. Closing his eyes, he pictured the familiar corridor, the walls and ceiling painted gunmetal grey, a floor of red tiles stretched into infinity. In his mind, he stepped forward, moving silently along the corridor; reaching the recess on the left he stopped, the door was white and emblazoned with images of pink horses cavorting over cotton wool clouds. Reaching out he grabbed the handle, the door held fast and he scowled as he tried again, slamming his heavy shoulder against the wood, his body echoing the shock.

'*Teach you!*' he screamed, attacking the door with both fists.

Rearing back, he felt blood pulsating through his head, hands throbbing with pain as he turned and stalked down the corridor to the next door. This one was coated pink and he watched in dismay, seeing the tiny fairy transfers come to life, fluttering back and forth over the woodwork.

His hand shot out, the palm slapped at the door, but the fairies skittered faster, taunting him, goading him; he could hear their faint tinkle of laughter. It said he was weakening again, his power ebbing away, soon he would be helpless and then...

'*No!*' he started to run, the doors flew by, an assortment of bright, vibrant colours that became a mad kaleidoscopic blur as he increased his speed.

His mind was in uproar and yet he couldn't put a name to this alien feeling, when he slammed blindly into the door he bounced back with bone-shaking force.

The door was painted black, the paint peeling in long dark strips.

Licking his lips, he tasted salt, his body coated with stale-smelling sweat; the grey walls of the corridor seemed to shrink around him until he became convinced that he was caught in the gullet of some enormous beast, the walls contracting like huge, powerful muscles, swallowing him whole, eating him alive.

Terror surged through his dark soul, lunging forward in desperation he snatched the handle, and suddenly he was back in the room with the ticking clock and lengthening shadows.

He staggered forward, arms thrashing at the air for balance and then he stopped as the truth hit him. The answer was so blindingly simple, so wonderfully straight forward. The power wasn't to be found in the past, memories were fragile and ultimately useless, no, he needed something permanent, something tangible.

'*Fresh meat,*' he hissed.

Gradually, his racing heart began to steady itself, his black mind making plans. For the first time in years he felt alive, his fingers rubbed at the trophy in his hand, his mind feverish with newfound expectation.

12

Marnie sat at one of the roadside tables, black coffee in hand, watching the stream of traffic flow past the front of the coffee shop. Closing her eyes against the sunlight, her mind was instantly filled with the usual nightmare images. Abby, her hair hanging, being carried off into the rain, the thunder crashing overhead; herself sprawled on the saturated ground, unable to help her sister as she was spirited away. Then her fevered mind conjured the skeletal arm of the mystery girl, the daisy ring on her finger, the bones suddenly clacked to life and began to crawl towards her, over the mash of wet, leaves. Marnie felt the remembered terror, as soon as she had seen the bones an image of her sister had rocketed into her mind and she had been convinced that she was looking down at the remains of Abby. When she had seen the little finger – intact – the relief had been palpable. She thought of Abby playing in the garden, it had been a sunny day and as usual their father had come home drunk and looking for an argument with their mother. Marnie and Abby had sneaked over to the open back door, clinging onto one another as their father shouted a tirade of abuse at their mum.

Marnie could remember Abby silently crying and she had slipped a comforting arm around her shoulder, the anger building inside Marnie's young mind. She could recall the hatred she felt for the man as if it had happened yesterday. The volume of abuse had risen and then her father had slammed the back door in drunken fury, the tip of Abby's little finger had been in the jamb. Marnie had reeled backwards, her sister screaming out in agony, her voice high pitched, the blood spurting over the patio flags, staining the pale stone red. The door had been slammed shut with such force that the end of Abby's finger had been sliced off.

Marnie could remember the commotion; her mother appeared at the door, her eyes wide in horror as her youngest daughter screamed. Two minutes later Marnie was in the car with her mum and a terrified Abby, her hand wrapped in a tea towel, bright red blood seeping through the white cloth. Their father had remained at home too drunk to comprehend what was happening. Six weeks later, Abby would wiggle the truncated little finger and smile as if all the pain had been worth it. Their father had left shortly after the "accident" and the two girls had grown closer, helping their mum pick up the pieces of her life. Finally, she pictured the goodie bag on the floor; Jenny Bell still missing, no more parties for her. Marnie had been one of the first officers on the scene, Jenny's phone had been in the gutter, her father's message on the voicemail demanding to know why his daughter wasn't picking up her phone.

Opening her eyes, she almost gasped aloud as sunlight chased the distressing images from her mind. Dipping into her pocket, she lifted out the cigarettes and lit up, drawing a frown from the woman who sat at the next table.

Marnie ignored her as she wafted an exaggerated hand in the air.

She thought of making an appointment with her doctor but that seemed extreme, besides in her line of work you couldn't afford to be doped, you needed to be on call twenty-four seven. She needed to find a way to get some sleep, a way to shift the nightmares that haunted her on a nightly basis.

She imagined a scenario, a break in the case and David Reese ringing her mobile as she slept on, buried under the duvet, lost in a world of drug-induced slumber.

With a shake of the head she flicked ash to the floor, drawing another look of disgust from the woman, who suddenly rose and strode away, leaving her coffee half finished.

'Get a bloody life,' Marnie whispered.

Picking up her cup, she tilted her head to take a drink and then suddenly stopped as she spotted the boy on the other side of the road. She frowned, watching him trudge along, head bowed; when he collided with a young woman weighed down with Primark bags the boy lurched back, arms held out in apology.

Marnie could see the woman's face, plastered with anger, barking out an insult and then striding away in a huff.

The boy lit a cigarette and walked away, shoulders hunched, his steps short and laboured.

Placing her drink on the table, Marnie rose to her feet and waited for a break in the traffic. Jogging across the busy road, she reached the other side, turned and followed at a distance, a frown of confusion creasing her brow.

The kid arrived at the busy junction and stepped off the kerb without even bothering to check the traffic; Marnie gasped, brakes squealed, a car horn blared, and the figure carried on walking as if in a trance.

'*Bloody bag head!*' the driver shouted through the open window.

Marnie ran forward and checked the road before crossing, the figure had made it to the other side, head still bowed, a trail of smoke drifting over his left shoulder.

'*Luke!*' Marnie shouted, but received no response.

Another junction approached and she sprinted forward, grabbing the sleeve of his sweatshirt just as he was about to step off the kerb.

He spun towards her, right arm thrown up ready to ward off a blow, and Marnie felt her stomach rise then sink in shock.

'*Luke?*' she repeated in a whisper of confusion. It looked like the boy she had dragged to the rain-soaked ground over two months earlier and yet it didn't.

He looked haggard, his eyes haunted; the cigarette clamped in his mouth gave him the appearance of an old man dressed in the uniform of a teenager – jeans, trainers and black hoodie.

'Jesus, Luke, are you OK?'

He turned away, but Marnie kept hold of his sleeve.

'Please let me go,' he whispered over his shoulder.

Marnie steered him, into the doorway of the old gas board offices – earmarked for swanky new apartments that would never materialise.

Luke glanced at her, but his eyes seemed restless, flicking left and right, seeing everything, seeing nothing, fear squirming in the blue depths.

'I haven't done anything wrong,' he whimpered.

'But you almost got yourself killed back there.'

He looked at her as if she were speaking a foreign language. 'Please, I have to go.'

'Go where?'

The tears welled and spilled over onto his cheeks. 'I don't know,' he panted, his voice cracked with emotion, his lips quivering in distress.

Marnie looked at the boy, shocked by his appearance, on the day she had arrested him for attacking the shopkeeper he had been upset, but now he looked crushed and broken.

'Are you heading home?' she asked.

Luke shook his head.

'So, where are you going?'

Tears continued to seep from his bewildered eyes. 'I don't know,' he repeated as the cigarette fell from his trembling fingers.

He tried to move forward, but Marnie spread her arms, blocking his exit. 'When did you last eat?'

The same blank expression remained on his face as if the question baffled him.

'Eat?'

'Right, come on you need something warm inside you.'

'But I don't have any money.'

'Don't worry about that.'

Despite the fear, Luke's mouth suddenly flushed with saliva and his stomach rumbled with want.

'What do you fancy, chippy or something from the pie shop?'

Luke wiped a shaking hand under his leaking nose. 'Chippy please.'

'Chippy it is then.'

She turned and waited, Luke glanced at her with uncertainty before stepping out of the doorway.

Marnie shortened her stride as Luke shuffled along beside her, one or two people gave them a strange look, the young woman with the long, brown hair, and the boy by her side dressed in scraggy clothes, his eyes downcast, his cheeks wet with tears.

13

The man wandered through the sprawling house as if trying to reacquaint himself with the layout of the place. Opening one of the bedroom doors, he dragged in a deep breath and stepped into the room. A double bed took up most of the space, with just a bare mattress, stained and dirty. In the corner of the time-worn room was an old, walnut-veneered gentleman's wardrobe, one warped door open, showing the few mouldy and mildewed clothes still hanging from metal hangers, a pair of cobweb covered brown shoes on the floor. The only other furniture in the room was an old ladder back chair next to the bed. The carpet looked threadbare, the colours faded; a net curtain hung over the fly-blown, curtainless window, the lace yellow with age. Every surface was coated in thick dust.

He looked around the room in confusion, he must have been in here before yet the place looked unfamiliar. The truth was, he had spent the last few years in his own room at the end of the long hall, only venturing downstairs to cook a meal or stand in the overgrown garden in the moonlight, trying to remember who he was before the void had swallowed him. The man moved back onto the landing, the walls oak panelled, the floorboards beneath his feet creaked as he moved along to the next door; when he tried the handle, he frowned finding it locked.

Looking down, the frown turned into a scowl as he saw the heavy key in the lock. Reaching out he turned it and pushed the door open, the man looked left and right along the hallway before stepping into the room.

When he saw the body on the bed, his dark eyes widened in astonishment, he strode across the room, fists' clenched, a look of bewildered puzzlement on his bloodless face. The girl was wearing a blue dress emblazoned with silver stars and matching shoes. She was lying on her side facing the door, her milk-white eyes were wide open. Her face was grey, a small patch of white fungus grew on her cheek, the skin pulled tight over her skull, teeth locked in a grimace of despair, fair hair spread out on the dirty linen sheet. Closing his eyes, he swallowed the sense of fear that crept through his mind, suddenly he was on an unknown street, his hands on the steering wheel of a black car, gliding slowly through the late afternoon sun. The man forced his eyes open and looked at the body, he must have taken her, must have been out there at some point trawling the streets looking for a lost soul. The realisation of the risks he had taken made his body shake with fear, the sweat standing out on his furrowed brow. Suddenly the whimpering sounds and fading cries for help made sense. He had assumed that the pleas had been inside his own tortured mind, now he knew the truth. He had taken the girl but then the confusion had seeped back into his soul, blinding him to the truth. He sniffed, the stink of corruption filled the air and then he shook himself angrily. Reaching down, he plucked the body from the bed, his eyes glittering as he carried her out of the room and down the stairs, the confusion pulling at his senses. Walking through the house, he made his way into the kitchen and then stopped when he saw the hateful light at the window.

Closing his eyes, his mind wandered, the girl in his arms felt as if she were made of straw. Behind heavy lids his eyes slid left, his brain conjuring an image of the boy hobbling along the landing of the old house. He watched with a sense of disgust as the boy stopped and leaned against the flower-patterned wall, his face wrought with pain and distress.

'Weakling,' the man whispered, seeing the child rub a hand across his tear-stained cheeks.

'Worm!' his voice dripped disdain, the young boy started to move again, his bloody feet shuffling over the worn carpet.

Slowly, he vanished into the fabric of the past, making the man shudder with anger.

'*Whippersnapper!*' he screamed in impotent rage, his eyes springing open.

For a few seconds, he stood swaying in the huge kitchen, he gripped the body tight to his chest, his teeth locked in anger. Sunlight lanced into the room forcing him to squint against the onslaught. He hated the sun, despised the spiteful glare, the burning heat; his best work had always been done in the shadows, when the darkness swept in to kill the abhorrent light, when he became invisible.

Standing in the vast kitchen, he looked out into a garden smothered with weeds. This had always been his favourite room, the grey walls, the stainless-steel worktops, the butcher's shop feel of the place. North facing, the light failed to penetrate the shadows, though he still winced when a shrapnel of sunlight ricocheted off the steel taps.

Seconds stretched into minutes. In his youth, he had been able to stay unmoving for as long as it took for the moment to arrive. That perfect feeling of synchronicity would slot into place, and he would attack with lightning speed.

The man felt the flutter of confusion trying to seep into his brain and he thrust it away with a grunt of loathing. He knew what he had to do to address the balance, he needed the surge of power, he was an empty vessel that needed filling to the brim.

The smile curled his lips, it was all about planning; if you prepared correctly then fate would do the rest. Though the dead girl in his arms was testament to how far he had strayed from the path of planning and control.

When he opened his eyes the smile widened, the light in the room had faded slightly, the temperature felt a couple of degrees cooler. Soon he would be able to move. And the hunt would begin.

Jenny Bell's fair hair hung down, her sightless eyes stared up at the ceiling.

'*Patience,*' he whispered, stepping back into the shadows.

14

Marnie watched as Luke demolished the fish and chips, shovelling the food into his mouth, eyes closed, grease on his lips and fingers as he chewed.

They were sitting on a bench outside the library, the pigeons strutting, waiting for scraps but Luke gathered the scratchings and wolfed them down before scrunching the chip paper into a ball.

Marnie studied him from the corner of her eye, his fingernails were chewed to the quick, hands smudged with dried mud as if he'd been digging at the earth, his hoodie stained, a rip on the shoulder revealed the thin, grey padding beneath, his jeans were filthy, the bottoms turned up over a pair of battered trainers.

'When did you get released from the Young Offenders' Unit?' she asked. 'Park View,' she added, seeing Luke's blank expression.

Luke wiped his nose with the back of his hand, his eyes still held a hint of fear. 'Five days ago,' he replied, his voice no more than a whisper.

'Where have you been sleeping?' Marnie asked.

Luke glanced up, and at last she saw recognition seep into his eyes.

'In the park,' he muttered.

'Things are bad at home?'

Luke shrugged. 'I hate it at home.'

'Because of your stepfather?'

Suddenly he was on his feet. 'Thanks for the food,' he said.

Marnie stayed seated, afraid that if she made a move he would bolt and vanish into the crowd of late afternoon shoppers.

Luke tossed the paper into the waste bin and then yawned – stretching his arms skywards – his hoodie rode up, and Marnie's eyes widened in shock as she saw the swathe of bruising on his torso.

Lowering his arms, he shivered before rubbing at his eyes. 'I gotta go.'

Marnie tried to think of something that would stop him, but her mind was still frozen in shock at the bruising.

Luke hesitated and glanced down at his feet, his face blooming with colour. 'You don't have a couple of quid spare, do you?' he asked, shamefaced.

Marnie thought before replying, the truth was she needed to know how Luke had come by the bruises but taking him in for questioning felt extreme, after all, as far as she knew he had done nothing wrong and yet she had no doubt he would run if she tried to get him to open up here on the street.

Standing up slowly, she slipped her hands into her pockets. 'I'll make you a deal, come home with me – I can cook you a proper meal – and then…'

'I can't do that,' Luke said, shaking his head rapidly and taking a backward step.

'Why not?'

He opened his mouth and nothing came out but a heavy sigh.

'Come on, Luke, you can get your head down for a few hours, get some proper sleep.'

'Why would you do that?' he asked, his voice fraught with confusion.

'Because you look worn out and sleeping in the park is no answer.'

'I can take care of myself,' he replied with a hint of defiance.

'I don't doubt it, but a few hours' rest and a hot bath sounds good, doesn't it?'

Luke thought for a moment. 'I guess so.'

'That's sorted then, I'm parked in the multi-storey, if we go now we can miss some of the rush hour traffic.'

Luke hesitated for a moment before moving forward with her. The trip back to the car seemed to take an age, Marnie having to shorten her long stride as Luke shuffled along beside her. Shoppers pushed and shoved and twice she had to take the boy's arm to stop him from being knocked off his feet. By the time they made it to the multi-storey the sunlight was fading and Luke's face was coated with sweat.

Pulling out her keys, she beeped off the alarm and pulled the passenger door open.

Luke suddenly looked nervous. 'You won't take me in, will you?'

Marnie rested a comforting hand on his shoulder and felt the muscle twitch. 'We'll get you cleaned up, and then you can leave if you want.'

Luke peered into her eyes, searching for a hidden agenda, and then he sat in the passenger seat, hands folded in his lap, eyes wide as if trying to control some unspeakable fear.

Closing the door, Marnie hurried around the car – half-expecting Luke to leap out and make a run for it. When she climbed behind the wheel, she let out a thin sigh of relief before starting the car.

'You OK?' she asked, turning in her seat.

Luke's face was deathly pale, his lips a thin bloodless line, but he nodded in acknowledgment.

Marnie flicked on the sidelights and backed out of the parking space, her mind full of concern, thinking about the bruising and the way he had backed away, arms raised, his face set with fear.

Luke moved his feet back and forth in the foot well as if, subconsciously, he was running away from something monstrous.

15

It felt monumental to be out in the darkness, yet the man couldn't dispel the fear, fear that later he would be unaware that he had ventured out of the rambling old house.

Pulling on to the deserted lane, his big hands gripped the wheel, his mind starting to fracture, the confusion seeping into his clotted brain. Driving around a left-hand bend, he pulled up to the kerb, leaving the engine purring; a fox broke cover and dashed across the narrow lane, disappearing into the protective trees on the left.

Closing his eyes, he tried to calm the rage within but his brain flashed with random snapshots of memory, faces from the past ballooned towards him and then vanished. The sound of screaming mingled with light, tinkling laughter echoed through his mind. He felt the shackles start to slip and he turned off the engine, thrust the door open and climbed out in an effort to keep hold of the here and now.

To his left, he saw the rusting park gate, set back amongst the trees. Walking to the rear of the Mercedes he opened the boot, the unknown girl lay curled in the small space, the smell of decay wafted into his face before dissipating into the night air. Reaching in, he lifted her from the boot and closed it before striding towards the gate.

As soon as the darkness enfolded him, he felt a sense of calm descend. The man sighed as he walked, the tension flowing from his anxious mind. This was his natural habitat – away from the streets and the endless stream of people living their pitiful lives. Taking a huge lungful of cool air, he let it out slowly and came to a halt, tilting his head to a sky ablaze with stars. The disappointment weighed heavily on his mind as he tried to calm the burning need inside. For the first time, he felt the passing of years, the strength he had always taken for granted was on the wane, he looked down at the girl and adjusted her weight, the scowl on his face growing deeper. Over the past few years, it had taken all his inner strength to try to hold onto his core being. Now, he was realising, during that time his body had slowly started to deteriorate; he could feel the effects of endless weeks and months sprawled on the bed staring into space as he fought the raging battle inside his own mind. It had to stop, he had to reassert his will otherwise the confusion would crawl back into his brain and he would languish again in a netherworld of confusion and doubt, locked in a limbo of torment. High above, a shooting star trailed briefly across the dark void before dying.

Hoisting the girl higher he moved forward, his long stride eating up the ground, the blood pumping through his veins, his face set in a scowl of dark intent. The tunnel of trees ended and he looked out into an open space of close-cropped grass; when he saw the bronze statue standing stark against the skyline he frowned. He had been here before, the memory raged through his failing mind. Suddenly, the confusion vanished and the man saw his younger self standing in front of the statue, gazing up at the severed head grasped in the statue's left hand, the snakes writhing as he held the sword aloft.

'*Perseus!*' he whispered, his eyes alight with fervour.

He had stopped many times to study the statue, a cloth sack thrown over his right shoulder, the bones rattling as he walked towards the trees.

The man watched his ghost image stride towards him, black hair swept back, his gait sure and confident. He had been in his prime and the man stood awestruck at the sight of his younger self.

A gust of wind blew across the open space and the spectre vanished into wisps of nothingness, the man turned and looked at the bank of trees and bushes.

That's where he had been heading, into the dark, deep into the trees. Grunting in satisfaction he followed the distant memory; dipping low to clear the branches, he walked confidently through the ankle-deep grass, his eyes gradually adjusting to the darkness as he weaved his way deeper into the woods. Occasionally, he thought he caught a fleeting glimpse of his ghost self in the shadows but then the image would vanish and he would grunt in disappointment.

The man had no idea how long he walked beneath the towering trees with the girl held in his arms, occasionally her long, trailing hair would snag on a bramble and he would grunt, tugging it loose. Eventually, everything faded until the only sound was the brush of his shoes in the grass and the blood thundering in his ears. When he reached the small stream he stopped, his mind seemed to refocus as he realised he had stood here in the past. The smile seeped onto his face when he saw the dark silhouette of the twisted oak standing on the opposite bank.

Stepping into the stream, he crossed, sure-footed, before striding from the water. He could feel the huge roots beneath his feet, roots that had burst from the ground, radiating out and anchoring the tree to the black earth. Falling to his knees, he placed the girl on the ground and then went to work with his bare hands, attacking the earth, pulling up the grass before delving deeper. After ten minutes his body was coated with sweat, he stopped for a moment, head tilted to the stars above, chest heaving, trying to regain his breath. Closing his eyes, he tentatively searched his mind, afraid that he would find the smothering confusion waiting in the shadows to draw him in. The smile crawled across his face, this felt right, it felt familiar and yet...

He attacked the ground again before the doubt could steal away the clarity, all that mattered was the here and now, the trees, the earth, the dead girl by his side. Time lost all meaning, he continued to delve, gradually widening the trough, huge hands ripping and tearing at the ground. Eventually he grunted in satisfaction before pushing himself upright. He let the cooling breeze sweep across his sweating face and then shook his head. This felt right and yet it didn't, he knew he had been here before and yet he couldn't imagine his younger, confident self delving into the earth with bare hands, couldn't picture him on his knees, the black earth caked beneath his fingernails. Somewhere in his mind, he heard laughter – rich and full – the sound held a mocking quality, as if the voice inside was laughing at his pathetic efforts. Snarling, he lashed out, his shoe thudded into the side of the girl and she rolled over; dry bones cracking she slid into the shallow grave.

Easing back down, he started to shovel the earth over the body, watching her sightless eyes look out at the world for the last time, mud filling her mouth, her fair hair snagged with brambles and leaves, her grey face disappearing beneath the dirt. Ten minutes later, he stood up and cracked his neck left and right before wiping his hands on the front of his jacket.

'*Fool,*' the voice whispered.

The man snapped a look over his shoulder, his eyes wide, expecting to find his former self standing right behind him, black hair slicked back, a sneer on his face.

'*Whippersnapper,*' he hissed into the darkness, trying desperately to hold on to the feeling of power, but already he could sense that it had been an illusion, a pale imitation of the real thing.

Rubbing his hands together anxiously, he looked around, the fear creeping out from the shadows as he realised he was lost, the darkness that had always offered concealment was now acting as a barrier. Fear clambered through his mind, he turned and set off running, branches slapped against his face, he felt the wicked pull of the brambles trying to ensnare him. He ran, splashing through the shallow water, before struggling onto the bank, his mind fighting for control as he staggered through the trees, a huge lumbering shape, the stuff of nightmares. He felt like screaming in anguish but his breathing was ragged, his heart slamming fast and furious. When he burst onto the path, he cried out in relief, then he turned right and staggered forward, his mind still smothered with confusion, the terror snapping at his heels.

Reaching the gates, he paused for a moment, trying desperately to reassert his will before walking unsteadily from the shadows toward the car.

Seconds later he was back behind the wheel, his body coated in sweat, the dread crawling over his skin.

'*Old fool,*' the voice inside his skull laughed.

The man scowled, unable to ignore the internal voice.

'*Did you really think you would simply bury the girl and then find the one you were looking for?*'

'I…'

'*Can you even remember the way it used to be?*' the voice asked with a sigh.

'Of course, I remember!' he spat in reply.

'*Somehow I doubt that.*'

'Silence!' he bellowed, his huge hands closing over the steering wheel with terrifying force, his eyes glaring through the windscreen, seeing nothing.

'*Think,*' the voice demanded. '*Think how it really was, not how you imagined it to be.*'

'But I can't!' his voice came out as a cracked whisper of despair.

'*You have to concentrate.*'

'I…'

'*LEDGER!*' the voice roared, the single word crashing through his stupefied mind.

The memory skewered his brain, he saw himself as a younger man, the same man who had strode across the grass with his bag of bones, only now he was sitting at a desk, head bent, as he wrote down the names, places, victims.

'Ledger,' he sighed in ecstasy, and then his mind lurched when he realised he had no idea where he had hidden the book.

'*Find it!*' the voice commanded.

The man nodded in understanding, when he slammed the car into gear his mind was already back at the rambling house, dashing from room to room, opening drawers and tipping the contents onto the floor. As he pulled away from the kerb, his ghost self was standing in the library, eyes widening at the walls lined with books of all shapes and sizes.

'Has to be here somewhere,' he started to pull books from shelves, the air filled with dust motes, the yellowing pages were checked before being hurled to the floor in anguish.

The car swept along the deserted road, the man making small corrections as he navigated the route, he was there yet he wasn't, his mind was back at the house searching for the final key – the one that would unlock *all the doors* – and then he would be complete and ready to move forward.

'Whippersnapper,' he mumbled, before smiling.

16

The filthy duvet moved, a few seconds later Christopher Hambling poked his head from beneath the cover, shivering at the cold. He sniffed and grimaced at the stink of the place, his eyes blinking into the gloom. When he heard the rats scuttling over the grit-strewn floor he reached out a hand and grabbed the chunk of wood by his side, slamming it on the floor. He listened, the scurrying increased before fading to nothing as the vermin ran for cover.

With a grunt of disgust, he sat up, keeping the grimy duvet wrapped tight around his shivering body; through the window he could see the moon hanging high in a clear sky glittering with stars. His stomach groaned and he wiped a shivering hand across his dry, cracked lips. Hambling tried to remember the last time he had eaten; it must have been over twenty-four hours earlier; he had ventured into the town centre to rummage through the bins behind the fast-food shops. Pickings had been lean and all he had managed to find was a half-eaten burger smothered in mayo. Despite the fact he hated the white gloop, he had wolfed down the food before heading back to the derelict house which was hidden by a smothering of ivy and woodland, the canal a few feet from the twisted front door. He thought back to his brief stay at the council flat, the central heating and warm comfy bed, the deep bathtub and endless supply of hot water. The thought set his body trembling with cold. He had been heading home from town the day the police raided the flat. Hambling had seen the cars pull up and the officers sprinting towards the entrance to the building. A lifetime of being in trouble with the law had made him turn and walk away, the sixth sense eating away at his mind, he'd glanced over his shoulder and looked up to see two people standing on the balcony of the flat. Hambling had turned and hurried away, back into the town centre, his heart hammering, his body suddenly tacky beneath the old parka. His mind had made the links with the missing girl, he had seen her on the television, her chubby, smiling face, staring out at him and now the police were looking for him. Left with no option, Christopher Hambling had gone into hiding. His time was spent within the four decaying walls of the house, huddled beneath the duvet, trying to think of a way to escape the nightmare that closed around him with every passing second. With a groan, he stood up and shrugged the cover from his shoulders. He needed to risk another trip to the town centre, he desperately needed something to eat and drink, though the thought of trying to remain hidden whilst scavenging for food made the fear inside writhe. He knew the police were looking for him and the passage of time would do little to change that fact, but the fear of being spotted by the gangs of lads that hung around Kirk head town centre was a more terrifying prospect. Hambling had been beaten up in the past – both inside jail and on the outside – and he knew that if he was identified on the street then there would be no warder there to put an end to the violence. Walking over to the window, he looked up at the moon and said a silent prayer before heading out into the darkness

17

Leaning back against the cupboard, Marnie watched through a cloud of cigarette smoke as Luke's clothes spun around in the washing machine, her eyes thoughtful, her mind thinking about Luke and the bruises.

As soon as they'd arrived at the house, she had sent him upstairs for a bath while she bundled his clothes into the machine. The dirty water sloshed back and forth, the machine drained then started to refill.

She couldn't square the circle of finding him in such a state. He had been dressed in the same bedraggled clothing that he had been wearing the day she dragged him to the rain-soaked ground. At sixteen, his luck had run out and he'd been sentenced to two months in a local young offenders' unit. Now, he looked like some street urchin from a bygone century. Yet it was more than the clothing, his face appeared haggard, his eyes constantly tear-filled and alive with fear. And then there were the bruises.

She had questioned Luke at his home on three separate occasions, each time his stepfather, Tony Oldman, had remained slumped on the sofa, seemingly unconcerned, as she explained about Luke's law-breaking habits. Marnie tried to imagine what it must have been like for the boy living in a house like that. Living in an environment where, at best, he was ignored, with no affection or parental guidance to keep him on the straight and narrow. When she pictured the bruises, she felt the anger flutter inside, perhaps Oldman had dished out the beating when Luke had returned home from his spell in Park View. She imagined Oldman – all six foot and sixteen stone of him – grabbing Luke and throwing him across the room as if he were made of straw, his face twisted with a snarl.

"*I'll fucking teach you, bringing the filth to this house!*"

It felt right, it made sense, no doubt Oldman had some dodgy scams going on, and the last thing he would want was the police turning up and snooping into his life, so he had made sure the boy had paid for his stupidity.

When she heard the heavy thump on the ceiling, she frowned before heading for the stairs. She took them two at a time, coming to a halt outside the bathroom door.

'Luke, are you OK?' she asked, knocking on the door.

'*Luke?*' her voice rose in concern.

No answer.

'If you don't open the door then I'm going to have to come in,' she warned.

Silence.

Seconds ticked into infinity and Marnie felt the tension rising. Bringing the boy to her house wasn't the normal course of action and she knew it wouldn't go down well with those in command but she'd had little choice, Luke Croft was damaged and needed help not a grilling.

Taking a deep breath, she cracked the door open, steam billowed out, the heat was stifling. Luke lay sprawled at the side of the bath; when Marnie saw the state of his body she jerked back in shock.

The bruises she had glimpsed on the street were only the start, his whole torso was mottled a deep yellow and brown, his legs were the same, his left thigh bloomed black.

'*Jesus,*' she gasped, wafting a hand to clear the steam.

Luke coughed and twisted his head, when he saw Marnie standing in the bathroom he scrunched himself into a ball, and she winced when she saw the bruises on the soles of his feet.

Reaching behind the door, she grabbed the robe from the hook before crouching down, and covering his wet, shaking body.

Easing him into a sitting position, she wrapped the robe around his shoulders, before slowly helping him to his feet.

'Luke, who did this?' she asked, catching sight of their distorted reflection in the steam-filled mirror – her face white with shock, Luke hunched, miserably, inside the robe.

'Fell,' he gasped as the water trickled down from his wet hair, mingling with the tears on his pale cheeks.

She could feel him trembling by her side as she led him onto the landing and into the spare bedroom.

It was like leading a small child, she even had to turn him around and put pressure on his shoulders to get him to sit down on the bed, then she took a step back as he lowered his head.

'Where did you fall?'

'Down the market steps,' he replied, his voice no more than a whisper.

'When did it happen?'

Luke gave the slightest of shrugs. 'Couple of nights ago.'

Marnie looked down at his bare feet, she could see three, small, red blisters, angry and inflamed, her mind juddered as she realised they were burn marks.

'Have you been to the hospital?'

'No.'

'Look, we need to get you checked out, I...'

'I'm not going to any hospital,' Luke glanced up at her, the familiar look of fear back in his eyes.

'But...'

'I mean it.'

Marnie eased down until she was eye level with the boy. 'Listen to me, I know you didn't get the bruises through any fall.'

'I did; I fell down the steps.'

'Luke...'

'I tripped and fell and that's what happened.'

He sounded like a child trying to convince himself that what he was saying was the stone-cold truth.

'You didn't get the burn marks on your feet from a fall down any steps,' she kept her voice low and calm, though inside she was seething as she thought of Tony Oldman sprawled on the lumpy sofa, the ever-present cigarette clamped between his nicotine-stained teeth.

Luke shuffled back on the bed, and dragged the robe down to cover his feet. 'Please, I just want to go home.'

'If that were true then you wouldn't have been sleeping in the park,' Marnie replied with a sigh.

He looked around the room as if trying to find an escape route, then he simply pulled the robe tight around him, his pinched face looking up at her, tears overflowed, he swiped at them, embarrassed.

'I promise, if you tell me who did this then I'll sort it.'

Luke shook his head, his lips clamped together.

'Was it your stepfather, did Oldman do this to you?'

The boy didn't move a muscle. 'Where are my clothes?'

'They're in the washer.'

'I want them; I've got to go.'

Marnie made to fold her arms and then stopped. 'I'm sorry, but they've only just gone in the machine, and...'

'I don't care; you can't keep me here.'

'No one is keeping you here, but I have to wait for the washer to finish.'

Luke folded his arms, chewing feverishly at his bottom lip. 'How long will they be?'

'About an hour and then I'll have to put them in the dryer.'

Luke shuffled further back on the bed.

'Are you going to tell me who did this to you?'

He shook his head again.

'You know I can't just forget it.'

'But...'

'I'm a police officer, Luke, I can't pretend it hasn't happened.'

'You *made* me come here. I told you I was all right on my own, a bath and something to eat you said, and now you're trying to *fuck me over!*'

Anger flooded his face and he scrambled off the bed.

Marnie stepped back in surprise. 'Calm down, Luke, there's no need to get upset, you're safe here.'

'*Safe, fucking safe!*' his voice rose, his face contorted in fury.

Marnie felt the confusion wash over her at his frightening change of mood, he glared at her with accusation bright in his eyes. 'Look, you said you got the injuries through a fall, two nights ago, right?'

Luke nodded. 'Yeah, that's what happened.'

'So, what about the burn marks on your feet?'

The boy seemed to shrink further into the robe, the anger in his eyes dying, leaving the fear behind. 'I...'

'Someone beat you, didn't they?'

Luke opened his mouth and his shoulders slumped. 'Someone jumped me in the park,' he admitted.

'Did you get a look at the person who attacked you?'

'No, I was asleep behind the bandstand and the next thing I know some bastard was laying into me.'

'And this happened the night before last?'

Luke nodded. 'Yeah,' he replied, wiping the sleeve of the robe across his eyes.

'How about the burns on your feet?'

'Did 'em myself.'

'Why?'

Another shrug and then he glanced away, his face flaring red.

'OK, listen to me, you're in no fit state to go back on the streets.'

'But...'

'I want you to stay here tonight, just get some rest and we can talk in the morning.'

'There's nothing to talk about I never saw the guy,' he paused, 'in fact there could have been more than one of them.'

Marnie opened her mouth to push the issue but changed her mind. 'Just try and get some sleep, if you need me then just shout, I'm only across the landing.'

Luke nodded and then yawned, showing a mouthful of fillings.

At the door, she stopped and turned but Luke was already on the bed, his head resting on the pillow, his body beneath the robe curled into a ball.

Stepping out onto the landing, she closed the door quietly and headed back down the stairs. Retrieving the cigarettes from the drawer, she lit one and looked at her reflection in the darkened window.

At first, Luke had said he'd fallen down the market steps and then he'd decided to come clean about the beating in the park. The trouble was Marnie didn't believe a word of either story.

She pictured the bruises, brown and yellow in colour, she knew that bruises altered depending on when they were inflicted. God knows she'd had enough of her own after a Saturday night on duty. She'd seen enough as well on the bodies of the battered women during her time in the Domestic Violence Unit. Fresh bruises were red and black, normally it took two to three weeks for them to fade to yellow and brown. She knew, from personal, painful experiences, some bruising – like on the shins – took much longer to disappear.

Marnie's face settled into a frown as she smoked the cigarette, there was no way Luke had been attacked in the last forty-eight hours.

Flicking ash into the sink, her eyes narrowed, following the links in the chain. Luke had been out of Park View for five days and yet the bruises were much older. She felt the anger ignite when she realised that Luke Croft hadn't been beaten on the outside, he'd received his injuries whilst locked up, locked up in a place that had meant to help the boy, not leave him terrified with a body covered in bruises and burn marks on his feet.

'*Bastards,*' she spat, dropping the half-smoked cigarette into the sink, the ember hissing as it was extinguished.

18

The fear of never finding the ledger grew, until it consumed him completely, eating away at the fragile barricades of his sanity.

He had started with a plan; he would search each room systematically, making sure he missed nothing. For the first hour, the plan had worked, he'd methodically lifted the books from the shelves, studying each one before dropping it to the floor and grabbing the next. The minutes ticked by, the fear and frustration had built, his movements becoming more desperate; the books flew left and right, flying through the dusty air and landing with a thump on the worn, carpeted floor.

In the end, the shelves had been bare and he had looked around the room, his face writhing with anger. He snatched the tie from around his neck and shoved it into his pocket.

'Not here,' he spat in desperation, turning and heading up the wide stairs.

It had taken him a further two hours to search the six large bedrooms, his face smeared with dust, the fear rampant as he thundered down the stairs and into the kitchen. Turning on the tap, he splashed his face with cold water in an attempt to cool down, though there was nothing he could do for his overheating brain.

Looking at his gaunt reflection in the window, he cringed when he saw the fear in his eyes, fear mixed with the dreaded confusion.

With a snarl, he spun away from the distressing image and stalked through into the beating heart of the house, the grandfather clock ticked in the corner – constant and eternal.

In the past, he would have found the sound comforting in the familiar surroundings, but not tonight, tonight he felt as if his brain was being cooked inside his skull.

Staggering to the Chesterfield sofa he slumped down, immediately his large hands started to shake and he crossed his arms, trapping them beneath his armpits in an effort to control the spasms.

The ledger was the key. He needed it to unlock his mind. Without it, his past would stay forever out of reach. Yet it wasn't in the house, he must have moved it to somewhere safe, though his grasping mind had no idea where.

His dark eyes flicked around the room in terror; when he spotted the small bookcase standing by the inglenook he stopped and held his breath – he could see the thin book lodged beneath for support.

Then, he was scrambling free of the sofa, arms outstretched he dashed across the room, his hands grasping at the fusty air. Falling to his knees, he reached out and snatched the book free, the case tilted forward before righting itself.

When he opened the book, the terror instantly fled, his eyes fell on the careful handwriting, the names leapt out from the page and the euphoria erupted, sending the fear and dread scuttling for the dark, shadowed places of his mind.

Holding the book, he grasped it to his chest, his head tilted to the ceiling, his face split by a wide grin.

'*Got you!*' his voice boomed out, to his ecstatic mind he felt the walls shake and the foundations shudder under the weight of his old self.

'*Happy now?*' the internal voice asked.

The man nodded. '*Oh yes!*' he cried, bursting into gales of uncontrollable laughter.

19

Marnie had left Luke Croft perched in front of the television, dressed in the same ragged clothes, though at least now they were clean. He'd promised to stay in the house until she got back; telling him to help himself to the ready meals from the freezer, she had headed across town to the station. Now, she watched the frown on David Reese's face deepening as she explained about finding the boy battered and bruised on the street.

Sunlight spilled into the office, the plant on the windowsill looked dry and withered.

'Do you really think it was wise – taking Croft to your home?' Reese asked, placing his elbows on the desk his brown eyes watchful, brow crinkling in concern.

'Look, he's harmless, and…'

'He's hardly that, he's just spent time in Park View for a violent assault.'

'Yes, but while he was there he was beaten black and blue.'

Reese held up a hand. 'According to you, he initially said he'd received the damage when he fell down the market steps, he then *changed* his story and said he was attacked in the park.'

'He's trying to keep the truth to himself, he's terrified.'

Reese sighed as he eased back in the chair. 'Have you had a doctor look at the lad?'

'No, but…'

'We need photographic evidence of the injuries, you know that.'

Marnie glanced through the third-floor window, she could see the town spread out below, a dizzying array of terraced houses interspersed with the occasional factory unit and shops.

She'd spent the night sprawled on the bed, wrapped in a throw, her mind too wired to sleep. It had been gone two by the time she drifted off, her eyes had pinged open at six, the room hot, the air still.

'Marnie?'

She turned away from the window, Reese was looking at her with eyebrow raised.

'I don't think he'll agree to photographs being taken, not yet.'

'Why not?'

'He's frightened, his body is smothered in bruises, and…'

'I know I'm playing the devil's advocate here but perhaps he's telling the truth, maybe he was attacked in the park by persons unknown. I mean, we know that place is a magnet for the drunks at night.'

Marnie shook her head. 'The bruises are yellow and brown, whatever happened to him took place a lot longer than two nights ago.'

Reese sighed as he loosened the tie around his neck. 'I know this is difficult, but we have to use everything at our disposal, and documenting the injuries is part of the process.'

'And if he won't?'

Reese closed his eyes for a moment and stifled a yawn. 'Look, we're stretched thin at the moment – you know that – we still have no idea who the remains in the woods belong to, I have four officers off with some bloody sick bug, I've got a mountain of files from three forces that need going through and Jenny Bell is still missing, not to mention that bastard Hambling.'

Marnie felt the guilt plucking at her senses, Reese was right, she pictured the parents of Jenny Bell desperate to discover the truth about what had happened to their child. She imagined Hambling – still in hiding – biding his time until he could strike again. Then she thought of Luke, battered and bruised. 'I still think this needs checking.'

Reese drummed his fingers on the desk, Marnie watched the flicker of annoyance pass over his face.

'Protocol has to be followed to make any case as watertight as possible. Now, it sounds as if the boy has had a tough time...'

'"Tough time" is putting it mildly, Luke comes from a bad home, his mother doesn't give a toss and his stepfather is a waste of space; he's used to a hard life – but this has broken him.'

Reese ran a hand over his tired eyes and Marnie felt a flicker of remorse as he sighed heavily.

'OK, what are you suggesting?' he asked.

Marnie thought for a moment before answering. 'The bruises are old, so I'd like to go to Park View and have a word with the person in charge.'

'That would be Gareth Walls,' Reese said.

Marnie looked on in surprise. 'You know the man?'

Reese pursed his lips. 'I know *of* him, and to be honest so should you.'

'Me?'

Reese nodded. 'Gareth Walls is the father of one of the three missing girls.'

Marnie felt the shock slam into her. '*Suzie Walls!*'

'Pam Oaks did all the follow-ups but so far they've found nothing new.'

Marnie felt the slight shake in her hands as she absorbed the information.

'I didn't realise her father was the Governor of Park View.'

'Yes, well, we've all been busy trying to piece things together,' he paused, 'in fact, I've met the man on a couple of occasions.'

Marnie looked up in surprise. 'What's he like?'

'Unblemished record, friends in high places.'

'Any hint of this sort of thing before?'

'Not to my knowledge.'

Marnie sighed, crossing her legs.

'Look, why don't you let the Witness Care Unit take over, Marnie, they're trained for this kind of thing, let them speak to Croft?'

'Not yet.'

Reese looked at her keenly. 'Taking the boy back to your house was a mistake, don't compound the problem.'

'I don't intend making things worse for Luke, but if I drag him in then any trust will vanish, and he'll run.'

'You're off shift today, aren't you?'

'That's right.'

'OK, here's the deal, get Croft to do the right thing, take him to the hospital. I want images of the bruises,' he paused, 'if he refuses then I'll have no choice but to involve the care unit.'

Marnie thought of arguing the point and then sighed. 'Fair enough,' she stood up, slid the chair back under the table and headed for the door.

'Twenty-four hours, Sergeant Hammond, and then I want you back, focused on finding Jenny Ball.'

Marnie stopped at the door and glanced over her shoulder. 'Understood,' she replied before leaving the room.

Reese rose and walked over to the window, the main road that passed the station was busy, a line of stop-start traffic heading into the town centre.

He pictured Gareth Walls, the last time they had met had been at a conference in Liverpool. Walls had been giving a keynote speech on the penal system in the twenty-first century. He had been impressive, though once or twice David had detected a note of arrogance in the man's demeanour. The truth was he had sounded more like a politician than the governor of a young offenders' unit.

Reese looked down as Marnie strode from the building, her brown hair swept over her shoulders, heading left to the car park.

With a sigh, he turned away and sat back at his desk, logging onto the computer he typed Park View into the search engine and started to read.

20

Hambling sat wrapped in the duvet, munching on a sausage roll, the stale pastry making him grimace, yet he shovelled the rest into his mouth, hunger pains gnawing at his innards. The journey into town had been fraught with terror, the streets crowded with people staggering in and out of the pubs. He had tried to stick to the shadows, hood pulled over his head, hands thrust into pockets as he cut left down the alleyway that led to the service road behind the shops. After half an hour scavenging through the bins, he had found a couple of pies wrapped in cling film and wolfed them down, crouching in the stinking darkness. The peppery pies left him with a raging thirst but after more desperate searching he had found nothing to drink apart from a bottle that, when he unscrewed the lid and took a sniff, made him recoil as the stink of piss wafted into his face. Emptying the contents, he had thrust the bottle into his pocket before heading back to the main road, nerves on high alert, he weaved his way through the crowds. Ten minutes later he had walked into the gents in the park; he swilled out the bottle, filling it with water and drinking the lot in one long swallow before refilling it. He'd looked at his reflection in the grimy mirror over the sink, his eyes red rimmed and haunted, his cheeks smothered with grey stubble. With a shake of the head he turned and walked out of the foul-smelling toilets and back into the darkness. The journey back to the derelict house seemed to take an age, he felt close to collapse as he stumbled back into the ruins. The rats had scuttled away into the darkness and Hambling had grabbed the duvet, shaking it before wrapping himself and laying down on the floor.

Now, he swallowed the sausage roll before taking a sip from the bottle of water. Through the broken window, he heard the low drone of an engine as a narrow boat chugged by. For some unknown reason, the sound brought tears to his eyes, the emotion welling inside his defences cracked and Christopher Hambling cried like a baby.

21

Marnie arrived home to find Luke sitting at the kitchen table, dressed in his clean jeans and hooded top, a cup of coffee on the go. When he saw her, his face blushed with embarrassment.

'I'm sorry for making a drink but…'

'You don't have to apologise,' Marnie smiled. 'Is there any hot water left in the kettle?'

'Er yeah, I think so.'

'I'll have coffee then, no sugar,' she said, slipping out of her summer jacket and hanging it over the back of the chair.

Luke hesitated, before rising and grabbing a cup from the drainer.

Marnie sat down, watching him make the drink before bringing it over and placing it on the table.

'I'm going to be honest with you, Luke, I've been to see my boss.'

He looked at her, though there was no real surprise in his eyes. Sitting down he hunched his shoulders in tight.

'What did they say?'

'Well, he was very understanding but we really need to have pictures taken of the bruises.'

'But why, I've already told you I never saw the ones who did it, I was asleep and it was dark, and…?'

'I realise that,' she paused, choosing her next words carefully. 'But being a police officer means I have to follow certain rules, now I can't make you help but it would make my life easier if you did.'

Luke glanced at her confusion in his eyes. 'But's what the point?'

'OK, you have no idea who attacked you but I noticed that some of the bruises on your back show the imprints of a shoe or boot.'

She watched as Luke licked his lips, his eyes watchful and bursting with nervous energy.

'Now, it's a long shot but if we can find a match for the tread then it would be a start and even if we don't then the images will be kept on file just in case.'

Luke wrapped his hands around the mug of coffee, his knuckles white as he held on tight.

'I mean, surely you want those who attacked you caught?'

Luke's face twitched, she could see the struggle in his eyes, the fear and indecision running rampant. Then he squared his shoulders and gave a brusque nod. 'OK, I'll do it,' he said.

Marnie took a sip from the cup and then smiled. 'Good. Now, as soon as you're ready we can head up to the hospital, it shouldn't take long.'

Tilting the cup, he drained it in one long swallow. 'I'm ready,' he said, wiping the back of his hand across his lips.

With a nod, Marnie rose, feeling like some duplicitous backstabber as they headed for the door.

22

The two boys dashed through the trees, every few seconds one of them would turn and raise their chunk of wood, firing wave after wave of imaginary bullets, cutting down a phantom army of zombies that shuffled towards them. '*Behind you, Billy!*'

Billy spun around and opened fire, his lips vibrating – making a brrrr sound – replicating the whine of the bullets.

The two boys grinned at one another.

'Thanks for the warning, Smithy.'

Smithy shrugged as if it was no big deal.

The boys moved deeper into the trees, the zombies momentarily forgotten about as the heat began to build.

'God, I'm thirsty,' Smithy complained, licking his dry lips.

Billy nodded in agreement, they'd set out early, both armed with drinks that had long since been supped, and now they were paying the price for their impatience.

Bright sunlight shafted down between the overhead canopy of leaves, trapping the heat at ground level.

They trudged along, side by side, the pretend guns in their hands, the sweat shiny on their skin, their feet shuffling through the swathe of fallen leaves.

Billy watched a grey squirrel zip up the bough of a tall beech tree, perch on a branch and look down, the bushy tail flicking.

Smithy pointed the makeshift gun upwards, drawing a bead on the squirrel. '*Bang!*' he shouted, grinning widely as the small animal vanished into the canopy of green.

'Good shot,' Billy said with admiration as they set off walking again.

When they came to the stream, both boys leapt into the shallow water, grinning at one another as their hot feet cooled off. Then Billy scrambled up the short bank and started to stamp his feet laughing as small jets of water shot out through the eye holes of his trainers. Smithy smiled, joining his friend on the bank; the boys stamped about, taking giant steps, their laughter ringing out beneath the trees, heads thrown back, sunlight playing across their faces.

Billy slammed his foot down and frowned feeling something crack beneath his trainer. He looked down, the smile falling from his face when he saw the small pale hand trapped under his foot.

The boy staggered back as his friend continued to goose step, flattening the grass and laughing.

Billy opened his mouth his eyes wide in terror. '*Zombie!*' He screeched.

Smithy stopped his stomping and looked at his friend, Billy had a hand clasped to his mouth, his face ashen. When he looked down and saw the hand poking out through the soil, Smithy leapt back in fright. The boys looked at one another, the horror emblazoned on their young minds; as one they turned and ran, leaping over the stream, their screams lancing out into the dry heat, terror spurring them on, they dashed away through the trees.

23

The man smiled at his reflection in the bathroom mirror, his hands plunged into the sink full of hot water. Now he had the ledger, he would be able to function as he did in the old days, the glory days. He had spent the afternoon going through the pages, at first each name had unlocked a memory long-since buried.

The list of girls' names had been longer than he remembered, each one providing him with a glimmer of the power he used to possess. Reaching the end of the ledger, he had studied the list of unfamiliar names, his brow knitted together trying to recall their significance. In the end, he had grunted in annoyance as the memories refused to be called forward.

'I was a busy bee,' he said, pulling the plug and watching the water swill away down the hole.

Placing his wet hands on the rim of the sink he leaned forward, tilting his head at the face that stared back at him. It felt strange to be looking at his reflection, it was something he used to do a lot of at one time, but as his mind started to falter he had avoided mirrors, afraid of what he would see staring back at him. He narrowed his black eyes and studied the image, his face no longer held the same strength as it had in his prime, the skin didn't cling tight to the cheekbones, his pallor was pale. Yet he still looked distinguished, the grey hair swept back over the high forehead, the eyes still glittered with the same dark light. He smiled again, all things considered he was satisfied with the reflection, the fear of seeing a frail old man hadn't materialised, the inner strength was still there if you looked closely enough.

He could feel the power returning slowly, forcing the confusion from his mind.

He blinked and suddenly he was back in the moment, the man turned and stalked through the house, moving from one room to the next, his stride confident, the smile locked in place.

When he reached the door that led down to the cellar he hesitated before twisting the handle and pulling the door open.

Pale light filtered down the flight of wooden stairs, the bottom remained lost to the darkness.

Reaching out, he pulled the cord to his right and a weak light pushed at the shadows. Slowly, he started to walk down, feet thumping on each step, the sound caused the memories to flare in his mind. He imagined his younger self taking the steps two at a time, the thought made him grimace as he held onto the rail and slowly edged down.

Reaching the bottom, he looked around the vast space littered with decades of junk, when he saw the huge Welsh dresser pushed against the wall on the right, his eyes sparked with malevolence.

Striding across the room he stopped, hands on hips, chest rising and falling, the excitement growing.

Grabbing the heavy piece of furniture, he heaved it to the right, muscles locked tight, a vein in his temple throbbed as he continued to shove the dresser along the dusty floor.

When the door came into view, he stopped and wiped the sweat from his brow with the back of his hand. Hot blood rushed through his veins, he grabbed the handle. The door squealed open and the fetid stink wafted out into his face. He breathed deeply through his nose relishing the stink, as if he were standing in a field of wild flowers.

'*Yes!*' he sang out, moving into the room.

Closing his eyes, his hand fumbled along the wall until he came to the hanging cord, tugging down he sensed light fill the room.

Slowly he cracked open his eyes, the heavy wooden table stood in the centre of the small space, the skulls lined up in a neat row exactly as he had left them.

Joy rose in his dark heart at the sight of them.

He moved forward on legs weak with rapture.

Reaching the table, the man stopped as he suddenly realised how lost he had been in the cauldron of his mind. He shuddered at the wasted years, years locked in confusion, growing old as he wandered around the house in a stupor, his mind unravelling.

How many times had he walked past the door to the cellar without noticing it, without realising the treasures held below?

Staggering from one dusty room to another like a child lost in an unforgiving maze.

Leaning forward, he planted his hands on the table, his muscles quivering with the fear of it.

He looked at the first small skull, the eyeless sockets were covered with cobwebs and he frowned as he reached out a hand and picked it up. As soon as his fingers closed on bone the thrill of electricity ran through his body, charging his brain with dark, firing neurons.

A scattering of spiders fell from the empty cavity and landed on the table, the man snarled and slapped his free hand on the table once, twice, three times, splattering the insects, grunting in satisfaction.

He lifted the skull up again and stared, tilting it back, a frown plucking at his brow as he looked at the teeth still lodged into the jaw.

'Too many sweeties,' he tutted, placing the skull back onto the table.

There were ten in all. Ten small skulls.

The smile on his face cracked into a wide, ghoulish grin.

'Monday's child, dead in a lake, Tuesday's child is mine to take, Wednesday's child is still in bed,' he paused to think for a moment, 'Thursday's child has lost her head,' he finished with a deep rumbling laugh of satisfaction.

24

Marnie stood in the back garden smoking a cigarette, she could hear Luke in the kitchen, the familiar sound of a spoon tinkling inside a cup drifted into the garden. After the photographs had been taken of Luke's bruised body, Marnie had sent him to the café with a five pound note while she hunted down the police pathologist.

Doc Kelly, was tall and lean he had a shock of dark hair that made his pale face appear even paler, he had smiled at Marnie before studying the images of Luke's bloodied and bruised body.

After a few seconds the smile had slipped from his face. 'Well, you're right about the bruises, there's no way they were inflicted within the past week,' he said, his voice still held a hint of Irish even though he had once told Marnie that he had been a kid when the family left Dublin.

They were sitting in his office, Kelly lounging his long frame into a chair that looked way too small for him.

'So, how long are we talking?' she asked.

Kelly pursed his lips. 'For the bruises to get to that colour – three to four weeks, possibly longer.'

Even though Marnie had suspected as much she still felt the anger crack in her mind to hear it confirmed.

'The boot prints are around a size nine, there are at least five separate injuries, though in my opinion they all came from the same boot.'

'So, one attacker?'

Kelly shrugged. 'More than likely, though of course he could have been held down by someone while another stamped on the boy. Though I can say that the bruises were not all inflicted at the same time. The variation in colour leads me to think that the boy was beaten on more than one occasion.'

Marnie sighed heavily at this latest revelation.

'In fact, I'm surprised there were no broken bones, but it seems as if the attacker concentrated on the torso and legs.'

'That makes sense,' Marnie replied.

Kelly raised a questioning eyebrow which arched even higher as Marnie explained about Luke spending time in Park View.

By the time she'd finished filling him in on the details, Kelly was the one sighing. 'It makes sense then, if he was beaten on the inside, the culprit would have left his face unmarked.'

Marnie nodded in agreement, hardly trusting herself to speak as she thought of Luke being systematically beaten by some faceless thug.

'I take it you'll be heading out to Park View to check this out?' Kelly asked as he slipped the images back into the folder and slid it across the desk to Marnie.

'Count on it,' she'd replied snatching them from the desk and heading out into the corridor.

'Can I borrow a cigarette?'

Marnie looked over her shoulder, Luke stood in the doorway, a steaming cup of coffee in his hand, his face blushing with embarrassment.

'Course you can,' she smiled, handing the pack over.

Her phone began to ring and she dipped a hand into her pocket, when she saw Reese's name flashing on the screen she tapped at the phone to answer it.

'Hello, boss, I was…'

Luke watched as the colour bled from Marnie's face, her left hand bunched into a fist as she listened to the voice on the other end of the phone. When tears sparkled in her eyes Luke lowered his gaze, shocked at the raw emotion in her gaze.

Two minutes later, Marnie was in the car and backing down the drive, Luke stood at the front door watching her drive away, his face etched with concern as he slowly closed the front door.

Half an hour later, Marnie was standing ankle deep in dry leaves, DCI Reese at her left side, both wearing matching looks of shock and anger as they stared down at the body of Jenny Bell.

Marnie couldn't take her eyes off the girl in the shallow grave, her unseeing eyes speckled with dark earth, her open mouth clogged with soil.

Reese cleared his throat, rubbing a hand across his eyes.

Marnie glanced at him before looking back down, she could see the silver stars on the blue party dress shining amongst the dirt. With a frown, she crouched onto her haunches, her eyes locked on the face of the girl, the skin drawn tight across the cheekbones, the fungus on Jenny's left cheek, a cheek that been plump and rosy just a few weeks ago but was now grey and hollow. Pulling on a glove she reached out and touched the sleeve of the dress, rubbing it between her finger and thumb before checking the glove for moisture.

When she heard the rustle of feet through the leaves, she glanced over her shoulder to find Doc Kelly walking towards them, his face unreadable. Marnie looked around, she could see several flashes of yellow as uniformed officers made a preliminary search of the area. She spotted Bev Harvey twenty feet away, the two women locked eyes until Bev turned away, her face blanched with shock.

Soon Marnie stood, flanked by Kelly and Reese around the make shift grave, like mourners, heads bowed as if in prayer. When Kelly looked at the face of Jenny Bell he scowled and shook his head.

'Bastard,' he mumbled.

'Feel the cloth,' Marnie said, suppressing her emotions, refusing to let them rule her.

Kelly looked at her before crouching to his haunches. 'Dryish,' he said with a puzzled frown.

'I want to know everything that happened to her, is that clear?' Reese said in a voice taught with anger.

Kelly looked up and nodded in understanding. 'As soon as SOCO have checked the scene, I'll have the body moved and get to work.'

Reese grunted an acknowledgement, his eyes still locked on the ravaged face that peered up at them from the dark earth. 'How long do you think she's been here?' he asked.

Kelly pursed his lips. 'Not long at all, like Marnie said the material is reasonably dry so chances are she didn't die here, and from the look of her face I'd say that she hadn't been fed or watered for some considerable time.'

'You think she starved to death?' the DCI asked through clenched teeth.

Kelly lifted his shoulders. 'It's possible, her skin has shrunk close to the bone, indicating a lack of fluid intake, but I'll know more once I've had a closer look at the body.'

Marnie slipped her hands into her pockets and looked at the huge oak tree, its branches stretched out above their heads, twisted and gnarled. Apart from the black scar in the earth, the rest of the ground was covered with leaves and patches of grass.

Marnie looked up at the sky, just visible through the new-leaved branches of the oak, these woods were attached to the park, the same park where she had found the skeletal arm of the unknown girl, the same woods that Abby had vanished in.

The thought made her heart race, she looked around at the trees and watched her fellow officers searching through the dappled undergrowth, looking for clues.

When Reese touched her arm she almost jumped in fright.

'You OK?' he asked.

Kelly flicked her a sympathetic look before turning back to the body.

'My sister went missing less than a mile from here,' she whispered.

Reese nodded in understanding. 'I know.'

'We've found a child's arm and now Jenny Bell in the same woods,' she turned and looked at her boss. 'What if there are more?'

Reese looked into her eyes, he could see the fear and anger of the unknown in the brown depths.

'Look, Marnie, this whole area will be searched but don't forget Hambling, he…'

'Hambling didn't take my sister, he didn't dump the arm in the woods.'

Reese nodded. 'I realise it's highly unlikely Hambling was involved in your sister's disappearance but until we have actual proof of anything we keep our options open, we cover all the bases.

Kelly stood up, grimacing at the ache in his back.

Marnie thought for a moment before answering. 'Hambling is on the run and if he's any sense, he would have left town weeks ago.'

'We don't know that,' Reese said, flapping a hand at a passing fly.

'Look, the doc's just said that the body hasn't been here for long, which means she was being kept somewhere else, somewhere warm and dry and…'

'Hambling could still be in town, holed up somewhere, he…'

'But his money's been stopped and he has no friends in the area so he has to be living rough. I mean, Hambling never even learned to drive so he can't have wheels and I doubt whether he walked through town with Jenny Bell thrown over his shoulder, he…'

'Is that some kind of sick bloody joke?' Reese asked, his eyes hardening.

Kelly looked at the pair of them, the warm air filled with tension, then he stepped forward. 'Marnie's right, if Hambling can't drive then how did he get the body here?'

Reese threw him a sharp look. 'Hambling could have been hiding in the woods keeping the girl hostage while…'

'No way,' Kelly said, with a shake of the head. 'If Jenny Bell had been forced to live out in the open for over nine weeks then her clothes would have been in tatters and soiled. Whoever did this kept her indoors.'

Reese looked from one to the other, his eyes flashing with impotent anger. 'We still need to find the man, he's still our main priority and I want him caught.'

Marnie nodded absently, her mind going through the facts, it was almost fifteen years since Abby had been taken, and the unknown bones in the woods had laid there for over a decade. Then there was Piper Donald, India Foster and Suzie Walls still missing, the years sliding by and no news for their distraught families. She looked around the woods again and shivered as if she were standing in the middle of an unmarked graveyard, the bodies waiting to be discovered, her sister's amongst them. The thought took her breath away, remembering Abby being carried away over the shoulder of the faceless man.

'*Whippersnapper.*' The word reverberated through her mind, bringing all the fear and loathing back in an instant.

When the two men approached through the trees dressed in white paper suits Reese turned to face them. 'I want her moving ASAP before the media circus gets here. I don't want those bloody vultures anywhere near her, and treat the young lass with respect, lads. She saw little of that in the last weeks of her life.'

The men nodded in understanding as Reese backed away from the grave. Marnie remained standing by the dislodged earth, Doc Kelly by her side, her mind a million miles away from this place of death, locked in the endless loop of grief and guilt. In her mind the sky darkened, the clouds gathered and the memory of thunder rumbled overhead. One of the SOCO team coughed, pulling her mind back from the nightmare.

Doc Kelly placed his hand on her arm. 'You OK?'

Marnie chewed her bottom lip and nodded before turning away and walking over to where Reese stood by the trunk of the huge oak.

'What do you want me to do?' her voice was barren of emotion.

'How did it go with Luke Croft?' Reese queried, thrusting his hands into his pockets.

Marnie looked at her boss in surprise.

The DCI raised an eyebrow. 'As you said, the bad guys are still out there and we have a job to do.'

'I never said that,' Marnie replied.

Reese gave her a cold stare. 'Look are you going to tell me or not?'

By the time Marnie had finished explaining that the bruises on Luke's body were at least three weeks old, Reese's eyes had hardened.

'Right, head to Park View, take Paul Clark with you and find out what the hell happened to the lad.'

'Are you sure?'

Reese threw her a tired smile. 'I know you, Marnie, you won't be able to concentrate on anything until you've checked it out.'

'Are you saying I can't do my job?' she asked, her eyes narrowing.

Reese held up his hand. 'That's not what I'm saying and you know it.'

Marnie felt the colour rise in her cheeks and then she nodded before turning and walking away.

Reese watched as she went in search of Paul Clark, within seconds she had vanished from sight.

When he turned, Kelly was walking towards him, his feet brushing through the dry leaves. 'You gave her something to do in case we find her sister, didn't you?' the doctor asked.

Reese sighed and nodded. 'I can't have her here when we start digging, it wouldn't be right.'

Kelly grunted in agreement, then Reese clapped a hand on the doctor's back. 'Right come on, we have work to do.'

25

L uke tried to block out the voices, but they wouldn't be
denied. He sat perched on the edge of the bed, fully dressed,
his mind in turmoil, his trainers shuffling back and forth
on the carpet.

"Make a sound and see what fucking happens, you little shit."

He chewed his lip in fear, remembering the hand pulling him
up by the hair, his tormentor's breath hot and sour as he pushed
his face in close.

It had been his first night in Park View and after a few short
hours locked up with Alby Roper, Luke had been left in a state of
terror, wondering how he was going to survive the next few days,
let alone weeks.

Closing his eyes, he pictured the sadistic thug, his broad face
smothered with acne and blackheads, his full lips drawn back in
a sneer of glee when he stamped down onto Luke's back while he
lay curled on the cell floor. The next two months passed in a haze
of never-ending beatings and torture.

The day he had been released, Luke had walked the five miles
home, his mind crammed with fear, his body broken. Twice he
had collapsed onto the quiet roadside verge, sobbing hysterically
in relief and fear. By the time he arrived home it was growing
dark. His mother had been at work, Oldman, his stepfather, had
been sprawled on the sofa, he hadn't even glanced at Luke as he
made his way slowly up to his room. That night the nightmares
had arrived, the terror so acute that Luke had been forced to run
from the house, convinced that there would be no refuge here if
Alby Roper came calling. He hadn't been back since and as far as
he knew no one was looking for him. No doubt Oldman was still

ensconced on the sofa and his mother had never cared what had happened to her only son.

"*You're safe here.*" DS Hammond's words came back to him. She had helped him, brought him to her home when he had no one to turn to.

Surely, he could trust her? His hands pulled at one another anxiously, the bitter voice in his head snorted at the notion. She wasn't interested in *him*, it said. All she wants is to get to the truth, to use him to catch his attacker. Luke tried to calm the doubt, but he knew the voice spoke the truth. He was nothing, just a means to an end, and when she had stirred the wasps' nest he would be alone again. Luke pushed himself up from the bed, the fear slowly engulfing him.

He tried to think what he would do, where he would go when it all came out, and the truth was he had nowhere to run. His so-called home wasn't safe, he pictured his bastard stepfather, Oldman, answering the door, a sour grin on his face.

"*The little bastard's in his room.*" Oldman would say, hooking a thumb towards the stairs.

Luke would be hiding under the bed as heavy boots thundered up the stairs, Luke's mother even got in on the act, standing in the corner of the bedroom, smoking a cigarette, as the hulking figure grabbed his legs and yanked him from his pitiful hiding place.

Luke gasped and looked around the unfamiliar bedroom, he had been mad to come here, what had he been thinking?

It was DS Hammond who had got him locked up in the first place, and now he had allowed himself to be brought back here because he had felt desperate.

She'd promised to help him, and yet she had conned him, making him think that she cared, that she gave a shit. When the truth was, all she had done was drag him over to the hospital to have photographs taken of his bruised body.

Luke had watched her take the call before dashing out to the car. Now his brain paraded the images through his fearful mind, she had dashed off because somehow, they had found the person responsible for his torture. Luke saw the scenario with such startling clarity that it made him feel physically sick. He shuffled from one foot to the other in agitation, wondering what madness had taken over his mind.

He tried to remain calm, but the demons were loose, he bolted from the room taking the stairs two at a time. Fear was running rampant, clinging to him and smothering his mind in a terror so intense that it drove all rational thoughts from his mind. Yanking open the front door, he ran out into the late afternoon sunshine, sprinting away from the house that had promised sanctuary but now felt like a trap.

The driver of a JCB watched as the scruffy-looking kid sprinted off down the street, feet flying as if the devil himself were giving chase.

'Bloody scally on the rob,' he thought, as he reached for his mobile phone.

26

Gareth Walls sat behind his desk dressed in a charcoal-grey suit, his black tie knotted to perfection beneath the collar of his crisp, white shirt. His dark hair was cut short, military style, his face stern, eyes watchful.

The air conditioning droned, keeping the stifling heat at bay, the solitary window stayed closed.

Paul Clark remained standing the freckles on his pale face standing out beneath the glare of the overhead light, Marnie sat facing Walls, the blue file on her lap, her eyes hard as she opened her mouth to explain about Luke Croft and the bruising that covered his body.

'Have you found Hambling yet?' Walls demanded, leaning forwards, and planting his elbows on the desk.

Marnie closed her mouth and looked at the man facing her, she could see the anger burning deep in his dark eyes, his lips a thin line.

'I'm sorry, Mr Walls, we haven't but...'

'Why not?'

'Let me assure you that we are doing all we can to...'

'You have a convicted child molester out there,' he jabbed a finger towards the window. 'You have no idea where he is yet you sit there and tell me you're doing all you can...'

'I'm sorry, Mr Walls, but that's not the reason I'm here,' she responded.

Walls frowned in sudden confusion. 'What are you talking about?'

Opening the file Marnie pulled out one of the photographs and placed it on the desk.

Walls's eyes widened slightly as he glanced down at the photograph.

'What the hell is this?' he demanded, slapping a hand down on the image.

'We have reason to believe that the bruises were inflicted on the victim whilst he was under your care,' Marnie replied, before explaining about the injuries and how they had brought her to Park View to get answers.

Walls closed his eyes for a moment, and Marnie could see the muscles in his jaw working as if the man were trying to suppress a rage that threatened to swamp him. 'So, how can I help?' he eventually replied in clipped tones.

Marnie eased forward in her chair. 'Tell me, Mr Walls, do you remember a boy named Luke Croft?'

Walls nodded sharply. 'I see it as part of my duties to know all the boys who are sent here.'

'And what did you make of Luke?'

Walls thought for a moment before replying. 'A quiet boy who liked to keep to himself, he caused no trouble, though I doubt whether he made friends easily during his stay.'

'You say Luke caused no trouble?' Marnie asked.

'That's correct.'

'So, I assume you have others who do?'

Walls drummed his fingers on the desk for a moment before easing back in the leather swivel chair. 'I'm afraid we don't have the *luxury* of picking and choosing who comes to the unit. There are some boys who really shouldn't be here due to their behaviour but I don't make the rules, I simply try to ensure that when they are here, the more volatile boys are monitored closely to ensure minimum disruption to others in my care.'

'Well, it seems as if this time the monitoring you speak of failed.'

Walls folded his arms and tilted his head. 'Over the past twelve months a reduction in funding has left this unit cut to the bone, I've tried to rectify matters though the money simply isn't there, we have to rely on part-time staff provided by an agency, now this is far from ideal but I work with what I have. All I can say is if this happened here then it was done without my knowledge.'

'Do the boy's share a room?' Paul Clark asked.

Walls flicked him a glance before nodding. 'Again, it isn't always ideal, some of the boys are fine sharing a room whilst others don't mix, and...'

'What about Luke Croft?' Marnie asked, sliding another image forward.

Walls held her gaze, ignoring the picture on his desk depicting more bruising.

Instead, he slid the chair to the left and started to tap at a keyboard.

After a few seconds the governor leaned forward studying the screen. 'On arrival Croft was placed in a single room, though three days later we had something of a surge of boys entering the unit and he was moved into a double.'

'I want the name of the boy he shared the room with.' Marnie demanded.

'Certainly,' Walls replied and tapped a few more keys before pressing enter. In the corner of the room a printer sprang to life; Walls rose to his feet and crossed the room to retrieve the paper.

'For the remainder of his stay Luke Croft shared a room with one Albert Roper,' he explained, as he sat back down.

'Unusual name for a teenager,' Clark commented.

'He preferred the name Alby,' Walls continued.

'What was he in for?'

The governor sighed as he leaned across the desk and handed her the paper.

Marnie looked at the printout, the sheet of A4 contained an image of Alby Roper staring out at her and her eyes widened in shock, he didn't look like a teenager but a fully-grown man, the lower part of his face was covered with stubble, his broad forehead peppered with angry-looking spots. Dark eyes glared out at her, hard and unflinching. Marnie began to read about Roper, her frown deepening as she scanned the catalogue of offences ranging from theft to assault.

'As I said, some of the boys shouldn't be here, they...'

'It says here he's seventeen,' Marnie said in disbelief.

'Looks older I know, and acts it as well, but as I said I don't make the rules,' Walls sighed heavily.

'I want to see him right now.'

'Not possible,' Gareth Walls replied.

Marnie frowned at the response.

'If you look at the final line you'll see that Mr Roper was released a week ago.' Walls explained.

Marnie looked back at the paper, she could feel the anger seething inside though now it had no outlet.

'Roper served his time and caused no trouble whilst here,' Walls said. 'I understand why you came but the boys were released around the same time and then Luke Croft is attacked. Now, I can't be one hundred percent sure that it didn't happen in here but I assure you that each and every one of the boys are told that my door is always open and if they are having problems then I want to know about it, and Croft never knocked on my door, he...'

'Perhaps he was too busy being beaten and trying to survive, he didn't have the time or the nerve to come knocking on your door,' Marnie replied in a cold voice.

Walls held her gaze, his own eyes sparking with anger. 'I have no idea about any of that, now, Roper's last known address is printed on the notes I gave you so perhaps it would be more prudent to speak to him.'

"*Prudent!*"

Walls nodded, ignoring the sarcasm completely. 'Of course, I shall be looking into things at this end but as I said, Luke Croft never complained and no members of staff mentioned anything about any problems between the two boys. If they had, then I would have taken direct action but I can only do that if problems are flagged.'

At her side, she heard Paul Clark sigh, he knew the conversation was over.

Marnie stood up and gathered the two images from the desk, Walls remained seated, she slid them back into the folder and then stopped, a frown plucking at her brow.

She searched through the pictures before pulling one out and slapping it down on the desk.

'Does the tread mark look familiar?'

Walls leaned forward studying the image, his mouth twisted briefly as he nodded. 'I will admit it looks similar to the standard issue footwear that we provide for the boys.'

'You see the thing is the bruises are old, I've had them checked and according to the expert they were inflicted a minimum of three weeks ago, and up until five days ago, this boy was still in this unit.'

Marnie felt a flush of satisfaction until Walls looked up at her, his face impassive.

'As I said, I know nothing about that but I can tell you that the boys who arrive often have little in the way of material goods. So, when they leave they are allowed to keep the footwear if they so wish.'

Marnie glared in frustration, there was something about the governor of Park View that she didn't like, a hint of insolence hidden deep in his eyes. The twist of his mouth when she had shown him the picture of Luke could have been one of shock but as she looked at Walls she suspected that it had been something more. Almost as if he had been playing some dark game, one in which he had all angles covered.

Snatching the picture from the desk she turned and gave Paul Clark the nod.

'So, can I expect to be kept in the loop about Hambling?' Walls asked.

Marnie slipped the images back into the file as she thought about Jenny Bell, her eyes open and mouthed stuffed with black earth and wondered how Walls would react when he discovered they had found the missing girl.

'I'm sorry for your grief,' she replied, 'but the chances of Hambling being involved with the disappearance of your daughter are slim and...'

'*Slim!*' Walls spat as he rose slowly from his chair, his face flushed.

Marnie nodded. 'I'm afraid so, of course once we catch up with Hambling then we'll know more but for now we have to keep an open mind.'

'People like Hambling are the scum of the earth, I mean, he'd already done this type of thing before and instead of being locked up for life he's let out to do it again!' Gareth Walls snarled.

Marnie looked at the man and sighed, she could see the anger in his eyes, anger and pain over the disappearance of his daughter. 'The day your daughter vanished Christopher Hambling was serving time so I'm afraid he wasn't responsible and...'

'What about Jenny Bell?' Walls hissed, planting his hands on the desk and leaning towards her.

'I'm sorry but I'm not in a position to comment about an ongoing investigation.'

Walls shook his head in disgust. '*Typical,*' he spat, turning away and walking over to the window, his back to the pair of them.

Two minutes later he watched Marnie and her colleague walk across the courtyard and climb into the car. His eyes grew narrow as she drove to the electric gates and spoke to the guard, then the gates glided open and she pulled out onto the country lane.

Walls remained at the window as if admiring the view, but the hands behind his back were bunched into fists.

'Little bitch,' he snarled, the car vanishing from view.

27

Reese stood ankle deep amongst the leaves, his face set in lines of sorrow as the remains of Jenny Bell were loaded into the rubber body bag; the flies buzzing angrily as their tasty meal was removed. When he saw the scattering of maggots squirming in the dark earth he felt the anger flair.

Looking around the woods, he could see yellow hi-visvests moving through the undergrowth, the team searching the area, thrashing at the brambles with white batons like an army of the blind.

Doc Kelly nodded to the two men who hoisted the body between them and set off walking through the trees.

'As soon as we get back to the mortuary I'll make a start,' Kelly said.

Reese nodded in understanding, watching a magpie hop along the ground before taking to flight.

Somewhere amongst the trees he heard a dog bark, there were three handlers searching the woods looking for clues that probably didn't exist.

Kelly clapped a hand on the DCI's shoulder. 'Catch you later,' the doctor said as he headed off between the trees.

Reese rubbed at his eyes trying to figure out what had happened. If what Kelly had said were true, then Jenny Bell had been kept somewhere warm and dry away from the elements. He thought of Hambling, a man on the run, a man who had never learned to drive and he grimaced as he realised that Marnie had been right. Whoever had brought Jenny Bell to the woods would had to have transportation. Unless Hambling had help disposing of the body. Reese shook his head dismissing the idea, all the reports into Hambling pointed to the fact that he was a loner, no family or friends, a man who had spent his life trying to avoid contact with the human race. As soon as he had become a suspect Hambling's bank account had been frozen, his benefits stopped which meant he would have no access to money and yet nine weeks later the man hadn't surfaced. Reese looked up at the huge oak, late-afternoon sunlight speared down through the leaves making him wince at the onslaught.

When the shout lanced out in the distance Reese snapped his head up, the dog started to bark again only this time the tone had changed, there was an urgency behind the sound. Another shout went up and Reese pinpointed the location and set off walking, when the animal started to howl Reese broke into a run, his skin crawling as more shouts echoed through the hot, still air. He weaved his way around the trees, dipping low under branches and snatching his feet free from the tangle of brambles that grew close to the ground. To his left and right he saw flashes of yellow, closing in on the area. Reese rounded another huge oak to find a group of half a dozen officers standing in a semi-circle. Striding forwards, he elbowed one officer to the side and then the shock hit him as he looked down at the scattering of white bones looking appallingly stark against the black earth.

28

As he cleaned the trophies time, lost all meaning. The man lovingly polished the bones with a soft, white cloth. All the cobwebs and dust had been removed and now he stood back to admire his handiwork.

Closing his eyes, he took a deep breath, tentatively searching his mind, afraid that the confusion would still be lurking in the shadows waiting to smother his thoughts.

He walked down the familiar mind corridor, except now, all the locked doors were open. Stopping outside the one with the prancing ponies he smiled as he looked into the bedroom beyond, the single bed complete with plumped pillows, the walls painted pink. He looked towards the small dresser by the side of the bed, littered with dolls and ribbons.

The man clapped his hands together in wonderment before snapping open his eyes and staring at the first skull.

'Hello, Samantha,' he whispered adoringly, closing his eyes again, instantly he was back in the tunnel of red and grey.

This time the fairies on the door were moving sluggishly over the wooden panels, reaching out he ripped one free, convinced that he could hear the tiny muffled scream as he closed his fist.

This room was similar to the first, the bed, the wardrobe, the walls painted in the subtle hint of pink that young girls loved so much.

Once again, he opened his eyes and glanced at the second skull. 'Piper,' he sighed, before moving to the next.

Each door stood open, revealing the room beyond, each one illuminating the name of the long-dead occupant.

'India, Josie,' he spoke the names like an incantation as he moved from room to room. 'Elizabeth, Ann, Suzie,' his heart sang as the names floated through his mind like butterflies waiting to plucked from the still air. 'Petra, Lucy, Marcie,' he finished and laughed a deep rumbling sound.

Closing his eyes again he strode down the corridor, when he reached the black door he stopped and frowned, the door was closed, the paint still peeling. The man looked down, his face twisted in confusion as he saw the water seeping out from beneath the door, he watched as it ran towards him before pooling around his feet.

His heart stuttered, the joy started to fade and he felt the old familiar sense of apprehension filter through his mind.

Reaching out, he grabbed the handle and pushed, when the door creaked open he gasped and took a step back, his eyes widening in astonishment.

There was no bed, no dolls, and no pink-painted walls. Behind the door, it was raining, tall trees groaned in the wind that howled like a hurricane.

The cinder path twisted away between the trees and the man stepped forward, the wind tugging at his clothing, the rain falling on his head and shoulders.

He looked down and shifted his feet on the rough path, the frown furrowing his brow, the thunder rumbling overhead.

What was this place, he pondered as his clothes became saturated?

'Abby!'

The word slammed into him and he snapped a look over his shoulder. The girl was sprinting down the long corridor, hair flying, her face fixed with fear; the man turned, his hands suddenly shaking as she tore towards him. Closer still and he could see he had mistaken the look on her face, it wasn't fear at all but hatred, a boiling, contemptuous look of pure hatred.

Suddenly, he felt the fear erupt inside the core of him and he lunged back and grabbed the handle, slamming the door shut with a gasp.

Seconds later, he heard the girl hit the panel with a dull thud. '*KILL YOU!*' she screamed.

He took two, faltering, backward steps and dragged his eyes open, he was back in the room of skulls, heart pounding, body coated in the sweat of terror.

His legs buckled and he fell hard to his knees, the sound of her hands hitting the door was still locked in his mind, mingling with the distant rumble of thunder.

Lowering his head, he tried to breathe, tried to steady his jittering nerves, a sliver of drool hung from his open mouth as he planted his hands on the hard, cold floor.

'*Abby,*' he whispered the name in hushed tones. 'The one that got away,' he snarled as the memories hit him in a jumble of chaotic thoughts. '*Whippersnapper!*' he screamed, his head tilted to the ceiling like a wolf howling at the moon.

29

The car hurtled along the country lane, Paul Clark held on tight to the seatbelt, his eyes widening in alarm as the car sped around a left-hand bend, the wheels clipping the grass verge, the stone wall looming large in the side window. Marnie sat hunched behind the wheel, her eyes narrowed, the anger tearing her up inside.

'*Easy, boss!*' Clark yelped nervously, as the car barrelled down the road.

Marnie never even heard him, her mind was a cauldron of turmoil, she could picture Walls's face, the insolence in his eyes, she thought of Luke – battered, bruised and afraid to open his mouth, terrified to tell the truth about what had happened during his stay in Park View.

The junction approached and Paul slammed his left foot down, desperately pressing an imaginary brake.

'*Boss!*' he bellowed.

Marnie blinked and hit the pedal, smoke poured from the tortured tyres, the car juddered before skidding to a halt.

Paul had his hands planted on the dashboard, his panicked eyes glaring out into the growing darkness.

'Are you OK?' she asked, turning in her seat.

'I thought we were going to end up in the bloody field.'

Marnie threw him a ragged smile before easing up to the junction and turning right, keeping a lock on her anger, and one eye on the speedometer.

When the two-way radio beeped, Paul leaned down and unhooked the handset.

'Four-seven,' he said, pinching the bridge of his nose between finger and thumb.

'Paul, is Marnie with you?'

Clark's eyes widened as he recognised DCI Reese's voice.

'She's driving at the moment, sir.'

'Right, well, tell her to pull over.'

Marnie immediately indicated and came to a halt on the left. As soon as she snatched the handbrake on, Paul handed the control over to her.

'I'm here.'

'We've found more remains.'

Marnie felt her heart stall, the sides of the car seemed to shrink, closing in around her as the first spots of rain hit the windscreen.

'They were found in a shallow grave about a hundred yards from Jenny Bell.'

Paul Clark sighed, a sound full of bitter distress; Marnie watched the rivulets of water trickle down the windscreen before closing her eyes. She thought of the images the Bells had provided of their daughter. In each of the photographs Jenny had been smiling, her plump cheeks rosy red and dimpled.

'Are you still there?' Reese asked.

Marnie opened her eyes. 'Still here.'

'We found a daisy ring on the finger of the left hand.'

Marnie jerked back in the seat, when she glanced at Clark he had his eyes closed, his big hands gripped together in his lap.

'We're on our way,' Marnie said, trying to absorb the information.

'I've had the area cordoned off and I was just on my way to the hospital to catch up with Kelly so meet me there.'

'The hospital, right,' she repeated automatically.

The radio beeped and Reese vanished.

Marnie sat hunched over wheel, her face set in grim lines of anger, the image of a smiling Jenny Bell branded onto the front of her mind surrounded by a scattering of old bones; and amongst the remains she feared finding one small fleshless hand, the tip of the little finger missing.

30

The man had the ledger open on the table, he sat going through the pages slowly, methodically, taking each word and absorbing it before reading the next.

He had rearranged the skulls into a horseshoe shape, drawing them closer towards him; the smile flickered as he glanced at the white domes, staring back at him with empty sockets.

Lowering his head, he looked at the name, Piper Donald, printed in his neat handwriting. Everything was there, her address, the name of her parents, John and Anne, the infant school she had attended, there were even details of her brother, Thomas.

He nodded in satisfaction as he continued to read, he had taken her in the park, but there had been nothing random about the act, it had been planned, by the time he had her he had known everything of value about Piper Donald.

'*You see now, don't you?*' the voice inside asked.

The man nodded a reply.

'*You've lasted this long because you planned everything, every detail.*'

Turning the page, he started to read about Samantha, reaching out he patted one of the skulls, the smile creeping ever wider.

Samantha Clove had been eight and just on the cusp of being ignored by the man but there had been something about her that had appealed to him, she had been small for her age, petite, the same light curly hair, the same spray of freckles on her cheeks.

He read the address and suddenly he was back on the deserted street as the sun sank slowly behind the houses. Samantha had been walking back from the shop, no doubt running an errand for her mother. The man absently ran a hand over his greying hair, her father had been killed at the steelworks where he worked, a freak accident the local paper had called it, he had been crushed when a sheet of steel had slipped from a forklift, SPLAT! He rumbled a deep laugh at the notion. As usual fate, had smiled on him – he had planned and she had been in the car in a matter of seconds, sprawled across the passenger seat, the bruise shining on her cheek as he spirited Samantha away.

It had taken four hours to get her back to the house, there had been jams on the motorway, holiday traffic cramming the lanes.

By the time he made it home he had been close to exhaustion, though he had taken the time to carry the girl up to the room with the hard, wooden bench. Samantha had been awake and paralysed with fear, he recalled standing over her, drinking in the emotion as tears trickled from her terrified eyes.

The temptation to stay and begin the fun and games had been immense, though he knew that if he gave in to temptation then it would have been over too quickly and all the carefully laid plans would be for nothing. Self-control was part of the process, so he had backed away, locking the heavy door before heading downstairs for something to eat.

Time passed, though in the windowless room he had no idea that the sun was heading slowly to earth, he remained with his head bent as he went through the list of names, absorbing every detail.

India had a birthmark on the back of her neck a fact that he had only discovered when removing her head with the hacksaw.

Petra's heart had stopped beating in terror and he sighed as he recalled trying to give CPR, desperate to keep her alive, but she had died with a gasp, leaving him furious.

He felt a flicker of the old power flowing through his veins, back then life had been good, he had felt immense in every way.

Closing his eyes, he pictured their faces, some were nervous as he leaned over them, others held nothing but trust in their innocent eyes. Later they had all seen his true face and he had loved the moment when the trust vanished and he revealed the monster behind the mask.

Turning another page, his face slipped into a savage twist of anger.

Abby Hammond aged eight, the address printed in his usual writing; mother, Susan, father, Richard, sister, Marnie.

He stopped as he pictured the girl running down the grey corridor, hair flying, the hatred flashing out as she flew towards him.

The man swallowed the sense of unease, jabbing a finger down at the name Abby he tried to concentrate, tried to think what had happened to her but the truth remained shrouded in the mists of time.

He felt the sense of confusion crackling at the boundaries of his mind, sliding his finger along the page he stopped again and the anger ripped through his body making him shudder under the impact, his finger had stopped on the name, Marnie.

31

Sally watched her husband slice into the steak, blood oozed, pooling on the pristine white plate as he studied the meat on the end of his fork before placing it in his mouth. The tension mounted as he chewed, his eyes closed, heavy jaw working from side to side; when he smiled, Sally felt a flood of relief.

'Good, very good.'

She smiled anxiously in return. 'The butcher said it was the finest cut.'

The knife sliced off another chunk of sirloin as he set about eating the meal.

'Carrots are a little overcooked,' he frowned, stabbing his fork into the orange vegetable.

'Really?' she asked, the nerves suddenly back.

'Took your eye off the ball, did you?'

Sally kept her mouth closed, the fear inside building with every passing second.

'Why would you do that, cook a wonderful steak to perfection, and then boil the carrots to mush and spoil the experience?'

Sally felt the familiar fear slither over her skin. 'I'm sorry, I thought you would have been home a little earlier, and...'

'So, this is my fault, is that what you're telling me?' he asked, arching a quizzical eyebrow.

'No, no of course not.'

Pushing the plate away – slowly – he folded his arms. 'You know I work in a stressful environment, don't you?'

Sally nodded rapidly in agreement, her shoulders slumped as if she knew what was coming next.

'I work hard, keeping the scum of the earth behind bars and then I come home to overcooked carrots.'

In any other situation, it would have been laughable, after all overcooked carrots didn't equate to the end of the world, but Sally knew better than to argue the point.

'Occasionally I eat at work, and yet I've *never* had carrots cooked like this. Now what does that say about you?'

'I could cook some fresh, I've got plenty and...'

'Don't bother,' he rose from the chair, his dark eyes flashing in anger.

Sally looked at him fearfully, he seemed to fill the room, his chin jutting, his brow furrowed. 'I can't stomach the sight of you, so I suggest you make yourself scarce.'

Sally didn't need telling twice, she lurched to her feet and turned for the door.

'So, you expect me to clear away the dishes?' her husband asked, sarcastically.

Sally stopped halfway across the kitchen, her eyes closed, her bottom lip taking a battering from her top teeth.

She turned slowly; he stood hands behind his back, eyes like chips of flint.

Sally started to clear up, gathering the plates with shaking hands.

'You really are pathetic, aren't you?'

She nodded in agreement as she grabbed the knives and forks.

'I'm going to my study because if I have to look at you for one more minute then both of us will be sorry.'

Sally felt the panic mutate into fear, it was a sentence she was familiar with, though she also knew that *she* would be the one who was sorry not him.

Crossing the room, she hurriedly scraped the food into the bin before placing the plates in the sink, her ears attuned for the heavy footfall of her husband. Convinced that any second she would feel his grip on her arms, and then...

Rinsing the plates, she hurriedly opened the dishwasher door; when the plate slipped from her hand and shattered on the floor, she yelped, her pulse racing, the fear clambering through her body as if her very soul was trying to escape the inevitable retribution.

Silence.

Sally remained hunched over, the dishwasher door open, fragments of shattered plate at her feet.

When she heard the kitchen door slam she spun around, to find the room empty.

Sally slid slowly to the floor the tears came, her face screwed up in anguish. She looked around the large kitchen, everything immaculate, though to Sally Walls it felt like one of the cells at Park View, and she was nothing more than one of Gareth's inmates, locked up and terrified.

32

Marnie had beaten Reese to the morgue and now she felt the tears prickling her eyes as she looked down at the body of Jenny Bell, Paul Clark by her side, his face pasty with shock.

'What did he do to her?' she asked in a voice thick with emotion.

Doc Kelly pursed his lips. 'As I suspected earlier she was starved to death.'

Marnie's hand went to her mouth in shock; Clark took a backward step and coughed.

'*Starved?*' she repeated in disbelief.

Kelly nodded, his face grave. 'The stomach cavity was empty and there was nothing in the intestines, you've seen the pictures of Jenny before she was taken?'

Marnie nodded.

'I'd say that she'd had no access to food for at least six to seven weeks.'

Marnie shivered at the revelation. 'What else?'

Kelly paused before answering as if gathering his thoughts. 'There's no evidence of sexual abuse, though there is some slight bruising around the lower part of her face but nothing on the rest of the body.'

'And you're sure she was kept indoors?' Marnie asked.

'Positive, the skin was completely dried out, I have no doubt that she was kept somewhere warm and dry away from the elements. I know the weather has been warm but temperatures plummet at night and that would have affected the body. I've checked the fingernails, if she had been in the outdoors there would have been earth beneath the nails, as it was I found some flakes of what looks like brown paint.'

Marnie flicked him a glance. 'Paint?'

'I've had it sent off for analysis but I'm pretty sure it was paint.'

Marnie closed her eyes, picturing Jenny in some locked room, her hands clawing at the door in an effort to escape, her cries growing fainter as her body weakened through lack of food and water.

'Why would someone take her just to let her starve to death?' Clark asked.

Marnie opened her eyes and thought about the question, Kelly lifted his shoulders in a shrug. 'God alone knows.'

Marnie cleared her throat. 'Reese said other bones had been found in the woods.'

The doctor looked at her and nodded. 'I'm expecting them here anytime soon.'

Marnie chewed her bottom lip in distress, the image of Abby pushing at her mind.

'As soon as they get here I'll get straight onto it,' Kelly offered, his dark eyes watchful.

Marnie managed to drag up a grateful smile. 'Thanks.'

'Soon as I know anything I'll let you know.'

Marnie took one last look at the remains of Jenny Bell before turning and walking from the room with Clark in pursuit.

Kelly watched her go before covering the body with the thin plastic sheet, a sigh of sorrow escaping his lips.

33

Alby Roper was steaming mad; he had been sprawled on the bed in the shitty flat, paper peeling off the walls, munching on a tasteless burger and taking gulps from his third can of cider when his phone had bleeped. Reaching out he grabbed it, his pitted face turning to stone as he read the message in disbelief, the sender's name had been withheld.

It stated that Luke Croft had been to the police and told them who was responsible for the beatings in Park View. The text ended with Croft's address.

Roper pushed himself up from bed as he tried to fathom who could have sent the warning text, then he smiled and grunted before grabbing his jacket and storming from the flat, his mind bubbling with anger, the scrawny face of Luke Croft branded onto his brain. Croft had grassed and now all that mattered was getting to the house and beating the shit out of the snidey little prick.

It took him an hour to walk across town, his mood darkening with every step, the disbelief clanging through his head.

Now, he watched as the man walked down the drive of the scruffy-looking council house. The sun had vanished, the warm air slowly cooling as the streetlights struggled to life.

The house reminded him of his old gaff in Liverpool, a shitty street with broken glass scattered across the potholed road. He counted three houses in the row boarded up, the gardens infested with weeds.

Draining a can of something cheap, the man tossed it into the overgrown garden of the house next door before walking away down the dimly-lit road.

Checking left, Roper flicked his hood up and jogged across the road, cutting onto the drive and hurrying alongside the house. The back garden was a mess, a shed skewed at an angle, half of the roof had caved in, the lawn rutted, the grass patchy and bare in places.

Moving to the back door he tried the handle, grimacing when he found it locked. Taking a step back, Roper lashed out his right foot, and the door bounced inwards.

Stepping into the darkened kitchen he sniffed, the familiar stink of stale booze mixed with the whiff of cannabis filled the air. Sauntering down the hall, he glanced into the empty living room, the sofa had a man-sized dent in the cushions, the television remote placed on the arm, three empty cans lay scattered on the floor, a glass ashtray full to overflowing on a small, battered coffee table.

Roper grunted and headed upstairs, the first bedroom contained a double bed, the duvet scrunched into a pile in the middle of the grotty-looking mattress, a wardrobe stood in one corner, the doors open to reveal a jumble of clothes.

Crossing the landing he peered into the bathroom, the floorboards bare, the shower curtain crawling with mildew.

The last door revealed a single room, the bed neatly made, the threadbare carpet free of clothing and mess. Roper smiled as he walked in and sat down on the bed, this was where the little fucker slept. The smile on his face widened as he imagined Croft coming home to find him sitting on his bed, no doubt the tosser would shit himself on the spot.

Alby Roper had tried most things in his young life, stealing cars, mugging people on the street; back in Liverpool he had set fire to a shed – knowing the old guy who had told him to bugger off his allotment was still inside. He'd spent almost half his life in secure units, and gradually over the years he had come to realise that on the outside he was a nobody. People would either look at him with distrust or ignore him all together, but inside four secure walls, he was a force to be reckoned with.

Truth was he preferred it inside, he got three meals a day, meals that actually tasted like food; when he'd been at home his mother had hardly ever cooked, and he'd lived on a diet of Pot Noodles and chocolate bars. Roper closed his eyes as he thought about the shepherd's pie they served in Park View, his stomach rumbled, and he sniffed as if he could conjure the delicious aroma from the stale air.

Since he'd been released, his diet had been reduced to greasy chips and burgers washed down with cheap cans of cider. He'd never had a job, but keeping order at Park View had felt like one, he'd felt like a bouncer working the doors, keeping order, and kicking the fuck out of anyone that took his fancy.

Suddenly, Roper craved to be back behind the reinforced doors of the unit.

The smile widened as his mind locked onto the single thought, if he *killed* Croft then chances are he would be locked up for years not months.

Alby Roper stretched out on the bed, the room dark around him, he felt like the big daddy bear.

'Who's been sleeping in my bed,' he rumbled in a dramatic voice, before breaking into a mad fit of giggles.

He would slaughter Croft, the messier the better, he started to work out a table of effects and consequences.

Strangulation, three years, stabbing four years, he smiled, setting fire to the little fucker was perhaps worth five years or more.

The minutes ticked into oblivion, and Alby Roper continued to daydream, he was back in his natural habitat, back at Park View, king of the fucking castle, and ruling with an iron fist.

Bliss.

34

Marnie sighed as she entered the kitchen and saw the half-full money jar standing by the side of the toaster. Slipping out of her jacket she draped it over the back of the kitchen chair her face laced with concern. After arriving home, she had dashed upstairs calling out Luke's name only to find the spare bedroom empty. The fact that the jar containing the money was still on the worktop pointed to the fact that he had left in a hurry.

Grabbing the clean ashtray from the drawer, she sat down at the kitchen table, and lit a cigarette.

Closing her eyes against the sting of the smoke, she tried to arrange her thoughts into something that resembled normality, then she sighed and lifted the chain from around her neck, eyes prickling with tears as she rubbed at the stone, her mind travelling back over the years.

Her mother had bought the matching crosses for her daughters and Marnie could remember the delight on Abby's face as her mother fastened it around her neck.

'Now listen to me, Abby, you do not sleep in this, OK?'

Abby had been looking down at the cross in awe.

'Are you listening, young lady?' her mother had asked.

Abby had raised her head, her young face serious. 'I promise, Mum.'

Susan had turned to Marnie. 'The same goes for you, Marnie, you can wear them during the day but when you go to bed you take them off.'

'We will,' Marnie had replied.

That night she had lifted Abby's long hair and opened the chain before placing it on the bedside cabinet.

Abby had turned. 'Now do yours.'

Marnie had smiled before doing as she asked.

Taking another pull on the cigarette, she tapped a finger of ash into the glass bowl, her mind aching with the vivid memory.

Marnie placed it on the table, the red stone shone in the overhead strip light, she turned it over, the letter M had been engraved on the back of the cross. Her mother had put an A on Abby's, telling them that they were her special girls and needed something special around their necks.

Years later, Marnie had come to realise that her mother had the letters engraved to make sure there were no arguments if one of her daughters lost their chain.

The cigarette continued to burn between her fingers, the smoke trailing upward and hanging in the air like grey ectoplasm.

She thought of poor Jenny Bell, starved to death over a period of weeks, her body growing frail, her mind filled with terror, crying out for her mother, feeling lost and abandoned. After death, she had been dumped in the same woods that Abby had vanished in all those years ago, along with the skeletal arm and now the fresh collection of bones. Marnie felt the pressure building in her head, the terror eating away at her resolve. When her phone rang, she jerked in her seat and snatched it from her pocket, Doc Kelly's name flashed up at her, suddenly she was terrified to listen to what he had to say. Then she steeled her nerve and tapped the screen.

'*That you, Marnie?*'

She cleared her throat as the fear tightened around her heart. 'Go on, I'm listening.'

'*They've found three sets of remains.*'

Marnie gripped the phone tight at the news. '*Three!*'

'*All the fingers on each hand are intact,*' he said.

Marnie slumped forward, resting her forehead on the table, her mind in turmoil.

'*We're running DNA tests to try and put names to the victims but I wanted you to know that none of them belong to your sister.*'

Marnie lifted her head and looked at the kitchen window, the dark pressed at the glass, seen through a blur of tears. 'Thanks, Doc, I appreciate that.'

'*No problem,*' Kelly replied, before ending the call.

Marnie dropped the cigarette into the ashtray, sat back and wiped at her moist eyes, her emotions swirled, a mixture of relief and terrible grief. She held her hands up, watching them shake, they had found three more sets of remains and perhaps there were more, perhaps her sister was still there in the woods waiting to be found. The thought reignited the anguish. She looked around the room, the fear erupting back into her soul. Pushing the chair back she lunged to her feet, she needed to get out of here, needed something to latch onto, something that didn't involve starving children and stark white bones.

Her mind shifted, she pictured Luke running from the house in terror at what the future would bring. The guilt pressed down on her, here she was standing in the kitchen of her nice, new house with a warm, comfortable bed waiting upstairs, and Luke was out there somewhere, no doubt in pain and full of fear, but alive. That single thought lanced through all the death, Luke Croft was alive and he needed her help, she couldn't help Jenny Bell or the others, she couldn't help her sister but she could at least try to help Luke.

She turned, her agitated mind clearing until all she could see was Luke Croft, his head bowed, shoulders shaking, his body bruised and battered, the fear alight in his eyes.

Striding across the room, she snatched her jacket from the back of the chair, half a minute later she was in the car and backing down the drive.

She tried to think where he would have gone to, he had no money so he would stay close to the town centre, try to find somewhere warm and dry to sleep.

At the junction, she paused as she tried to decide which way to go, and then she thought of Luke's mother and stepfather, and her anger sparked and caught. Both had left the boy to his own devices, and as far as Marnie was concerned they shared the blame for what had happened to him at Park View.

She thought of Luke, wandering the streets, trying to remain hidden, perhaps desperation would drive him back home.

It seemed unlikely but ultimately what choice would he have? Eventually the need to eat and sleep would force him back to his mother, though Marnie knew it could be days or even weeks before he risked going back to the house that had never been a home.

Mind made up, she spun the wheel left and headed off down the road, her frustration turning to anger, her face livid.

35

The man stood in the doorway to the huge house, watching as the barn owl flew low to the ground, silent white wings shimmering in the darkness; when it lunged to the ground he smiled.

It had been a momentous day; he had found the ledger and his mind had soared as the key unlocked the doors. The hidden room in the cellar had felt like home, surrounded by his girls and reconnecting with the past.

Yet despite all this, the vile confusion still plucked at his mind as he tried to fathom the mystery of the girl named Abby. An image of the running girl scuttled through his mind and his brow furrowed in concentration. She had been sprinting towards him down the long corridor and somehow the sight of her had sent a bolt of real fear into his heart.

He shook his head in anger, the owl took to the air, prey clamped between cold talons.

In his brain the image shifted and twisted, teeth gritted as he pictured the girl running, only this time she was sprinting away, her hair streaming out as she threw a look of terror over her shoulder.

He grunted in satisfaction at her fear, then his shoulders slumped, he looked down at the gravel drive, the thoughts, and images becoming entangled, the frustration building.

Stepping from the doorway, he strode out across the unruly lawn, a thin wind blowing in his face as he walked down the three, worn, stone steps. Reaching the towering oak, he stopped and looked at the ancient tree, he could picture the boy lashed to the trunk, the rain falling, the wind howling.

'*Spineless whippersnapper!*' he spat, his hands grasping at the air, his face blasted with anger.

He turned slowly and looked back towards the house, his eyes narrowed, studying the upstairs windows. When he saw the flash of a pale face looking down at him he felt the anger transform into hatred, he blinked and the image vanished.

'*Whore!*' he hissed, turning left and striding further into the shadows.

The grass grew taller, brushing his knees, his mind stark with raw emotion.

Reaching the double garage, he snatched the doors open, the sleek black Mercedes gleamed as moonlight filtered into the space, lighting the chrome and reflecting the black paintwork. A sudden image flitted through his mind, he had been parked in some nameless town when the man with the gruesome comb over stopped to admire the car. Dressed in an expensive suit and reeking of aftershave, the man had bent down to the open driver's window.

'You don't see many of these old beauties in such good condition,' he said with a smile.

Gripping the steering wheel, he had smiled back, showing a set of perfect teeth. 'Well, it is getting on a bit but still rides well.'

'Is she a sixty-three or four?'

'Sixty-three,' he replied, the false smile still locked in place.

'Have you ever thought of selling her?'

'Her?'

The man had patted his ridiculous hair, the smile still wide and warm. 'I always imagine these cars to be female, odd I know but there's something about the curve of the bodywork, elegant, feminine even.'

Suddenly, he wanted to reach out, grab the man by the back of the neck and slam his face into the door. 'It's just a car to me,' he replied, his dark eyes shining.

'Ah but it's not just any car, it's a classic,' dipping a hand into his pocket the car lover handed over a card. 'Classic cars bought and sold,' was stencilled on the front.

'If you ever change your mind, then…'

'I never change my mind.'

'I can offer you a great price.'

The man had wound the window up without uttering another word and at last the smile fell from the would-be buyer's face; he scowled before turning and stalking away.

In the moonlight, the man recalled the memory, sometimes the fates would come together perfectly.

Closing his eyes, he thought about the man who had tried to buy the Mercedes, half an hour after closing the window he had seen the same man again, only this time blood was flowing from his mouth, his eyes wide in pain.

'Kismet,' pulling the car keys from his pocket he moved into the garage and unlocked the car.

Sliding behind the wheel, he reached across the seats and lifted the leather gloves from the passenger seat, the smile lighting up his face he slipped them on.

'At last,' he muttered, as everything slotted into place.

36

At the sound of the front door slamming, Roper cracked open his eyes and squinted into the darkened room. He'd been dreaming of Croft and the things he would do to the little bastard, in his fevered mind the blood had flowed, the screams had been filled with terror and pain. Suddenly he was wide-awake, the smile leaching onto his pock-marked face.

Rising, he crossed the room and eased the door open, from below he heard the familiar sound of a ring pull being yanked back, the hiss followed by a heavy sigh of satisfaction.

Roper scowled as he realised it wasn't Luke downstairs, it had to be the guy he had seen walking from the house before he broke in.

Dipping a hand into his pocket, he pulled out the knife and unfolded the serrated blade moving silently along the landing. At the top of the stairs he paused, he could see light below spilling from the living room and into the hallway.

When he heard the opening credits of Top Gear blaring from the room, he grinned as he made his way down the stairs, he thought back to Park View, sitting in the rec room watching endless reruns of the programme.

Reaching the hallway, he squared his shoulders and took a deep breath before striding into the room, the man lay sprawled on the sofa, the remote control on his whale-like stomach, a can in his hand. Roper could even see the bald spot on top of his head.

On the television screen Jeremy Clarkson was driving some open-top car at speed, his mouth open and flapping as the wind tore into it.

The man on the sofa laughed, and Roper stepped forward and slammed the handle of the knife into the top of his head.

Tony Oldman screeched and tried to lunge upright, but his stomach made it an impossible task.

Leaning forward Roper placed the knife against the man's throat. '*Where is he?*' he hissed.

Oldman swallowed, the keen blade nicked his skin, making him gasp in fear. His mind befuddled with booze and bad dope, his senses reeling.

'I don't know who…'

'Where's *Luke?*' Roper demanded.

Oldman wanted to twist his head away but the blade lay hard and cold against his fevered skin. 'I haven't seen him in days.' he gasped, his eyes screwed shut, heart pounding.

'You'd better fucking tell me!'

'*I don't know!*' Oldman wailed, lager-infused sweat oozing from his pores.

Alby Roper felt the frustration surge as he realised the man was telling the truth. 'He lives here; you must know where he is.'

'Honest, he only came home for one night after he was released from the nick, I don't know where the little shit is.'

Roper snarled, he had broken into the house convinced that he would soon have the little bastard at his mercy, and now this fat tosser was telling him that Luke had vanished after coming out of Park View.

'Where would he have gone?' he asked, pressing down on the blade.

Oldman screeched. 'He has no friends, he's a little fucker and…'

'*Liar!*' Roper bellowed, the spittle flying from his gash of a mouth.

Tony Oldman started to cry, he tried to hold onto his bladder but the fear had to have an outlet and he felt the warmth leaking into his jeans as he tried to shrink himself down into the sofa.

'Please, I don't know what to tell you, but when I get my hands on the shit I'll…'

Alby Roper pressed down hard and Oldman gasped in terror, his tongue poked out from between his trembling lips as his life hung in the balance.

Alby Roper paused for a moment trying to think what to do, then his face hardened and the anger flooded his system.

'*Fuck it,*' he hissed, swiping the blade across the exposed throat in a savage sweep.

Tony Oldman's arms shot into the air as the blood sprayed from the gash in his neck. Thrashing his body, he managed to roll off the sofa; clattering to the floor, mouth open, he tried to scream out the pain, but his vocal cords had been severed, suddenly, with a gurgle, his mouth filled with blood.

The can of Special Brew fell to the floor, the lager spilling, mixing with the blood that continued to rain down from the gruesome wound.

Alby Roper watched, fascinated, as the man writhed on the floor, his right leg shot out and hit the coffee table, sending it skittering across the room.

Oldman jittered, his chin tucked to his chest as if trying to close the ghastly wound.

Roper licked his lips, the thrashing slowly began to subside, seconds later Oldman slammed face first to the floor.

For as long as he could remember Alby had wondered what it would be like to kill someone, it was a fantasy that had filled his dreams, leaving him feeling thrilled and disappointed in equal measure. Reaching down, he wiped the blade on the shoulder of the man's T-shirt before picking up one of the cans and pulling the tab; emptying it in one long swallow, he tossed it to the floor, belched loudly and smiled. Suddenly he felt lighter, as if some weight had been lifted from his shoulders, he imagined this is what a striker must feel like having broken his goal-scoring drought.

'I killed the fucker,' he said, before burping again.

Slowly the feeling of euphoria began to dissolve; Croft was still out there somewhere, taunting him, goading him.

Roper tried to think of a plan, but the truth was he didn't have an idea in his empty head.

Then his eyes widened, he fumbled the phone and charger from his pocket, looking around the room he spotted the socket, plugged the phone in and grabbed another can from the floor. Slumping back on the sofa, he placed his feet on the body sprawled on the floor and opened the can before taking another glug.

On the screen, Jeremy Clarkson continued to gurn for the camera.

'*Fucking gormless wanker,*' Roper growled, and took another drink.

37

Marnie pulled up outside the house, headlights illuminating the woman walking along the pavement. When she recognised Luke's mother, she snatched on the handbrake and yanked the seat belt off before pushing the door open.

Karen Croft had a carrier bag in her right hand, the tell-tale clink of glass bottles rattled from inside.

'I want a word with you,' Marnie said, stepping onto the kerb.

Karen looked up, her face scrunched in annoyance, she had the same narrow bone structure as her son, the same pale eyes, her hair was straggly, hanging to her shoulders, looking like it needed a good wash. 'Whatever our Luke's done, I don't want to know,' she said, coming to a reluctant halt.

'What makes you think he's done anything?'

'Because you wouldn't be here otherwise, now I'm tired so say whatever it is you have to say then I can get in the house.'

Marnie felt the anger squirm in the pit of her stomach. 'You do realise that Luke was released from Park View a week ago, don't you?'

Karen Croft shrugged. 'I told him he'd get banged up if he kept nicking stuff.'

'Why didn't you visit him?' Marnie snapped.

'And why would I do that? He made his bed, he bloody lies in it.'

'What you mean is you couldn't be bothered.'

Croft huffed and tried to move forward but Marnie didn't budge an inch.

When she looked into Marnie's hard, brown eyes she frowned. 'Are you going to move or what?'

'While your son was inside, he was beaten by another inmate…'

'Knowing Luke, he probably got gobby and rubbed someone up the wrong way.'

'And that's all you have to say, is it?'

'He goes his own way, always has – he's not a little kid, he's old enough to suffer the consequences.'

'Someone stubbed cigarettes out on his feet, they beat him black and blue and you never moved a muscle to find out how he was.'

'I didn't know anything about that,' Karen snapped, though there was still no concern in her eyes, just a total lack of emotion.

'*Why* didn't you know?' Marnie stepped forward until she was mere inches from the woman's sour face.

'I…'

'You make me *sick!*' Marnie hissed. 'You don't give a toss about your son, you haven't seen him in months, and you never thought to contact us to find out where he is.'

'Like I said, he's not a child. Besides he's probably staying at one of his mates.'

'Oh yes and which *mate* would that be?'

Karen moved back a step, the bottles in the bag clinked. 'I don't know which mate, but he must be staying somewhere.'

'The fact is, your son doesn't have *any friends*, but then again why should you be expected to know that, after all he's no concern of yours, is he?'

'It's up to him where he goes, besides he's never listened to me, he's always been an ignorant little sod.'

Marnie tried to keep control of her anger but every word Croft uttered was like pouring fuel onto a roaring fire. 'I've just told you that your son was *beaten black and blue and burnt with cigarettes,* and yet you stand there as if we're talking about the weather.'

For the briefest of moments, Marnie saw something resembling hurt in the woman's eyes and then it was gone, replaced with the usual disdain.

'I've been at work all day; so, if you've finished then I want my tea and a bath.'

'What about your *son?*' Marnie shouted in her face.

Karen didn't bat an eyelid. 'Lay one finger on me and I'll make sure everyone knows you attacked me for no reason.'

The two women stood facing one another, their eyes firing anger back and forth.

Reluctantly Marnie stepped to one side, and Karen threw her a look of triumph, but as she passed Marnie grabbed her arm and Luke's mother winced at the pressure of the grip.

'If, by some miracle, Luke turns up here then you ring the station and tell us, is that clear?'

Karen snorted a laugh, as if the notion of wasting phone credit ringing the filth was the best joke she had heard in years.

'If you don't and I find out about it, then I'll come back here; and then you'll know what it's like to have someone beat *you* black and blue.'

Karen glared, though there was also a flicker of doubt in her eyes; Marnie clamped down on her arm and Karen felt the strength there and the fury.

She snatched her arm away and strode up the garden path, the bottles rattling like a bag of bleached bones.

Marnie fumed as she watched the woman fumble the key from her pocket and thrust it into the lock.

Karen Croft threw her a final look of hatred and defiance before slamming the door.

Marnie felt the frustration battering her senses. Luke would never come back to this place; he would sooner spend a lifetime on the streets than see his mother with her heart of stone and twisted bitch sneer.

Marnie turned for the car; suddenly the door to the house slammed open and Karen Croft reappeared, only this time she was running and screaming; the plastic bag fell from her hand, the sound of shattered glass muffled by her screams.

Marnie bolted forward and snatched her as she tried to dash past.

'*He's dead!*' Karen screeched.

Marnie felt her stomach plummet and then she was running for the front door, her hair streaming as she dashed into the house.

Glancing up the stairs she moved down the hallway, her heart racing as she stepped into the room, her mind trying to prepare itself for finding Luke Croft dead. When she saw the bulk of Tony Oldman on the floor she felt a guilty sense of relief flood through her system. Three long strides took her to the body and she grimaced as she took in the pool of blood that had spread under the sofa and bled into the lager-stained rug. She could see the cans strewn around the floor. The air felt charged with sudden death, the stink of spilled blood filled the air. She looked around the threadbare room, dust covered every surface, wallpaper was peeling from the walls, the overhead bulb throwing out a pitiful cone of nicotine-tinged light. She thought of Luke living in such bleak surroundings, trying to find his place in life while his mother ignored him and his stepfather barked at him to grab another can from the fridge.

With a heavy sigh, she headed back into the hallway and glanced into the kitchen before taking the stairs at a rush. She grimaced as she looked into the double bedroom, the place stank of sweaty feet and old sex. Back on the landing she took a couple of seconds to look into the bathroom and shook her head before coming to the single room. The door was ajar, the single bed, neatly made, stood under the window, the rest of the small space taken up by a flimsy wardrobe and a bedside cabinet. Compared to the rest of the house, the room looked neat and tidy, and Marnie felt her heart ache as she pictured Luke trying to build his own oasis against the harsh realities of life. She could almost see the boy perched on the bed, the door closed, his ears plugged with headphones as he tried to block out the gruelling monotony of his existence.

Stepping back onto the landing, she took one last look at the room before turning and heading back down the stairs.

The front door was still open and she glanced out into the night, Luke's mother was standing by the front gate, her face buried in her hands. Pulling the phone from her pocket, Marnie called the cavalry before turning and walking into the kitchen. The worktops were covered with an assortment of pots, pans and plates, a packet of Corn Flakes lay on its side on the small kitchen table. Walking over to the back door, she frowned when she saw it was open slightly.

Reaching out, she flicked it wide with the toe of her shoe and looked out into the darkness, the garden was a mass of smothering shadows, a length of blue washing line vanished into the darkness. Glancing down, her eyes widened in surprise, the shoe print was clear to see on the red painted door. Marnie eased down for a closer look, Luke had been wearing trainers, this tread was large and broad. She pictured the bruise high on Luke's shoulder, and her eyes widened further as she recognised the tread.

'*Roper,*' she hissed.

38

The man parked the car in front of the scruffy parade of shops and turned the engine off, his eyes locked on the houses opposite, when he saw the state of the gardens he grimaced. He tried to think of the last time he had parked here and looked across the road watching the girl playing in the front garden.

'*It's been years,*' the voice inside whispered.

He shook his head at the notion, it was ridiculous, preposterous, it couldn't be so long since he had last been here.

When the voice tried to insist, the man slammed a hand into the side of his head as if trying to dislodge some annoying tic.

Then he thought of the ledger, every detail written in his no-nonsense style. He went through the list of names in his mind, each one a wonderful memory, except for two.

The one called Abby had been in his grasp and yet somehow, she had eluded him, he scowled at the thought. His hands rested on the steering wheel as he closed his eyes. The fact that he couldn't remember what had happened to the girl didn't mean she had escaped. He sighed but the memories remained hidden from him and then he opened his eyes and glared at the house opposite, he could see light shining behind the grotty curtains, the grass a foot tall, the rickety garden gate standing open.

Mandy Farmer had been the last name in the ledger, all the usual details were there, address, parents' name, school attended, though the man also knew that he never finished the job. His hands tightened on the wheel, the leather gloves creaking. Why hadn't he finished the job, he asked himself but his brain was starting to misfire again, the thoughts jumbling like bricks in a cement mixer, clattering together, the sound increasing.

The faces of the dead girls twisted his mind, morphing into one another, blending until he felt the confusion cram his head, squeezing his brain ever tighter. He gasped and thrust the car door open before leaping out into the cool, night air.

The parade of shops at his back were in darkness, the street deserted.

Standing with one steadying hand on the car door, he tried to breathe but his chest felt clad in iron, his mind turning to mush as the thoughts continued to lash at his senses.

Glancing left, his heart juddered as he saw the woman walking along the road moving from one cone of light to the next, she was dressed in jeans with a white padded jacket, her high heels clicking on the pavement as she strode along holding the hand of a child dressed in red.

When she reached the house opposite they turned onto the path, the girl glanced over her shoulder as if she somehow knew she was being observed.

'*Mandy Farmer,*' he mouthed the two words, his eyes widening in astonishment.

A memory flashed through his head, the last time he had seen her she had been wearing red, her hair in pigtails just as she was now.

The man turned and slumped back into the car, his body shivering with a mixture of joy and incredulity.

How can it be, how can it be *her*?

He watched as the woman and child walked up to the door, when they vanished inside the house, he felt like screaming in despair.

Slamming the door, he leaned forward and rested his sweating brow on the steering wheel. His chest rose and fell rapidly, his hands – trapped inside the gloves – felt tacky.

In the dark swirling mess of his mind he saw Mandy Farmer, the voice had told him that it had been years since he had last been parked here watching the girl playing in the garden and yet tonight he had seen her again with his own eyes unchanged by the years. Time had stood still and she had remained exactly as she was, it was a sign, it had to be, a sign to finish what he had started.

He grunted in agreement. This was fact, the girl was here, waiting to be taken.

'*Not yet,*' the voice whispered.

The man snarled in anger though he knew the voice was right; the time would come and he would be ready.

Starting the engine, he took one last lingering look at the house before driving away. His mind still stuttering but at least now he had a plan, something to concentrate the mind, something to look forward to.

'All mine,' he rejoiced, as the car glided down the street.

39

Luke hovered in the empty shop doorway, trying to quell the sense of fear that ran amok through his mind. At this time of night Market Street was deserted, most of the pubs were closed, even the takeaways were shutting up shop. With a heavy heart, he stepped out of the doorway and set off walking down the darkened street, his feet throbbing with every step.

As soon as he caught the scent of kebab meat and frying onions, his mouth flooded with saliva, his stomach groaned. When he saw the man across the road, toss a half-eaten burger into the litter bin, he glanced left and right before making his way over.

Luke felt the shame burning his face as he dipped a hand into the bin and snatched the burger before taking a huge bite.

He kept his head bowed and moved away from the bin, the food held between both hands. Seconds later it was gone, and he licked his lips, tasting ketchup and mayonnaise.

His stomach ached as if the small amount of food had woken a hungry beast inside. Another roadside bin approached, and he stopped to glance down into a mangle of wrappers and plastic bottles, reaching down he snatched a half-full coke bottle free. Spinning the cap, he took a drink and glanced over his shoulder, Market Street was still deserted, light from one or two shop windows illuminated the pavement, leaving dark patches of shadows that bled into the road.

Two minutes later he had rummaged in three more bins. The last one revealed a tray full of warm chips and gravy, to Luke Croft it tasted like the food of the gods as he walked down the street, shovelling the chips into his mouth.

Reaching the junction, he stopped and waited for a gap in the traffic before crossing. As he walked, he thought about DS Hammond and felt a shiver of guilt but with a desperate shake of the head he crushed it before the feeling had time to grow.

He had to forget all that and concentrate on getting away from this place. Deep down he knew the only way he would manage it would be to grab some cash. An image of the shopkeeper entered his head, falling sideways as Luke lashed out then grabbed the money from the till before running from the shop. Five minutes later, DS Hammond had dragged him down to the leaf-littered floor and the nightmare had begun.

The thought of having to risk the same fate a second time made him weak with trepidation. Gradually the road began to grow steeper, and his pace dropped to little more than a shuffle. With each painful step the despair grew until he came to a staggering halt, his feet refusing to take him any further.

Turning, he looked back down the hill, Market Street was deserted, he felt like the last person alive on the face of the planet.

Luke sighed as the road continued to climb, looking like an insurmountable mountain guaranteed to break him.

He started to walk again, the cigarette burns itching inside his scruffy trainers. A large apartment block appeared on the left, and he hesitated as he reached the narrow opening that led to its private car park. To the right, he could see three large industrial bins pushed up to the wall. Licking his lips, he made his way over, all three bins had lids propped open with the rubbish inside. When he spotted the mattress, wedged upright between the bins and the wall, he stopped.

It wasn't what you would call warm, but it was dry and close to the town centre. Luke knew he would have to stay near the shops and litterbins if he wanted to eat, simply walking out of town and into the open fields was appealing but ultimately pointless. If he wanted to survive then he had to stay local, it was as simple as that. Sliding behind the bins he nudged them forward slightly before dragging the single mattress to the floor, then he flopped down, exhausted. Within minutes he was asleep.

40

Reese stared down at the slumped form of Tony Oldman, face down on a floor sticky with spilled beer and blood.

Doc Kelly heaved the body onto its back and leaned in close like some gangly vampire ready to drink his fill.

Marnie glanced at Reese who was busy shaking his head at the sight. 'OK, what's the score? And don't say he's dead because I'm not in the mood for gallows humour.'

Kelly glanced up from the body, 'Serrated blade,' he said. 'One cut left to right.'

Reese grunted in acknowledgment before looking around the room, the place stank of booze, dope and sweaty feet, mingling with the smell of dark blood and tart urine. Turning to Marnie, he flicked his head towards the doorway.

Sliding her hands into her pocket, she followed him down the hallway and into the kitchen.

'You were looking for Luke Croft?' he asked, with a dark frown.

Marnie nodded. 'It was a long shot but I wanted to make sure he hadn't come back here.'

'The truth is, you should have been at home getting some rest, we have Jenny Bell plus three sets of remains to investigate and I need you alert, not half asleep looking for some kid on the run.'

Marnie kept her lips clamped together as Reese carried on talking.

'I know this is hard for you, but if you can't concentrate and give one hundred percent then I need to know right now?'

She opened her mouth to fire a retort but Reese snapped up a hand.

'Anyway, maybe Luke Croft was here, perhaps he's been and gone?' Reese added, his voice heavy with innuendo.

Marnie walked to the back door and, opening it, pointed to the print on the paintwork. 'Luke Croft owns one pair of trainers and they are falling to pieces, and at a guess I'd say a size six or seven at a push.'

Reese pursed his lips as he eased down to his haunches, his eyes fixed on the tread mark.

'I came here in the hope that Luke would have come home, but there's no way he would have come here. I spoke to the mother before all this happened and she really couldn't care less where he is or what's happened to him.'

Reese stood up slowly. 'Did you get to speak to Gareth Walls?'

Marnie took a deep breath and started to talk, she explained about Luke sharing a cell with Alby Roper and Walls's denial about any violence that was taking place at the unit.

'And you think this Roper character was the one who beat Croft?'

'I know it's a young offenders' unit but Roper looks older than you,' Marnie smiled slightly when Reese raised an eyebrow. 'His record is one of violence and mayhem, and we also know that he left Park View wearing the standard issue trainers, trainers that had that tread,' she pointed at the door. 'So yes, I think he was responsible for the beatings.'

'What about an address.'

Marnie nodded. 'We have one, in fact I was going to check it out...'

'Were you now?' Reese said, folding his arms.

Marnie had the good grace to blush.

'What I don't understand is, if Roper is involved then why the hell would he come here in the first place?' Reese asked.

Stepping back Marnie eased the door closed. 'He came to find Luke, he...'

'Yes, but why? If Roper did beat the boy in Park View then you would imagine that was the end of it, why come to the house? Why kill the stepfather?'

Marnie pursed her lips, Reese was right it made no sense. No doubt Roper was a bully and thug but people like that normally just moved onto the next victim, after all there were dozens of Luke Crofts in Kirk head, kids with no hope, easy pickings for someone like Roper. Then a thought flashed into her mind, one that made her eyes spring wide open in surprise.

'Roper came here to take care of Luke, right?'

Reese gave her a quizzical look and then sighed. 'OK, let's hear it but bear in mind all this could have nothing to do with Roper, it's speculation at best.'

Marnie slid her hands back into her pockets. 'Luke can be cocky and mouth off, but what happened to him in Park View broke his spirit.'

Reese waited for her to continue, arms still folded.

'Now, if it was Roper then something must have wound him up, the address Walls provided is about five miles away on the other side of town.'

'He could have jumped on a bus, Marnie, it would have cost next to nothing and he could have been here in less than half an hour.'

'Yes, but *why* would he do that, what would drive him to come over here and kill Luke's stepfather?'

'Again, we don't know that for certain, Oldman could have been into anything, he could have been in shit so deep that...'

'Roper came here looking for Luke and he would only have done that if he somehow knew that we were involved,' Marnie said hurriedly.

Reese stepped back in surprise.

Marnie held his gaze as he ran a hand over his eyes. 'Guesswork, Marnie, and you know it.'

'It's the only thing that makes sense, we have a print on the door...'

'That could have been since the year dot.'

Marnie ignored him and ploughed on. 'Luke never pointed the finger but the bruises are at least three weeks old, Doc Kelly confirmed that fact. I went to see Walls who denied any knowledge of the attack but less than twenty-four hours later Luke's home address is broken into and his stepfather killed.'

'You're saying that Walls – a man whose daughter could turn out to be one of the piles of bones we have – contacted Roper and gave him this address?'

Marnie sucked in a gulp of air and then nodded.

Reese shook his head as he looked out of the kitchen window, into the smothering darkness. 'But you still haven't said why? Why a man who has given keynote speeches on the penal system would do something so bloody stupid?' Reese turned to face her. 'Think about what you're suggesting, I checked the facts and Walls has a bloody long list of glowing recommendations from some heavy hitters, he's been in charge of the unit for ten years and in all that time there hasn't been a whiff of anything dodgy going on.'

Marnie felt the weight of Reese's words bombard her, he was right, it sounded ridiculous, but then she gritted her teeth and straightened her shoulders.

'Someone must have pressed Roper's buttons, he wouldn't…'

The DCI snapped up a hand again. 'I've heard enough, you are meant to be a detective, not fabricate theories to make the facts fit your suspicions.'

'But…'

'No, Marnie, we do this the right way,' he said. 'SOCO should be here any minute so we let them do their job, we do not make things up to suit ourselves, is that clear?'

Marnie kept her shaking fists lodged in her pockets. 'Perfectly.'

Reese grunted in satisfaction. 'Now, this time when I tell you to get home and rest I expect you to do it.'

'But what about Roper?'

Reese stepped towards her, his eyes flaring in anger. 'I'll have the address checked out, now just do as you're told for once, get home and get some rest!' his voice rose in annoyance.

Marnie spun on her heels, not trusting herself to reply as she stormed down the hallway and out into the darkness.

She could see people out in the street, neighbours trying to find out what was going on.

As she climbed into her car she spotted Karen Croft, her arms waving in the air as she told a group of neighbours exactly what had happened, her face animated, her eyes alight with fervour, loving every second of the attention.

With a snarl of disgust, she drove away, her emotions swelling, the anger steaming to the surface as she thought of Luke, out there on the darkened streets, unaware that he was being hunted by a hulking man-boy with a knife dripping with blood.

41

The flame in the paraffin lantern flickered, throwing shadows around the room, the skulls catching the light, the bones shining. The man sat in the chair, his eyes moving from one skull to the next as he tried to calm his mind. The confusion was still there but somehow just having the girls close was enough to bring a semblance of calm to his mind.

The plan remained the same, he would watch the house, Mandy Farmer's house and as soon as the chance came he would take the girl and bring her back to the cellar, only then would he be made whole again.

Closing his eyes, his head started to drift as the heat in the cellar began to build, he tried to remember when he had last slept but found that he couldn't. His brow furrowed, his life seemed to consist of waking hours only, days, weeks, months that had stretched into years in this strange limbo.

His chin touched his chest and the decades rolled back, the boy was there, waiting, though now he had grown, tall and rangy, his hateful, narrow face framed with black hair. The man's hands closed over the arms of the chair, gripping tight as he watched him walk through the darkened house, though this time there was no shuffling but a confident stride.

The perpetual look of fear was no longer evident in his eyes, instead there was a dark malice, fury burning in the depths.

He followed the boy, his eyes locked on the figure ahead, his hands opening and closing like mechanical grabbers.

Stopping at a door on the left, the boy eased down to his knees and leaned forward, his eye staring through the keyhole.

In the room of skulls, the man growled like some wild beast, his eyes moving rapidly behind closed lids.

The perspective changed and suddenly he saw *her*, she was standing under the shower, her wild hair tamed by the water, her breasts were no more than a slight swelling, her body blooming with shivering goose bumps.

The boy reached down and fumbled his growing member free as she turned and looked toward the door.

It was as if she could sense him, as if she knew exactly what he was doing.

When she smiled, the boy licked his lips, his hand pulling and tugging in excitement and disgust.

Suddenly she opened her mouth and screamed, the sound echoing around the large, tiled bathroom.

The boy lurched back in terror, somewhere close by a door slammed open and he snapped his head left to see the man storming towards him, his fury writhing around his head like some filthy, black cloud.

He tried to scuttle back, at the same time stuffing his member back into his trousers.

Then the man was on him and the pain began.

In the flame-flickering cellar, he snapped awake with the scream on his lips, his quivering member grasped in his right hand, the loathing slithering through his body like a living thing.

42

Gareth Walls sat at the kitchen table, a glass of single malt grasped in his right hand, his face creased with annoyance. After being grilled by Hammond the anger inside had grown, she had looked at him with disdain as if she hadn't believed a word he had said about Croft and Roper.

'*Bitch*,' he spat, before draining the glass and refilling it with a shaking hand.

What right did she have to sit there and question him about Park View? He had thought she had come to give him the latest update on Hambling and yet she had brushed it aside as if it was of no real concern to her. Suzie had been taken by someone like Hambling, a stinking, filthy pervert, he was sure of it. Yet the bitch, Hammond, had left him in the dark, worse than that, she had questioned him about Luke fucking Croft.

Hammond had no idea about the way to run a prison and that's exactly what it was, the fact that it was for young offenders didn't change the realities. The boys were locked up, guards patrolled the corridors; they were criminals simple as that and it was his job to make sure they were punished. He pictured Luke Croft with his sly, weasily face, the face of a scally, someone who was used to breaking the law and getting away with it. Walls smiled as he recalled leading the boy to his cell, Roper had been sitting on the bunk, a hulking figure who dwarfed the diminutive Croft.

Taking another sip from the glass, the governor of Park View eased back in the chair, Roper was an animal, though Walls knew the boy trapped in the man's body had his uses. Fools like Hammond didn't have a clue about the real way to run a unit, she probably thought the little bastards got along, all smiles with not a cross word between them. When the truth was the exact opposite and that's where the Ropers of this world came into their own.

Walls emptied the glass and sighed again before rising to his feet and heading through the kitchen and into his study, bottle in hand.

Slumping down in the swivel chair, his face sour as he pictured Hammond again, her eyes full of loathing, slapping down another image of the bruised and battered Croft on his desk, each one an accusation.

Yes, well if things worked out as planned, Croft would think twice in future before going to the police about the conditions at Park View.

'Little bastard,' he mumbled, before reaching out and firing up the laptop.

His heavy fingers stabbed at the keys, he grunted in annoyance, hitting the wrong letters, then he pressed enter and leaned forward, elbows on the walnut desk.

Moving a finger over the mouse pad, he tapped on one of the links, the image springing to life.

He started to read, his eyes gradually widening in surprise.

'Well, well, it's no wonder you have a chip on your shoulder, you slut.'

A smile plucked at his full lips and then he tapped again but the smile slipped as he read the latest local news.

The headline leapt out at him, he lunged forward, his hands suddenly shaking. '*Local man stabbed to death in his home*' the tagline screamed.

Walls scrolled down until he came to a piece of footage, he pressed the play button, the palms of his hands slick with sweat.

The image of a woman jittered and then she was talking to camera, in the background he could see a multitude of swirling blue lights, a policeman in a bright yellow vest stood guard at the gate of a tatty-looking council house.

'It's believed that the victim, named as Tony Oldman, lived here at thirty-five Foxton Drive, and was found by his partner, Karen Croft. According to MsCroft he had been stabbed in the throat. Although the police have yet to confirm how the man died it appears to have been a violent death and...'

The clip ended and Gareth Walls felt the study close in around him, bolting to his feet he looked down at the image on the screen in disbelief.

'No, no he can't have,' he said, rubbing a hand over his stricken eyes.

The walls continued to shrink as he ran from the room and across the kitchen, the fear slamming through his head as he burst out into the darkness.

The air was cold and he felt the sweat on his brow cooling as he stood beneath a million stars, his heart thumping with terror.

'*Calm down,*' he hissed, licking his lips and tasting the expensive single malt, now laced with fear.

His brain – normally so cool and calculating – felt like an out-of-control runaway train steaming down a mountainside.

Closing his eyes, he gasped as the image of Marnie Hammond lurched to the forefront of his raging brain.

This was all her fault, if she hadn't come to Park View with her stupid photographs of Croft then he would never have sent the text.

Gareth Walls staggered forward in the darkness as he realised the enormity of what he had done. After the bitch had questioned him the anger had built, growing minute by minute until it consumed him utterly.

He was the governor, the *governor* and yet she had made him feel like a fraud, as if she had seen through the mask he wore to the heart of the man beneath.

The fury had exploded in his mind, and he had fired off the text, sitting in his office with a smile on his face as he thought of Roper punishing Croft for daring to tell tales.

Walls shook his head, and tried to gather his thoughts, Roper would have gone to thirty-five Foxcroft Drive, no doubt with the intention of giving Croft another beating, and yet the reporter on the news had named the victim as one Tony Oldman. There had been no mention of the boy, Walls glared up at the sky, his mind cluttered with questions. He thought of Roper – all sixteen stone of him – going to the house with the intention of teaching Croft a lesson, but what if Luke hadn't been at home?

Walls shivered as his mind slowly joined the dots, Albert Roper wasn't the kind of thug who thought about his actions, that much was obvious, his record proved that, he had been in and out of childrens' units all his life. He had started with the usual shoplifting, petty crime that had quickly escalated into assault and ending with Roper setting fire to a shed that was occupied by a seventy-year-old pensioner.

The fear suddenly increased into outright terror, in the unit Roper had been easy to control, easy to manipulate, but now he was out and if the news bulletin was to be believed, he was responsible for the death of Tony Oldman.

Walls remembered the flashing blue lights of the police cars and vans parked at the front of the house. No doubt they would be going over the place like a plague of locusts, he thought of Hammond, the cunning look in her eye. She was no fool and Walls had no doubt that she would want to know what had sent Roper to the house in the first place and then…

Gareth Walls cringed, convinced that he could hear the distant wail of sirens, his mind full with swirling blue lights.

If the police made the same links, then they would be out there looking for Roper and when they caught him, Walls had no doubt that the young thug would simply shrug his shoulders as he admitted to killing Oldman and then he would hand the phone over, showing Hammond the text.

He had been careful to withhold the number but now the doubt raced around his mind as he thought of some IT geek getting to the truth and then it would all be over.

Walls stood swaying in the darkness, the desperation squeezing his heart.

If Roper had failed to find Luke but killed Oldman, then he would still be out looking for the boy who had grassed him up; after all what did he have to lose?

Roper had been at the unit for nine months and Walls had sudden flashbacks, Roper in the gym lifting heavy weights the smile locked in place, Roper in the television room laughing at some inane comedy on the screen. He saw him outside sitting on the grass topping up his tan, in the refectory eating a shepherd's pie with gusto.

When the realisation hit him it almost knocked Walls off his feet. On the outside Roper was a nothing and a nobody, just another teenager with no prospects, no money and a criminal record but on the inside, he was a force to be reckoned with, someone who could use his physical strength to rule the roost.

'*Oh my God,*' Walls groaned, as he realised the ramifications that were unfolding.

Roper didn't care about being caught, the fact that he had murdered a man wouldn't bother him in the slightest. The only thing he would care about now was finding Luke Croft and finishing the job, after that he would happily spend the next twenty years behind bars, content and happy with his lot in life.

Spinning on his heels Walls ran back to the house, the fear with him every step of the way. Slamming the door closed, he leaned back against the woodwork, eyes wide, sweat running down his terrified face.

In the hallway, the clock chimed, the seconds ticking away into infinity.

43

The incident room was awash with whispers and sighs; Marnie was sitting with Paul Clark and Bev Harvey as they waited for DCI Reese to put in an appearance.

'And you're sure there was no sign of Roper?' Marnie asked.

Paul shook his head. 'The place was a dump, empty cans everywhere, the usual shit but no sign of Roper.'

Marnie sighed in disappointment. By the time she had made it home it was gone midnight and she'd fallen asleep on the sofa, her mind crammed with images of Oldman, the gruesome gash in his throat opening wide as Doc Kelly rolled the body onto its back. She thought of Luke, out there in the dark, unaware that his stepfather had been slaughtered. As usual Abby floated to the surface, the rain hammering down as she was carried away into the mist.

Marnie whimpered in her sleep and five hours later she had been climbing into the shower, trying to shake the nightmare as she got dressed and headed out into the early morning sunshine.

When the door banged open the room fell silent, Reese stormed into the room his face serious, his brow furrowed.

Heading behind his desk, he stopped and turned, a black file clasped in his right hand.

Marnie held her breath as he flicked it open.

'I've just received this from the North Wales force, they've found a match for one set of remains in the woods.'

One or two people gasped at the news, others remained grim faced, Pam Oaks narrowed her eyes and crossed her legs.

'The girl's name was Josie Roberts,' Reese sighed as he studied the file. 'Aged seven, she vanished in two-thousand and one, the family lived in Conwy and Josie attended a local school. The day she went missing, the class had gone down to the beach – twenty-four children – with two teachers to keep an eye on them. According to records, the kids were looking in the rock pools and Josie simply vanished. It was believed at the time that she had somehow wandered away from the group and had possibly slipped on the rocks and fallen into the sea,' he paused, 'we now know that wasn't the case.'

Glances were exchanged, the air charged with tension.

Marnie grabbed her ponytail, her fingers pulling and tugging.

'Now, we're trying to identify the other remains found in the woods and a search of the area will continue until we're absolutely sure that there is no one else to be found.'

One or two heads turned in Marnie's direction but she ignored them, choosing to keep her eyes locked on the DCI.

Reese looked around the room, his face grave. 'The fact that a daisy ring was found on two of the victims indicates that they were killed by the same person and at this juncture it seems prudent to assume that the others were all murdered by the same hand.'

Heads nodded in agreement.

'I want *all* records pulled on any local paedophiles, I know this has already been done but I want them checking again and this time you're looking for any links with North Wales.'

'Was Josie taken in the summertime?' Pam asked.

Reese slid his hands into his pockets. 'July.'

'So, the beach would have been busy?'

Reese sighed. 'Correct.'

Marnie thought for a moment before flicking up a hand.

Reese looked at her, his face haggard, his eyes red rimmed. 'Go on, Marnie?'

'If it was the height of summer then it could have been someone who worked in the area during the busiest months.'

'Such as?' Reese enquired.

'Well, perhaps on the fair, cafes, or one of the tourist shops. I mean, in that kind of work you see people coming and going all day, so it would be easy to target an individual without raising suspicion.'

Pam Oaks flicked a glance at Marnie before smiling and nodding in agreement.

Reese leaned back and folded his arms. 'OK, good thinking. Right, so we all know what we are doing, I want everything checked and then checked again, we have the name of one of the victims so it's up to us to find the links.'

Chairs were pushed back and people headed for the door but Marnie remained in her seat, her face impassive, though inside she was agitated.

As the last of the stragglers left, Reese turned to Marnie and raised an eyebrow.

'Before you ask, I'm waiting for fingerprints to get in touch, they dusted the Croft house so if this Roper character was there then we should know soon enough.'

'What about Walls?' she asked.

Reese tilted his head slightly. 'I thought I made it clear last night we leave Walls alone, and don't say you don't like the man because there are plenty of people I don't like but that doesn't mean I can lock them up and throw away the key. Besides, one set of remains could turn out to be the man's daughter, so for now we wait to see how this unfolds.'

Marnie remained in the seat, arms folded as Reese pushed himself away from the desk.

'Listen to me, Marnie, Oldman was murdered and Roper is a suspect but trying to tie him in with Gareth Walls is a step too far. For all we know there could have been unfinished business between Roper and Luke Croft.'

'Unfinished business?'

Reese sighed. 'Come on, if Roper is as bad as you suggest then he could simply have wanted to carry on with the abuse on the outside. He gets on a bus heads across town looking for the boy but finds Oldman there instead, now...'

'Even if that is the case, it still leaves Luke out there, clueless as to what's happened, and if Roper did murder Oldman as soon as he catches up with Luke he'll kill him and we will have done nothing to stop it.'

As soon as she uttered the words she knew she had gone too far.

Reese's scowl turned into a look of burning anger. 'Are you saying I'm not doing my job properly, Sergeant Hammond?'

Marnie chose her next words carefully, fully aware that her boss was close to losing it big time. 'Luke doesn't deserve to have an animal like Roper hunting him down, yes he broke the law, yes he's been a pain in the arse but it still doesn't alter the fact that he was sent to Park View to learn a lesson but not...'

Reese snatched the file from the desk and thrust it forward. 'Josie Roberts was seven years old when she was taken, she wasn't shoplifting or trying to steal a car, she was *playing on the bloody beach*! I thought you of all people would have been all over this like a rash and yet you sit there as if this means nothing!' He shook the file in his fist, the rage flashing in his eyes.

Marnie stood up slowly. 'Josie Roberts has been dead for nearly two decades, my *sister* went missing fifteen years ago, now I have no idea if any of this is linked but the truth is I gave up any hope that Abby was still alive years ago.'

Reese eased back, the fury subsiding, caution taking its place. 'Listen, I'm sorry, that was out of order but...'

'They're dead but Luke Croft isn't,' she replied, straightening her shoulders and standing ramrod stiff.

Reese held her gaze before turning away and dropping the file to the desk. 'Every patrol working the streets knows about Croft and Roper and if they see either one of them then they'll be brought in. Now, if you think I'm overlooking anything or shirking my duties in some way then I'm sorry but my priority is catching the animal who took Josie Roberts and cut her up before leaving her in the woods, the same animal that killed the other unknown girls and was possibly responsible for starving Jenny Bell to death, so if you think I'm in the wrong, then tough shit.'

Marnie felt the anger writhe inside, her hands closed into fists, the sound of remembered thunder rolled in her head as Abby looked at her with the cold, hard accusation flashing from her long, dead eyes.

'I need you focused on this, Marnie, you have to give me one hundred percent.'

'I always do,' she barked back.

Reese held her gaze, he could see the anger in her eyes, the fury burning deep. 'Just take a look at the files, if there's anything there then you'll find it.'

Marnie glanced at her shoes before nodding. 'No problem,' she said, crossing the room and closing the door quietly as she left.

44

Sally Walls stood at the bedroom window, one hand rubbed absently at the tender spot high on her left leg, her other hand clutching the teddy to her breast, it had been Suzie's favourite and the ache for her missing daughter forced the tears from her eyes.

During the night, she had lain in the dark listening to Gareth clattering around downstairs, occasionally hearing him bark out in anger, the fear rising as she watched the luminous dial on the bedside clock; by two o'clock fatigue took over and despite her best effort she had closed her eyes and drifted off to sleep.

Her eyes had sprung open when she'd heard heavy footfall on the stairs, as if her slumbering mind had remained on high alert, waiting for the sound that brought instant fear roaring back into her head. When the door opened, light from the landing had spilled into the room and she held her breath. The tension in her head crackled, hearing him grunt and kick off his shoes made her shiver under the duvet in fright.

'*Bloody bitch,*' he muttered.

Sally felt the sweat break out on her body, when she heard the whisper of his belt sliding through the loops she tensed.

'How *dare* she, how fucking *dare* she!'

Sally had whispered a silent prayer, hoping that her husband would simply climb into bed and fall asleep.

The room fell silent; she could feel the warm breeze filtering in through the open window.

Gareth Walls grunted as if in answer to some internal question.

When the duvet was whipped back, she kept her lips clamped together.

'*Teach you to question me!*' her husband bellowed.

Sally felt her soul shrivel, the sound of the leather belt whipped through the air. When it lashed across her thigh she almost cried out, though bitter experience had taught her to remain silent, if she was quiet then maybe he would be satisfied with hitting her a couple of times. If she made a sound, then it seemed to enrage him further, and the lashings would continue until her screams echoed around the room.

The belt hit again, the pain in her side exploded in a welt of fire, then Gareth had slumped down on the bed.

Sally felt him drag the duvet over them, she had lain still, waiting, listening, the minutes ticked by, somewhere in the dark she heard an owl hoot.

'*Slut,*' Gareth snorted then almost immediately he started to snore, the stink of whisky almost making Sally gag.

Now, she stood at the window watching as her husband climbed behind the wheel of the Range Rover.

Suddenly she started to cry. She tried to see a way out of her life, an escape, yet she knew that Gareth would never allow it. He was a man of standing, well thought of by the great and the good, and the last thing he would want was a wife going off the rails.

Besides she had committed the greatest sin of all, she had lost their daughter, failed to protect her, and Suzie had been spirited away leaving Sally in a never-ending limbo of crushing guilt. She thought back to before their daughter had been taken, even back then Gareth had been cutting with his remarks, nothing she had ever done had been good enough. After Suzie's disappearance, her husband had pinned the blame directly on her, and every day he made her pay for it. Over the years, Gareth had screamed at her, terrible words of accusations and then he had started to lash out, starting with slaps and gradually the attacks had increased in ferocity as all her husband's anger and hatred had spewed forth.

The tears slid down Sally's cheeks as she watched her husband drive away, knowing that there would be no happy ending, and most definitely no release date for her.

45

Bev placed the cup of coffee by Marnie's elbow before sitting down opposite her. Even with the window open it felt hot in the small room, the fans in the computers whirring in an attempt to cool the machines down.

Closing yet another file Marnie rubbed at her tired eyes. Bev glanced at her before looking down at the papers on the desk. 'I still can't believe how many perverts there are in a town this size,' she said, shaking her head.

Marnie nodded in agreement, they had been searching through the files for over ten hours and the light was starting to fade on yet another fruitless day. She knew that other officers in the building were doing the same, heads bent as they read one distressing tale after another, stretching back over twenty years.

She also had no doubt that one of her colleagues would be reading about the disappearance of her sister, pouring over the details of the day Abby vanished. The thought made her grimace, she took a sip from the coffee and lifted another file from the pile to her left.

'So, how are things with you and the undertaker?' she asked, in an effort to lighten the mood.

Bev pulled a face. 'Don't ask.'

Marnie raised an eyebrow. 'Why, what happened?'

'I left school twelve years ago, and I know people can change a lot in that time but when he was at school Sam was captain of the football team. While everyone else caught the bus to school he ran all the way there without breaking sweat.'

Marnie opened the file but kept her eyes on Bev. 'So, he liked to keep fit there's nothing wrong with that.'

'Keeping fit is fine but when I met him the other night he was like some muscle-bound freak,'

'A sted-head?'

Bev sighed. 'It was like sitting down for a meal with the Incredible Hulk. I kept thinking he was going to split his suit and turn bloody green on me.'

Marnie smiled at the image and then she thought of Luke Croft and the smile slipped.

'Well, better luck next time,' she said, looking at the file on the desk.

She started to read about Steven Cox, a local man, who had been questioned about having sex with an underage girl years earlier.

Charlene Reynolds had been fourteen, Cox had been in his mid-twenties and working on a travelling fairground. Marnie frowned, her eyes skimming through the file, the case had gone to court and, according to the record, Cox hadn't turned up so a warrant had been posted for his arrest.

Marnie's eyes widened as she read that he had been picked up in North Wales still working for the travelling fairground.

Seeing the date of his arrest, she felt her heart skip a beat, Cox had been working in the area at the same time Josie Roberts had gone missing.

She looked up, Bev was just taking a sip from her coffee.

'Look at this,' Marnie said, sliding the file across the desk.

Bev wiped her lips with the back of her hand before spinning the file around.

Outside, air brakes squealed as a truck pulled up at the traffic lights.

Bev snapped her head up, Marnie nodded in acknowledgement then stood up.

'There's a local address in the file, it needs checking.'

Bev followed suit, the air suddenly charged as they grabbed their coats and headed out of the room. They hurried down the corridor, by the time they exited the station they were running for the car.

46

The man woke and grunted, climbing slowly to his feet he grimaced at his aching muscles. The skulls on the table seemed indistinct, pale blobs mingling with the shadows. Turning, he walked from the small room and into the cellar, the pitiful cone of light did little to force the shadows back. The man trudged up the steps, his head still clotted with sleep and bad memories.

Reaching the top of the cellar stairs, he opened the door and stepped into the large, oak-panelled hallway.

Running a hand across the back of his neck, he made his way into the lounge, the clock ticking in the corner, the air still, dust motes filtered through pale shafts of dying sunlight.

The man made it to the Chesterfield sofa and slumped down, the years of doing nothing had left him weak, drained. Everything was an effort now, everything needed planning carefully.

Plumping one of the threadbare cushions, he placed his head down and closed his eyes, confident that he would wake when darkness filled the room, then he would go back to the house and continue his vigil, waiting, watching until…

He started to snore, this time there were no bad dreams sweeping through his dark mind, this time he slept like a newborn baby.

47

Luke woke with a start, for a few seconds he stared at the red brick wall convinced he was back in Park View, the drab wall inches from his face, the lumpy mattress beneath his bruised body.

He shot to his feet, the fear rising. When he heard the cars passing on the road, the terror peaked and then began to subside, leaving him shaking with cold and fear.

He stood unsteadily on the sprung mattress before squeezing out from behind the bins. A thin breeze blew under the canopy, and Luke dragged a hand across his tired eyes.

Half a minute later, he emerged onto the main road and looked right, he could see the town centre lit up, people walking on Market Street moving from pub to club. Unease crawled over his skin, thirst and hunger gnawed at his stomach. He must have slept the day away behind the bins, like some hibernating animal simply wanting to sleep and forget about the harsh reality of life.

Flicking up the hood of his sweatshirt, he set off walking, his face creased with tiredness and distress, his feet throbbing with each painful step. A taxi went flying by, the windows open, the sound of laughter unravelling into the early evening air. Luke felt a strange twist in his chest, he had never had a night out in town, never even ridden in a taxi. He went everywhere on foot or if, on the rare occasion he had money, he caught the bus.

He thought of the wasted years spent hanging around with the older teenagers, trying to impress, trying to be something he wasn't and getting a police record in the process. He remembered laughing at some of the kids in school, the ones who always looked neat and tidy with their new bags and shiny shoes. While he was trying to find ways to get out of doing any work, they would be sitting at their desks, heads bent, working hard to get good grades. In his five years at secondary school Luke had never done a scrap of homework, never read a book; only now was he starting to realise that he had been the fool.

He had no doubt that those who had done the work would now be at college, some would move onto university and get jobs, proper jobs that paid a decent wage, while he trudged the streets with nowhere to go and no chance to escape this drab town and the threat of violence. Suddenly, every step felt as if a weight were being added to his shoulders, his breathing sounded laboured, his body started to sweat. He tried to fathom how things had turned out like this, what made him different to the kids at school who had done well and tried hard, and suddenly he knew the real reason, they came from a loving family and he didn't.

Was it really that simple? Luke realised that he could have done the same as them if his mother had encouraged him and helped him. She had never asked him about school, never made sure he did his homework or helped him study, so Luke had lost interest and now, here he was homeless, penniless, no qualifications, just a police record, walking down the street with taxis ferrying people to the town centre for a night of fun with friends, groups of young people laughing and shouting, going from pub to pub. And himself on the outside, looking in.

The other kids at school had never bothered with him, why should they when they had their lives mapped out and he was like some train wreck waiting to happen?

He had hit the buffers at Park View, a buffer named Alby Roper who had smashed his fists and boots into Luke's battered body with glee.

When he looked up, it was to find the pavements crowded with people; coming towards him were three girls, arms linked, their heads thrown back, laughing, a group of lads eyeing them from across the road.

Luke stopped in disbelief; he had been so lost in the misery, so closed off from reality that he now felt the panic rise as he found himself on the crowded street.

His eyes flicked from one face to another, scared to hover too long in case they looked his way and noticed the scruffy boy in the shabby clothes and tatty trainers.

The girls continued to laugh, Luke glanced over his shoulder but the pavement behind was full of people walking towards him, the boys dressed in clean jeans and designer tops, the girls with flowing hair and high heels.

Luke staggered into the doorway of the Oxfam shop, one of the three girls looked at him and smiled, Luke felt his soul shrivel as he saw the look of pity in her eyes.

Lowering his head, he shuffled back until he hit the door, suddenly the air was filled with the sound of singing, laughter and merriment, the cacophony drilled into his head. He tried to think when he had last laughed but he couldn't remember, the thought crushed him in exactly the same way Roper's boot had as it slammed into his back.

48

'We're on our way over there now,' Marnie explained as she changed up a gear and checked the mirrors, her right hand holding the wheel in a light grip.

'*So, what else do we know about this Steven Cox?*' Reese's voice came out of the phone placed in the holder.

Marnie eased down on the gas as she explained about Cox being arrested in North Wales two weeks after Josie Roberts had vanished.

At her side, Bev watched the world go by through the side window.

'*Right, I'm just leaving now so I'll make my way over to the house and meet you there.*'

'No problem.'

'*I should be there within the hour depending on the traffic.*'

'OK.'

'*Oh by the way, I've heard back from forensics about the fingerprints, Roper was in the house, we've got clear prints from two empty cans of lager.*'

Marnie felt the tension inside tighten. 'I bloody knew it.'

'*I've got a couple of officers keeping an eye on his flat, if he goes back there then we'll have him.*'

'And if he doesn't?' Marnie asked, her voice brittle with pent-up emotion.

Reese sighed. '*Look, Kirkhead isn't a big town, so he can't hide forever.*'

'He doesn't have to stay hidden forever, he's already killed one man and he knows that we'll catch him, so all he will be concerned with is making Luke pay.'

'*I...*'

'I was the one who went to Park View and questioned Walls, Luke never pointed the finger but Roper won't care about that, he'll…'

'We've already been over this and we're doing all we can to catch Roper but the world doesn't grind to a halt, Marnie, we have a lead on the murder of Josie Roberts and I expect you to follow it.'

'But…'

'I expect you to do your job, so for now you concentrate on this Cox character!' the DCI's voice went up a notch, the anger evident in every word.

Bev glanced at Marnie, she had her eyes narrowed, her teeth clamped in anger as she pulled up to the red traffic lights.

Her phone beeped, the DCI had hung up.

Bev folded her hand in her lap, her eyes locked on the road ahead.

Marnie closed her eyes for a moment, inside she was seething at the latest news. When she opened them and saw the figure, dressed in scruffy jeans and sweatshirt with the hood up, walking past the front of the car, she felt the breath hitch in her throat, instinctively she slammed a hand on the horn.

The man jumped and snapped his head around and Marnie let the disappointment out in a long sigh as she realised it wasn't Luke.

Bev gave her a quizzical look, the lights changed and Marnie sighed before moving forward.

'Don't worry, boss, we'll find the lad.'

'I know,' Marnie replied, as the roadside lights came to life. 'I just hope he's still alive when we do.'

49

The man strode from the house, brain buzzing, his thoughts clear as crystal.

For the first time in years everything was there, instant recall, the room in the cellar, the skulls, the ledger and the names written in his neat handwriting.

Turning left, he breathed in the evening air, the dying sun brushed the sky in raspberry swirls of colour, his shiny shoes crunched the gravel.

It was cool in the shade of the hulking house, the blackened windows passing to his left, the smell of dark earth wafted on the night breeze as he made his way to the garage.

Once behind the wheel he went through the same ritual, sliding hands into gloves, checking all the mirrors before starting the engine and turning on the lights; then he frowned as the memory flittered through his mind.

With a grunt, he pushed open the door and climbed out, walking around the car checking the lights, then he placed his foot on the brake and glanced over his shoulder, watching the red lights flare against the garage wall.

Satisfied, he sat back behind the wheel, a smile hovering around his lips.

'Ready,' he mumbled, driving out of the garage and along the snaking driveway, finally emerging onto the tree-lined lane.

Flicking the lights to full beam, he eased back in the sumptuous leather, his hands held on the wheel at ten to two, his eyes burning with dark desire.

50

arnie lifted a hand to knock on the door just as the
terrified scream erupted from inside the small semi-
detached council house.

The sound was abruptly cut off and Bev gasped.

Marnie slammed a hand against the door and the screaming
started again, loud and piercing.

'Jesus, what the hell's going on?' Bev said, placing a nervous
hand on her baton.

Stepping back Marnie lashed out her right leg, her foot
slammed into the lock, the door shook but held fast, meanwhile
another muffled scream echoed inside the house.

'*Fucking useless bitch!*' the voice bellowed.

Marnie kicked out again, putting every ounce of strength
behind the blow, this time the door bounced inwards.

'*POLICE!*' She shouted, sprinting down the hallway, to her
right she heard a young child wailing, the sound high-pitched
and animal-like in the confines of the house.

'*Check in there!*' Marnie fired over her shoulder before racing into
a kitchen that resembled a war zone. The fridge and table had been
overturned, a carton of milk lay on its side, the contents glugging
across the floor, mixing with the yolks of half a dozen smashed eggs.

A young woman in her early twenties lay sprawled against
the front of a washer on fast spin, her breasts jiggling from side
to side to the rhythm, eyes wide, her lips smeared with blood
that dripped down onto her Bart Simpson onesie. The machine
clattered, Marnie crouched on her haunches, her anger flaring.

'Are you OK?' she asked, as the woman dragged a hand across
her bloodstained mouth.

'Bastard hit me with the frying pan,' she managed to mumble through a froth of blood.

Bev Harvey arrived in the kitchen with a child held in her arms; the girl looked to be around six or seven, she rubbed at her eyes, her hair a tangled mess, bottom lip quivering. As soon as Bev spotted the woman looking bloodied and dazed a look of anger flashed across her face.

Marnie heard the yelp of pain coming from the garden, and bolted to her feet; snatching the baton from Bev's belt, she stormed to the kitchen door in time to see a darkened figure clambering over the fence.

She blasted across the patio, sprinting through the long grass, she leapt into the air, clearing the weed-infested border and hitting the fence hard. Scrambling to the top, she saw the man dash through the fading light, barging his way past a children's slide and swing before running for the side gate.

Marnie landed in a crouch, flicking her wrist the baton sprang open as she dashed across the garden and through the open gate.

The attacker was running down the side of the house, his long legs eating up the ground.

With a look of ferocious determination locked on her face, Marnie took a deep breath and sprinted after him. By the time she made it to the front gate he was halfway across the street. He glanced over his shoulder, seeing Marnie closing him down he snarled, before snapping his head around and setting off again.

At the junction, he turned sharp left down a narrow alleyway, his boots ringing out on the cobbled stone, sweat coating his brow, slick and warm.

Marnie let the fury take control, she sprinted forward, her feet moving over the ground – sure-footed – closing the gap.

The alleyway led to an open field of scrub grass and she watched the man scoop down to pick up a blackened chunk of wood from the ground, a remnant from a November bonfire.

Skidding to an abrupt halt, he spun towards her, his face smeared with hatred, his lips drawn back, crooked teeth on show.

Marnie didn't hesitate, and at the last second, she saw the man's eyes widen in surprise.

Raising the length of wood, he swung it sideways in a wide arc, determined to slam it into the side of her head.

Marnie beat him to it, the baton whistled through the air and slammed between his legs.

A split second of silence, the world stopped turning, everything paused – then the pain hit. The man screamed in agony, any thought of violence vanished, his head snapped back, and the make shift weapon fell from his grasping fingers.

He hit the ground hard, his scream peeling away into the growing darkness, both hands clutched between his legs.

Pushing the hair from her eyes, Marnie looked down at him writhing on the ground, his T-shirt riding up, revealing an expanse of pale flesh.

Easing onto her haunches, she peered into his glaring, pain-filled eyes.

'*Fucking bitch,*' he managed to snarl.

Marnie smiled, though there was no hint of humour in her dark-brown eyes. 'You're nicked, dickhead.'

Cal Wilson closed his hate-filled eyes and continued to groan.

51

The man felt the confusion press against his mind as he watched another police car pull up in front of the house, blue lights flashing, siren wailing, sending a bolt of fear through his heart.

When the doors opened and two officers jumped out, he reached for the gear lever, convinced that they would sprint across the road to where he was parked in front of the scruffy parade of shops.

He sighed in relief when they headed up the garden path and vanished inside the house.

Glancing in the wing mirror, he saw a man standing in the doorway to the newsagents, smoking a cigarette, watching the drama unfold across the road.

Seconds later he pushed the car door open and climbed out, heading towards the smoker.

'Never a dull moment around here,' the shopkeeper said, taking another pull on the cigarette.

'I wonder what's happened?' the man asked over the noise of an ambulance screeching to a halt outside the house.

'See the bloke they're loading into the back of the meat wagon?'

The man looked across the street to see two officers flanking a thin-faced man with short, white hair, being manhandled into the back of a van.

'What about him?' he asked.

'That's Cal Wilson and let me tell you the man is a tosser, always kicking off at anyone who gets in his way, how that young lass puts up with him is beyond me.'

The man turned and they both watched the paramedics run up the path and into the house. 'Regular occurrence I take it?' he queried.

'You could say that, the coppers are never away from the place, called out at all hours they are, because of the screaming and shouting, and then Wilson has put her in hospital at least twice – yet he's still there, bold as bloody brass. I tell you it stinks.'

The man glared across the street, his dark eyes shining.

'The world's a bloody mess,' the shopkeeper continued, flicking the cigarette to the floor. 'I feel for the mother and the little girl, I mean, imagine living in a house with that animal?'

The shopkeeper's words seeped into his mind, the anger howled through the core of him.

He thought of the girl, frozen in time, trapped in a house of violence and his face twitched in anger.

'Anyway, what can I get you?' the newsagent stepped back and pushed the door open.

The man had his gloved hands in his pockets the fury writhing inside.

'Are you OK?'

He turned and managed to smile before nodding. 'Do you sell milk?' he asked.

'We sell bloody everything,' the man replied, vanishing in the shop.

Taking one last look across the road he entered the shop, pulling out his wallet while the door closed behind him.

52

Half an hour later, Marnie was standing in the living room listening to Mandy Farmer's sister lose her rag.

The ambulance had arrived and Mandy had been taken to hospital, her boyfriend Cal Wilson was sitting in the back of a police van at the front of the property, spitting and cursing about police brutality.

'So, this has happened before?' Marnie asked, as Dawn held young Emma Farmer in her arms.

'All the bloody time,' Dawn replied. 'I'm sick to death of telling our Mandy to leave the bastard but she always bursts into tears and says she *loves* him!'

Marnie sighed, it was the same old story; an abused woman making excuses for her partner and when all else failed they fell back onto the tried and tested 'I love him' cliché.

'If I wasn't here to pick up the pieces then Emma would have been taken into care months ago,' Dawn said with a sigh. 'I tried for seven years to have a kid, three lots of IVF and nothing. Then you have my sister who's had two abortions because the "time wasn't right" and now she has a child and couldn't give a toss.'

Marnie kept her mouth closed as Dawn fumed at the injustice.

'Well, from now on she can forget it,' Dawn looked at Marnie, her eyes alive with anger. 'She's had plenty of chances, if she wants to carry on living with that prick then that's her choice, but there's no way she's getting her hands on Emma, she can fuck right off!'

Marnie pursed her lips before clearing her throat. 'I'm just glad we turned up when we did.'

Dawn scowled as she continued to stroke Emma's unruly hair. 'Hang on, what were you doing here in the first place?'

'We came looking for a Steven Cox, we had this as his last-known address and...'

'Cox is dead and good bloody riddance.'

Marnie's eyes widened in surprise. 'Dead?'

'As a doornail,' Dawn replied.

'You knew him?'

Dawn snorted. 'Of course I knew him; he was my father.'

Marnie took a step back as Emma buried her head into Dawn's shoulder, the child had a thumb plugging her mouth, tears glistening on her closed lids.

'When did he die?'

'Six years ago – he worked on the fair and got trapped in one of the rides.'

'I see,' Marnie felt the disappointment clouding her head, she had come here with the intention of questioning Cox and now that particular door had been slammed shut.

'Neither me nor our Mandy had seen him for years, and I thank God for that.'

'He was a bad father?'

'The worst,' Dawn replied, her eyes full of anger. 'He made our mother's life a misery. She died ten years ago of cancer, towards the end she went into a hospice and that bastard turned up and moved in here as if nothing had happened.'

'I see.'

'He never went to see her, never asked how she was; he just saw this as a place to stay rent free, I wouldn't mind but my mother worked all hours God sent to buy this place.'

'But I take it he moved out?'

Dawn sighed heavily and nodded. 'Eventually. You see there's not much call for travelling fairgrounds in the winter, that's why he came here, but as soon as spring time came around he buggered off. The following year he turned up again but this time we were ready for him and wouldn't let him step foot in the house. He tried to barge in but we managed to slam the door and then we rang your lot but by the time someone showed up he'd done a runner.'

'And that was the last time you saw him?'

'Yeah.'

'Do you know where he went to stay?'

Dawn shrugged. 'I know he had a small caravan at the fair but don't know any more than that.'

Marnie took a step closer to Dawn. 'Did your mother trust him?'

'God no, she…'

'I meant did she trust him around you and your sister?' Marnie asked.

Dawn's eyes widened, her face flushing with colour. 'Why do you ask that?'

Mindful of Emma being in the room, it took all of Marnie's ingenuity to explain the situation without little Emma repeating any words.

Dawn sighed and lowered her voice to a whisper as she placed her free hand over Emma's ear. 'Look, he never laid a finger on me or Mandy but my mother never left us alone with him, now, that could be because she didn't trust him to look after us properly or it could be that she thought he was a creep.'

'A creep?'

Dawn nodded slowly. 'That winter he came to stay I didn't feel comfortable, he used to walk into the bedroom without knocking and he always seemed to be there when I was wrapped in a bloody towel.'

'So, you didn't feel safe?'

'It was like having a complete stranger in the house, we hadn't seen the man for years and then suddenly he's there all the time. Let's just say I made sure our Mandy slept with me while he was here.'

Marnie nodded in understanding.

'I can see him now, sitting in that chair, his eyes following me across the room, he made my skin crawl.'

Reaching out, Marnie ran a hand over Emma's hair letting one of the curls wrap around her finger, an image of doing the same thing with Abby's hair flashed through her mind and she felt her heart ache at the memory.

'What happens now?' Dawn asked.

Marnie blinked and stepped back. 'Wilson has been arrested, so hopefully…'

'Mandy won't press charges, she never does.'

'Well, let's take things one step at a time, in my experience women in your sister's position all have a point where they say enough is enough.'

Dawn shook her head. 'I know I seem like a heartless bitch but I worry about her and I'm terrified what it's doing to Emma, she shouldn't be in an environment like this, it's not right.'

'I agree,' Marnie said. 'So, are you taking Emma home with you?'

'I know she'll be safe with me.'

'Good,' Marnie walked with Dawn along the hallway and watched as she carried Emma to her car and tenderly strapped her into a booster seat.

Dawn raised a hand and climbed behind the wheel.

Marnie felt the need for a cigarette grow and then she sighed as DCI Reese screeched to a halt in front of the house.

'Typical,' she mumbled, walking out to meet him.

53

The man eased forward in the seat, his eyes widening as he saw the woman carrying Mandy down the path before placing her in the back seat of an estate car.

His heart started to thud as the woman climbed behind the wheel, seconds later the headlight sprang to life and the car pulled away from the kerb.

Grunting, the man slotted the Mercedes into gear and pulled out onto the small service road, his eyes flitting nervously towards the house. When he saw the woman walking through the garden gate his thumping heart almost stopped.

Hitting the brakes, he watched her talking to a tall man with short, dark hair, suddenly he was back in the room with the tall trees, the wind howling, the rain lashing down, the girl running towards him, her hair flying, her mouth stretched wide as she dashed through the downpour.

'*Abby!*' the word blasted out and the man shook his head, in an effort to dislodge the image.

The engine of the big car purred, he waited at the junction, his mind in chaos, when the woman glanced across the street towards the car the spell was broken. He pulled right and drove down the street, his bewildered eyes kept flicking to the interior mirror in disbelief.

Then he faced front, the taillights of the estate car were mere smudges of red in the distance.

'*Concentrate,*' the inner voice insisted.

'Yes, yes, concentrate,' he repeated, easing down on the accelerator.

54

M arnie watched the black car drive away into the darkness, a frown plucking at her brow.

'So, Cox is dead?' Reese asked with a sigh.

She turned and nodded. 'Dawn and Mandy are his daughters and according to Dawn he was a total waste of space as a father.'

Reese looked annoyed as he glanced towards the house. 'Right, we need to know more about the man, I want to know his movements over the past twenty years.'

Marnie opened her mouth and Reese snapped up a hand. 'Don't worry I've got people checking already and DI Oaks is cross-checking the movements of the fair that Cox worked for.'

'If we can prove that Cox was working in the areas that the girls went missing it could provide the answers we're looking for.'

'Precisely.'

Marnie gave her ponytail a tug as Reese tilted his head to the night sky.

'I know it's probably not politically correct but I hope to God Cox was responsible. I know it would be hard for the parents but at least it will allow for some closure,' he said.

'Yes, but Cox can't have taken Jenny Bell.'

Reese sighed in understanding. 'I realise that, so we have to keep looking, we have to follow the threads.'

Marnie thought of her sister, the possibility that Cox could have been responsible for her being taken was a bitter pill to swallow, especially with the man dead. In her darkest moments, she had always imagined a scenario where she found the one responsible and made him pay for all the years of heartache and despair.

'Listen, Marnie, I've been thinking about what you said about Roper and Croft.'

She looked at her boss with a keen glimmer in her eye. 'And?'

'I think you could be onto something.'

'What about Walls?' she asked, trying to keep her voice calm and level.

Reese arched an eyebrow. 'When you went to question the governor, how many people knew about Luke Croft being beaten?'

'Apart from you and me there was Paul Clark and Doc Kelly.'

Reese nodded his face thoughtful. 'Well, someone had to have pressed Roper's buttons for him to turn up at the house and kill Oldman.'

'Agreed,' she responded.

Reese checked his watch. 'OK, first thing in the morning get back to Park View and have another word with Walls, make the bugger sweat but don't overstep the mark.'

'No problem.'

'In the meantime, if we get any news on Cox then I'll give you a call so keep your phone on.'

'Right.'

Reese looked at her and smiled. 'Off you go then.'

Marnie headed over to her car and climbed in, as she drove away she could see Reese in her mirror diminishing until he vanished into the darkness.

55

'Are you OK?'

Luke glanced up from the doorway of the Oxfam shop. A girl stood in front of him, the same one who had smiled when she walked passed. But now there was a look of compassion in her eyes.

'I'm fine,' he mumbled, lowering his gaze.

She stepped closer and he caught her scent, sweet and fresh, Luke was aware of his own odour – a tart smell of sweat and fear.

When she lifted the purse from her pocket and snapped the clasp, he jolted back as if she had pulled a loaded gun on him. When she held out the ten-pound note Luke shook his head.

'Go on take it, you look hungry and thirsty.'

Luke stared at the money, he felt wretched and cursed this simple act of kindness, reinforcing how low he had sunk in his pitiful life.

'No thanks,' he muttered.

The girl tilted her head slightly, her hair seemed to glide from one shoulder to the other. 'It's not much, but I want you to have it.'

Luke's hands began to shake, the battle inside raged, one voice screaming to take the cash, the other begging him not to.

He shook his head again and the girl smiled, showing perfect teeth, Luke blinked, looking at her properly for the first time.

The last time he'd seen her she had been sitting two desks to the left in maths, her head bowed as she effortlessly scribbled answers on the white paper; Luke had signed his name at the top of the sheet and then sat back with his arms folded.

'*Sarah,*' he whispered her name and she nodded, the sadness in her eyes deepening.

'What happened to you, Luke?'

The fact that she knew his name stunned him into silence; he had always thought she was stuck up, always with her head in a book, never acknowledging him as they passed in the corridor.

'Please, take the money,' she repeated.

If Luke had felt wretched before, he suddenly felt a thousand time worse, the fact that she knew him somehow made the feeling of humiliation more acute.

'*I can't,*' he gasped, tears flooding his eyes.

Sarah took a step forward as Luke hunched his shoulders and lowered his head.

'Have you been sleeping rough?' she asked in a quiet voice.

He shook his head, the emotion thick in his throat, a solid lump that seemed to expand and fill him to the brim. 'I've got to go,' he managed to mumble.

Sarah didn't move and Luke hovered in the door unsure what to do.

'Please, let me help you, I...'

As soon as she uttered the words Luke barged forward. '*Can't help me!*' he gasped.

She grabbed his sleeve but he snatched his arm free and broke into a run.

'*Luke wait!*' she shouted after him.

Within seconds he had sprinted to the junction, turned left and vanished. Sarah looked down at the money in her right hand before slipping it into her coat pocket with a heavy sigh. When she glanced across the road she saw two police officers in shiny yellow vests talking to a group of girls.

She thought of Luke and the panic in his eyes, the desperation as he turned and sprinted away.

Mind made up she headed across the road, her hair swaying, her face set with determination.

56

Before leaving the house, Roper had rifled through the pockets of the dead man, when he found the thirty quid in his trouser pocket he had grinned in delight before going in search of more cash. He'd found another twenty pounds in a drawer upstairs along with a handful of loose change. Now, he stood on Market Street munching on a hot dog smothered in greasy onions and tomato ketchup.

He watched as people walked back and forth, some already pissed, others well on the way to joining them.

When he spotted the two coppers on the right, he angled left and lowered his head before taking another chunk from the hot dog. The air laced with the whiff of cheap perfume and fast food.

Making his way down the street, his mind bubbled with anger as he scanned the faces looking for Croft, feeling the disappointment rise when he came up with yet another blank. When he banged shoulders with a girl she snapped her head around and frowned.

'Hey, watch where you're going.'

'*Fuck off, bitch,*' he hissed in reply.

Her eyes widened and he sneered before stalking away.

Reaching the junction, he hesitated for a moment trying to fathom where the little shit could be hiding. Glancing left, he saw the bulk of darkened trees in the distance leading to open parkland. If he was in Croft's shoes then the park would be a good place to hide, close enough to the town centre yet at this time of night it would be quiet, offering plenty of places to get your head down.

Roper grunted, turned left and headed down the road; the sound of the revellers shouting and bawling slowly faded as he left the busy street behind.

Pushing the last of the hot dog into his mouth, he dropped the paper napkin to the floor, licking the ketchup from his fingers with a sigh of contentment.

It felt good to have cash in his pocket, all he needed now was to find Croft, and all would be well with the world. After he had killed the little bastard he would try and avoid the police until the money ran out, then he would hand himself in and admit to the crimes. As he walked Roper smiled, it was the perfect plan – kill the kid and spend years in the safety of the unit.

Gradually a spring came into his step as he thought of what the future would bring. He imagined a world where he lived in his own cell with an endless supply of tobacco and good food, working for Walls, taking care of business from now until the end of time. He started to whistle the tune to Top Gear, his stride growing longer, his chest puffing with pride. Coming to get you Croft he thought, as he barrelled along the street.

57

Twice the man thought he had lost the car in front, both times the fear had rippled through his brain and then he had heaved a sigh of relief as the lights appeared in the distance. His mind seemed to lurch from joy to terror, his leather-clad hands shaking on the wheel.

He thought of the woman who had been standing at the front of the house, when she turned to look at the car the confusion had speared his brain.

Now, he increased his speed, closing in on the car in front, the car that contained his Mandy, his little girl trapped in time.

He thought of what the man in the shop had said about all the times the police had been called to the house and about Wilson, a violent man, a man who cared little for others.

'*Teach you!*' he snarled, as he followed the car, his mind conjuring dark images of Wilson writhing in agony. '*Teach you the error of your ways.*'

The car turned right onto a side street and he felt the excitement rise, turning the wheel, his eyes narrowed as the car pulled onto a driveway.

Mind buzzing, tension rising, he pulled up on the left and leapt out to the pavement. The street was deserted, blinds drawn against the night, he caught a glimpse of the woman opening the rear door, the interior light clicked on and the breath caught in his throat as he saw the child being lifted from the seat.

He hesitated as she pushed the door closed with her hip before walking up the drive. Moving forward he reached the gate and peered into the darkness to see the woman heading down the side of the house and suddenly everything clicked into place. All the fear and anxiety fell away as he ran towards her, the years of confusion torn away by this sudden clarity of thought.

The side of the house was smothered in shadow, a bank of trees to the left grew tall and thick. He was six feet away when the woman started to turn as if sensing something was wrong, he saw her mouth spring open and he lashed out, his right hand slammed into the centre of her face and she staggered to the right, crashing into the wall of the house.

He grunted in satisfaction as he watched her slump to her knees, the girl still locked in her arms, seemingly asleep.

Reaching down, he tried to pull her from the woman's grip but she refused to let go.

'*No!*' she gasped through a froth of blood.

'*Give her to me,*' he hissed.

Dawn shook her head in despair as she felt his hot, sour breath in her face, his monstrous shadow loomed over her and still she refused to give Emma up.

'*Teach you,*' his voice rose as if he were unaware of his situation.

Reaching down he grabbed the woman by the hair and cracked her head against the brick wall, yet miraculously she tightened her grip on the child, his child, his trophy.

Moving left, he grabbed her head in his huge hands, thumbs moving in the darkness he felt for the soft twin orbs.

'*Whippersnapper!*' he spat, the eyeballs exploded under the immense pressure as he drove the thumbs forward.

Dawn Farmer's legs thrashed in the darkness, her arms finally sprang open and Emma tumbled to the floor and immediately started to cry.

As soon as he heard the sound the man grunted and released his grip, Dawn slumped to the ground, her face running with blood, her body shaking in shock.

'Teach you,' he snarled, slamming his foot down on the back of the woman's head, driving her face into the concrete, then he grabbed her legs and dragged her under the privet hedge, the wreckage of her face leaving a long smear of blood and gore on the pale flagstones. Turning, he looked at the child before swooping down, picking her up, he clamped a hand over her mouth before walking back down the path.

Reaching the gate, he checked the street left and right, before striding towards his car, his face dripping with sweat, his balls tight in fear and excitement.

Opening the passenger door, he placed the child in the seat, Emma Farmer's eyes were screwed shut, her mouth plugged with her thumb.

The man closed the door quietly before walking around the car and getting behind the wheel. Looking at the blood-smeared gloves he peeled them off, dropping them onto the girl's lap.

'Hello, Mandy, long time no see,' he said with a smile, before pulling away from the kerb.

Emma shivered, her eyes still closed in terror as they drove away.

58

L uke sat on the riverbank, legs drawn up, knees and elbows throbbing, adding to the waves of pain that swept through his shaking body.

After his chance meeting with Sarah he had set off running, ignoring the pain in his feet, the crippling shame driving him on. Five minutes later he had sprinted through the park gates, crossing the open field only stopping when he came to the river that weaved its way through the park and the town centre.

Now he looked at the deep moonlit water, a dark, slow-moving ribbon seen through a sheen of burning tears.

The small internal voice informed him that he was going to die in this town; there was no escape, no help to be found. He tried to push the thought from his mind but he knew it would happen. Luke had hated the unit, every second had been filled with fear, he had spent almost two months in the place but Roper had broken him in the first week. He pictured the thug revelling in the fact that he was confined in a place with locked doors and barred windows – and why shouldn't he be? Three warm meals a day and a never-ending supply of people he could torture whenever he felt like it.

Without even realising it, Luke shuffled to the edge of the bank.

He thought of DS Hammond, and tried to weigh up what would happen if he simply went back to her house. Could she help him; would she even try?

Luke could tell his story but who would believe him, a scrawny kid who had been in trouble with the police on countless occasions, or the governor? Luke knew the answer well enough.

No one. Nobody would believe him and he would be locked up again, but this time Walls would make sure he died in his cell.

His feet dangled in mid-air, the dark, beer-coloured water six feet below.

His mind scurried around, searching for an escape route that didn't exist.

Suddenly, the weight of his situation bore down on him and his shoulders slumped in hopelessness. He had nothing to carry on for, nothing to live for, his mother didn't care and his stepfather was nothing but a bastard.

Looking out into the darkness, his mind threw up an image that made his soul shrivel. An open grave, a cheap pine box. A thin, cold wind blew across the gloomy cemetery; he was vaguely aware of tilted gravestones on the edges of his petrified mind. He saw hands lowering the casket into the ground, and he knew that he was inside the box, his body battered and broken, torn and unrecognisable.

On the riverbank, Luke lifted his hands to his eyes in an effort to block out the image. The box hit the ground with a dull thud and the view pulled away showing a looming figure reaching for the spade, no one else stood by the side of the grave as he began to shovel earth onto the box.

No one had bothered to turn up to see him laid to rest, his mother had stayed away, unwilling to spend money on the bus fare to come and say goodbye.

Luke closed his eyes and everything went dark, yet the terror remained. When he opened his eyes, it was as if he were inside the box, inside and still alive. His lips quivered in a terror so blinding that it drove him to the edge of madness. Inside the box, he screamed, his elbows cocked, his hands hammering on the inside of the lid.

When he heard the low rumble of laughter, he suddenly knew who the gravedigger was. Alby Roper shovelled another spadeful of dry earth onto the oblong box. His chin jutting, his thick lips curled back in a maniacal grin of dark triumph.

Luke could hear the earth raining down on the lid, he screamed but there was no one to hear, no one to care. He edged forward on the bank, his legs kicking at the air in horror. Then he heard another scream but this one was low and deep, but nonetheless filled with agony. In his mind's eye, he saw Roper staggering back, blood spurting from the ghastly wound in his head. Then he heard the spade hiss through the air but wielded by another, the top of the Roper's head was sliced off above the eyes, the gory cap of skull, blood and brains spun away into the air, and he toppled back like an oak crashing to the ground, his eyes wide and staring in agony.

Luke blinked and DS Hammond was standing at the graveside, the spade held in one hand, when she jumped down onto the casket Luke screamed. And then he was back in the moment. The dark water beckoned and he gasped, lunging backwards onto the bank.

Up above, stars shone in the darkness as Luke realised he had come within a second of falling into the river. When he thought of the dark, cold embrace he shivered in fear; the spark of life caught and suddenly Luke Croft wanted to live. He was sixteen and he didn't deserve this life of torment.

Grabbing handfuls of coarse grass, he pulled himself along the ground, desperate to be away from the water's edge. He propelled himself forwards like some primordial being squirming away from the swamp of life, his breathing laboured and frantic.

After half a minute, he came to a halt and glanced over his shoulder; the river had vanished into the darkness and he sighed in relief, collapsing back to the ground.

Closing his eyes, Luke pressed his face into the damp grass, his body shaking, his mind stuttering with fear. Deep inside the flame burned, flickering as if caught in a hurricane blast – still burning, still alive.

59

The man eased the black car into a lay-by, concealed by large conifers to the right providing a barrier against the road and a stone wall to the left leading to woods of ancient oak and beech.

He had intended driving straight home but the enormity of emotion wouldn't allow it.

Looking in the interior mirror he smiled, the minute he had grabbed the girl the years had rolled back until the face in the mirror resembled his old self, his true self. The look of confusion had vanished from his eyes, his skin looked taut, clinging tight to the bone beneath, he ran a hand across his head, even his hair looked darker. His smile widened and he turned to look at Mandy, she looked exactly as he remembered her and the realisation was bewildering. She had remained unchanged throughout the years and now her magic was rubbing off on him, morphing him into the man he used to be.

The girl still had her eyes closed, her mouth sucking on the thumb, her hair a tangled mess of curls and corkscrews, the sight of it made the smile slip from his face.

He thought of the one called Cal Wilson, being loaded into the back of the police van and the fury stormed through his mind. Mandy had clung on to life despite having to live with a man who had mistreated her. The thought that she could have died at the hands of Wilson in the missing years made him quake with anger.

Fate had saved the girl, kept her in a timeless, insular bubble just waiting for the moment when he discovered her anew, though the truth was she had lived in the balance hovering between life and death at the hands of Wilson.

In his mind, the fact that he intended killing the girl was irrelevant, she was his passage back to the glory days but Wilson would pay for leaving Mandy in a world of turmoil and hurt.

The shopkeeper had said it himself, the police came to the house on a regular basis, Wilson was a thug, a bully, a *whippersnapper* and the man hated the very idea that he continued to breathe.

In the passenger seat Emma sat stock-still, her heart racing with fear, her mind slowly closing down as if she somehow knew what was to come and her soul couldn't stand the strain.

The man sighed, he was attuned to her fear and it helped to wash away the last of the confusion in much the same way a sandblaster will scour the old, dirty stone leaving the surface pristine and shining.

The engine purred, the stars above shone down, the last of the pieces fell into place – synchronicity.

60

The thought of going home to sit in an empty house had been too much to bear, so Marnie had headed into town to grab a coffee from the drive-thru Starbucks and she now sat on the car park, steam fogging the windscreen, cigarette smoke filling the car. With a grimace, she slid the window down and wafted a hand as the smoke trailed out into the night.

She thought of Dawn holding young Emma in her arms telling Marnie about their father and his wastrel ways. Her sister being carted off to the hospital while her thug of a boyfriend was taken in for questioning. Marnie felt the anger twist in her guts, Wilson would probably be back out within a few hours, back to the house where Mandy would dutifully return for another beating.

She felt the presence of Luke Croft pushing at her mind, waiting to gate-crash the never-ending parade of morbid thoughts. Flicking ash through the window, she lifted the cup from the holder and took a sip.

She pictured Gareth Walls sitting behind his walnut desk, all the time appearing helpful though there had been something about the man that Marnie hadn't liked. He made all the right noises, had all the excuses ready, the cuts to the budget, the lack of fully-trained staff. Reese had said that Walls had an unblemished record, no complaints in the past about the conditions at Park View, so, would someone in Walls's position really contact Roper to tell him about Luke Croft?

Marnie took another pull on the cigarette, the idea seemed preposterous but when she pictured the hidden look in his eye, the insolence when responding to Marnie's questions, she suspected that Governor Walls would do exactly that. She had the feeling that Walls thought she had no right to even be in his office asking questions, he was above that, above the law; that's the impression that had been lurking beneath the façade of helpfulness.

They now knew that Roper had been to the house and no doubt he was responsible for the death of Oldman. Something, or someone, had wound Roper up like some thuggish clockwork toy, knowing he would go to the house to make Luke pay, but Luke had been absent from the house, so Roper had taken out his fury on Oldman.

Marnie licked her lips nervously, she could feel the clock ticking, time running out for Luke and yet she felt helpless to do anything about it.

She closed her eyes in an effort to block the distressing thoughts but there was no solace behind closed lids only more guilt at her inability to change the past or influence the future.

She slotted the cup back into the holder as her phone rang, lifting it from her pocket she frowned when she saw Reese's number flash up.

'*Are you at home?*' he asked, without bothering with the pleasantries.

'Not yet, I'm in the drive-through having a coffee.'

'*Right, I've just had Susan Romney on the phone, she's on duty in town with Keith Barnes and a girl approached them; apparently, she'd bumped into Luke Croft and…*'

'Where, when?' Marnie asked, sitting up straight, one hand gripping the wheel tight.

'*If you stop interrupting I'll tell you,*' Reese growled.

Marnie waited for him to continue, her emotions stretched to breaking point.

'*The girl went to the same school as Luke and he was standing in the doorway to Oxfam. She stopped when she recognised the lad but she said he seemed nervous and when she offered him some money he scarpered.*'

Marnie pictured the scene trying to imagine what it must have been like for Luke seeing someone from his old school, and then having her open her purse and lift out the money. Marnie somehow knew that simple act of kindness would have crushed him.

'Did she see which way he went?'

'She said he turned left off Market Street heading towards...'

'The park!'

Reese sighed again at the interruption. *'Yes, Marnie, towards the park.'*

'Right, I'll head over there and take a look.'

'I thought you might; I've asked Romney and Barnes to take a look as well, so keep your eyes open for them.'

Marnie felt a sudden thrum of tension, if Luke saw the two officers in their yellow vests walking through the park then he would run and vanish again.

Turning the key, she started the engine before tapping the screen on the phone, clipping the seatbelt into place she pulled out of the parking space, her senses on high alert, her hands damp on the wheel as she sped away.

61

L uke trudged across the open stretch of parkland, the moon had vanished behind a smothering of cloud, the temperature dropping. His brain insisted on parading an image of Sarah in front of his eyes, taunting him with her white-toothed smile, fresh, clean skin and her immaculate clothes. It was as if they came from different planets, one full of laughter and light, and ten-pound notes to be handed out to the people who occupied the other world. One made up of darkened alleyways and houses devoid of affection. HHHHe wondered if Sarah had ever been afraid to go home, ever spent time sheltering under a market stall canopy while the rain lashed down or slept on a mattress that someone had thrown out.

As he hobbled along, he pictured a bedroom full of light, a bed in the corner with clean sheets and plumped pillows. The smell of home-cooked food filled the imaginary air and Luke felt the despair mounting with every step. When he came to the bench he slumped down and rubbed at his tear-filled eyes.

He looked out at the park and blew out a heavy sigh, he would go and see DS Hammond and tell her the truth about what had happened at Park View. Tell her all about Alby Roper smiling as he stubbed the cigarette out on his bare skin, tell her about the first time he had set foot in the place and Roper had lashed out while Governor Walls stood nonchalantly with his hands behind his back as Roper laid into him. The small voice inside tried to warn him that it would do no good but for once he managed to ignore it, holding onto the small flame that flickered inside, the flame of hope. He had spent a lifetime trying to stay below the radar, trying to survive in a harsh world. Luke thought of his mother and the string of men that had passed through the house, some he had never even bothered to learn their names, somehow knowing that they wouldn't be around long enough to make a difference.

One or two had tried to get to know him but his mother had sent them packing or they had walked out and never returned.

The truth was his mother was a slut, he had always known it as he listened to one man after another grunting and groaning in the next bedroom, Luke covering his ears in an effort to block out the sounds of the creaking bed.

Then Oldman had turned up and he'd been there for over three years, treating Luke like the hired help, there only to bring him another can from the fridge and clear up after the slob.

He tried to think back to happier times but his searching mind couldn't grasp one single thought of when he had felt content with life. All roads led to misery and a sense of hopelessness that he couldn't shift. Head in hands he felt the bitter sting of tears prickle his eyes again, his mind lost in the torment.

When he heard the tuneless whistling coming from his left he turned his head, but the path beneath the trees was hidden in darkness. Luke suddenly felt his hackles rise, and then he was on his feet leaning forwards slightly as he tried to penetrate the gloom.

The whistling stopped and he heard someone cough – a heavy chesty grunt – and Luke's mouth fell open in terror. He was back at the unit, Roper had him pinned in the corner of the room, the cigarette hovering above Luke's right foot.

Alby Roper had taken a long pull, the end of the cigarette glowing, and then he had started to cough, the same heavy, racking sound that floated out of the darkness.

Then the whistling started up again and Luke recognised it as the Top Gear theme tune. Suddenly, the fear blasted through his senses, it couldn't be Roper, yet somehow, he knew that it was Alby Roper stalking along the path. At the last second, the paralysing spell was broken, and Luke dashed around the bench before slipping into the trees.

Grabbing the thick trunk of an old oak, he shuffled behind it as the sound of heavy boots on loose gravel arrived out of the shadows.

Luke Croft held his breath in fear, afraid to move afraid to breath, in case...

The heavy footfalls came to a halt, the whistling stopped, and Luke became convinced he could hear the sound of his own galloping heart.

The cough came again, and then Luke heard the sound of someone hacking up and spitting out, it was yet another sound that made him cringe, the voice inside screamed the word *Roper*, and Luke hung on to the gnarled tree.

Finally, he heard the satisfied sound of someone sitting down on the bench.

Time seemed to slow down, the darkness grew deeper, darker; and Luke couldn't move a muscle.

'*Come on you fucking little bastard, where are you?*' the voice growled.

Luke felt his sanity slip, he tried to keep the terror at bay but it crowded in around him, a shadow darker than all the others, like a living entity that clung to him and seeped into his pores, filling him utterly as his worst nightmares were realised.

62

The man kept one eye on the speedometer, the big car locked at thirty miles per hour as he drove onto the ring road. He glanced towards his passenger, the child was asleep, chin resting on her chest, perfect face obscured by a mass of tangled hair.

His eyes flicked to the mirrors before moving back to the road ahead. Reaching the round about, he slowed down and waited for the truck to branch off left before moving forward.

He felt in complete control, his brain firing on all cylinders, though the fury burned deep within, lighting his dark eyes with an unfathomable malice.

He had the girl now and he would keep her forever, eventually she would join his collection in the cellar but not now, not yet. He would savour their time together, using her fear to quench the thirst that raged inside.

When he caught the flash of blue in the wing mirror, his eyes narrowed, his heart picking up speed, the fear flashed out threatening to take control, as the sound of a siren split the late-night air.

The temptation to plant his foot on the pedal was overpowering, the light in the mirror increased, the siren growing louder by the second, at the last minute he indicated and pulled over to the left, his eyes flicking to the right, teeth gritted as the car flashed by.

He waited, watching the car speed down the road before vanishing around the corner. A taxi went by and still he waited, the indicator ticked away the seconds and he blew out a sigh of relief, engaged first gear and set off again. He glanced at the girl and smiled at her sleeping form.

'Don't worry little one, we'll soon be somewhere nice and quiet, somewhere we won't be disturbed, doesn't that sound like fun?' he asked.

When he received no reply, he frowned.

'Whippersnapper,' he mumbled, turning his attention back to the road.

63

Marnie shot around the corner, lights flashing, siren bellowing. Slowing for the traffic lights she glanced left and right, accelerated across the junction, moving quickly through the gears, her eyes narrowed, picturing Luke in the park and spotting the two shapes moving towards him in the darkness, forcing him to run like a startled deer. He would vanish into the trees and they would be back to square one.

The thought that they would miss this chance and Roper finding him first was too terrible to envision, though Marnie knew more than most that life wasn't made up of happy endings. Life was hard and often the guilty went unpunished while the innocent suffered and were forgotten about. The car sped right at the round about, her hands gripping the wheel tight as the tyres fought for control.

She thought of Piper Donald's parents trying to live lives that had no real meaning, their hearts ripped out the day their daughter vanished. Marnie had recognised the twin looks of despair in their eyes, after all she saw it when she went to visit her own mother, saw it when she looked in the mirror.

The injustice of life gnawed at her and she somehow knew that Luke had come to symbolise all her fears, including the fear that once again she had tried to help someone and had fallen short of the task.

Gradually the houses fell away and fields took over, the street lights ended and she flicked on the main beam before turning off the siren and flashing lights. If Luke was in the park, then the last thing she wanted to do was announce her arrival.

Checking the mirrors, she started to slow down, dropping through the gears; when she saw the squad car parked at the gates she felt the frustration tug at her senses. Pulling alongside, she snatched on the handbrake and reached over to the glove compartment to retrieve the heavy metal torch, she clicked it on and off checking the batteries, before pushing the door open and climbing out into the darkness.

The ornate park gates were standing open and Marnie walked through, peering into the dark, her eyes moving left and right searching for a flash of yellow in the darkness. If her colleagues had arrived with whistle and bells blaring, then Luke would be gone by now.

With a heavy sigh she set off, reluctant to turn on the torch, within seconds she had vanished into the darkness.

64

L uke clung to the tree, he could see the hulking shape in the darkness, could hear him mumbling words that he couldn't make out, though he knew that had been another of Roper's traits; incoherent mumbling. When the lights went out in the unit, Luke would lay in the dark, huddled beneath the thin cover, his heart racing, the fear twisting his guts. Roper would start to grunt and mumble as if holding a conversation with some inner demon, perhaps discussing new ways to torment the weaker boys in the unit.

There had been something horrific about listening to the nocturnal ravings, occasionally Roper would bark out a laugh and Luke would hear the madness in the sound.

Time stretched out and Luke's legs began to shake with tension, his arms tightened around the trunk as if he were hugging a lover in the darkness.

Tears leaked from his despairing eyes and he realised that he couldn't stay here, he became convinced that if he didn't move then Roper would smell the fear that oozed from his open pores.

Suddenly, Roper lurched to his feet and Luke almost screamed at the rising shadow, then the thug leaned forward as if peering into the dark.

'*Stay where you are!*' the voice blasted out across the moonlit park.

Alby Roper tensed and spun away, this time Luke did yelp and all of a sudden Roper was peering into the trees right at him.

Everything seemed to stop, time itself freezing as the two boys looked at one another, Luke's eyes filled with terror, Roper's flickering with disbelief as if unsure what he was actually seeing.

'*Stop right there!*' the voice shouted again.

Luke saw the exact moment when Roper knew this wasn't a dream but reality, he seemed to expand with anger, his face twisted with fury.

Luke lunged away from the tree and spun around, his feet slipping in the leaves as he tried to gain traction.

'*Fucker!*' Roper screamed, blasting forward.

The sound of branches snapping and cracking spurred Luke on though he knew it was hopeless, Roper was big and no doubt he could run while Luke felt the fatigue of living on the streets, his body battered and bruised. Yet inside, a small flame still burned so he gave it his all, dashing around the trees, his eyes wide and frantic, the night full of shouting voices, though they all blended into one horrific cacophony of sound.

Luke Croft ran for his life.

65

As soon as Marnie heard the shouted warning to 'stop' she snapped the torch on and sprinted forward.

Over to her right she saw twin lights bobbing in the darkness, she angled towards the light, her legs eating up the ground at a ferocious pace, her hair flying.

More shouted warnings and then the torchlights flickered randomly as they entered the trees. The grass beneath her feet felt bone hard, every step transported her back over the years until she was eleven again and fighting for her sister, fighting to keep Abby from the "bad man".

Marnie's lips drew back in a snarl, as the demons of the past screeched through her tortured mind.

She could hear her own breathing light and fast, the trees grew closer and then she reached the boundary and plunged into the undergrowth without breaking stride.

A thin branch whiplashed into her face and she winced at the vicious sting, up ahead she could see the torchlights lancing out, bouncing off the thick trunks of ancient trees.

Suddenly the air was split by a single piercing scream and one of the lights ahead was extinguished, Marnie increased her speed, ducking and weaving under the low hanging branches, as she closed in on the remaining light.

She caught of a flash of yellow and blasted forward to find Susan Romney kneeling in the grass over the slumped form of Keith Barnes.

Marnie came to a halt and trained the light towards the ground, when she saw the red seeping through the yellow of Barnes's jacket she felt her stomach roll.

Susan looked up, her eyes saucer wide. 'He stabbed Keith,' she whispered in disbelief.

Within seconds Marnie had her phone out, her hands shaking as she called for help, Susan tore open her jacket and pulled it off. Dropping to her knees, Marnie slid the zipper down on Keith's jacket before taking the bundle from Susan and pressing it down on the wound.

'What the hell happened?' she asked, as she bore down.

Susan Romney eased back on her haunches before dragging a trembling hand across her brow.

'We came looking for...'

'Luke Croft, I know,' Marnie snapped in reply.

Romney nodded. 'Someone was standing by one of the benches and when we shouted for him to stop he bolted, so we gave chase and we were closing him down but then he turned and lashed out and Keith went down.'

Marnie closed her eyes and said a silent prayer before she asked the question. 'Was it Croft?'

'No way, this guy was too big to be Luke Croft.'

'Are you *sure*?' she asked, twisting her head to look at Romney.

'Positive.'

Marnie felt the relief flood through her body and then she grabbed Susan's hand and placed it on the jacket.

'Chances are the ambulance will come down Bush Lane, I'll make my way to the gates and flag them down, we don't have the time to wait for them to find us.'

The young PC nodded, her eyes suddenly infused with determination.

Rising to her feet, Marnie gave her ponytail a savage tug. 'Will you be OK?' she asked.

'Just go,' Susan paused, 'I'll be fine.'

Marnie set off, dashing through the trees, the fury rising as she ran.

66

L uke hit the stone wall and snapped a look over his shoulder, when he saw Roper blasting towards him he cried out, scrabbling up the rough-cut stone; his body screaming in pain he managed to clamber to the top.

'*Cunt!*' Roper bellowed, leaping into the air.

Luke felt the big hand grab at his leg and for one terrifying second he felt himself being pulled back, then he yanked his leg free, falling the six feet to the pavement beyond.

Landing on his side he screamed in agony, rolling sideways and forcing himself upright, his legs almost buckled again as he staggered forward.

'*Got you now!*' Roper screeched.

Luke threw a look over his shoulder as he continued to lurch forwards; Roper stood atop the wall, a monstrous shape, his face smeared with a grin of madness, right hand brandishing a knife that dripped red.

Luke felt the flame of hope die, he was seconds away from being slaughtered on this deserted stretch of road and he felt his soul shrivel at the prospect.

Turning, he tried to break into a run but his body was exhausted, the fear taking the last of his diminishing strength, he hobbled into the road. He heard Roper grunt and then the thud of his feet as he landed on the ground.

'*Mine now!*' the voice was right behind him and Luke came to a stop and waited for the inevitable feel of the knife slamming into his back.

Then the night was filled with twin supernovae and Luke tried to look towards the lights though even that simple task was beyond him, he staggered on and the sound of tortured rubber on tarmac ripped through the air.

The car screeched to a stop but not before it had nudged into Alby Roper sending him to the ground in a jumble of arms and legs, the front wing of the car clipped Luke's trailing leg and spun him around, he lost his balance and fell to the floor crying out again in pain.

Silence apart from the purring of the engine and Luke's ragged breathing.

'*Fucking bastard!*'

Luke managed to raise his head to see Roper gain his feet, his eyes locked on the car, his rage filling the air.

'*Twat!*' he roared as he stabbed the knife into the bonnet of the black car, dragging the blade across the gleaming paintwork.

The driver's door opened and Luke watched the dark shape step out.

'*I'm going to kill you, you old cunt!*' Roper spat, as he stormed towards the man.

Luke wanted to shout out a warning, wanted to scream at the driver to run for his life but his throat constricted, making it hard enough to breathe let alone voice his fear.

Roper's right hand shot out with the intention of gutting the man, his mind infested by the urge to kill then he felt his wrist gripped, felt the strength in the tightening hand and the first flutter of surprise rippled through his mind.

When the hand tightened further, his eyes sprang wide and he found himself looking up into the face of the man who suddenly loomed towards him.

Alby Roper couldn't recall the last time he had felt anything like fear but he felt it now. The man yanked down on the arm and suddenly Roper was a seventeen-year-old boy not a man, nowhere near being a man.

'*Let go!*' he screeched, his voice high pitched with fear.

'*WHIPPER,*' the man's left hand shot forward, the index finger extended. '*SNAPPER!*' he screamed and plunged the finger into Alby Roper's left eye.

Roper jack-knifed straight, his left hand shot into the air, his scream of agony blasted into the night sky, he staggered back, blood gushing from the ruin of his eye.

The man stepped forward and Luke watched, unable to move, as he gripped Alby Roper's head between his huge hands – then Roper was screaming again.

'*Teach you!*' the man roared, thumbs plunging into the eye-sockets.

The man lunged down and started to smash Roper's head into the ground, lifting it and slamming it down repeatedly.

Luke tried to gain his feet as a chunk of skull blasted away to the left and brain matter spewed from the back of Roper's head; but he couldn't move, could hardly breathe as he watched the destruction of his tormentor.

The man slammed down again though this time there was no thump just a wet splat. Alby Roper's skull crumpled and Luke screamed as the face seemed to slide away from the bone beneath.

When the man turned his gaze towards Luke he felt his heart stop; there was nothing in the eyes, at least nothing human, just a monstrous black void leading to...

'*You!*' The man roared and Luke felt his bladder twitch as the man took two long strides towards him.

Luke sat in the hulking shadow, unable to move, his body shaking uncontrollably. The figure reached down and grabbed his sweatshirt.

Then Luke was snatched up from the ground and felt the hot, sour breath in his sweating face.

'*I'll teach you, I'll teach you the error of your ways,*' he snarled.

Luke felt his feet leave the ground and the man opened the door of the black car and tossed Luke across the rear seat before slamming the door closed.

He closed his eyes against the terror, his mind slowly closing down against the horror of what he had witnessed.

Back behind the wheel the man began to laugh, shoulders shaking in merriment, Luke took the sound with him as he spiralled away into the darkness.

67

Marnie emerged from the trees, dashing through the park gates she snapped her head left peering along the deserted road in the hope of seeing Luke, she sighed in despair, looking right the sigh turned to a gasp seeing the figure slumped in the middle of the road.

She ran over, her mind trying to block out the damage done though her eyes insisted on taking small snapshots of the horror spread-eagled on the road.

Marnie felt the bile rise as she looked at the huge bloodstain glistening on the black tarmac, slivers of white bone shone in the darkness, when she looked at the face she felt the true horror slam into her.

When she saw the bloody knife on the ground she frowned in confusion and then her eyes sprang wide as she tried to join the dots. Ten seconds later she heard the distant wail of a siren followed by flashing lights in the distance. Moving to the centre of the road she raised the torch and started to flick it on and off.

The lights on the ambulance flicked to main beam and she narrowed her eyes as they drew closer before pulling up on the left.

Only when the two men jumped out and hurried over did she lower the light.

'Jesus, what the hell happened here,' one of them said with a shake of the head.

'Forget him the one you want is in the trees, take the path for two hundred yards and shout out, the injured officer is to your left about fifty yards in.'

'We should check this guy out first, he...'

'His brains are smeared all over the bloody road, in fact you're standing in some now, he's dead and if you don't get a move on my colleague will be joining him, so shift your arses!' Marnie barked as she pointed the torch towards the gates.

The two paramedics looked at one another and turned and ran, leaving Marnie in the middle of the road, her arms dangling by her sides.

By the time they had vanished into the darkness she had turned and was looking back down at the body, what remained of the skull had warped out of shape leaving the gore-covered face twisted beyond recognition.

Moving carefully around the body, she trained the light down from the head over the scruffy-looking denim jacket – now stained red – to the black jeans, when she reached the shoes she frowned before easing down to her haunches and shining the light on the soles of the shoes. Suddenly she pictured the bruises on Luke's back, the same zig-zag tread had been stamped into his flesh.

'*Roper,*' she whispered, as more sirens blasted out into the night.

68

Fifteen minutes later the road had been cordoned off, police vehicles parked left and right to stop any late-night traffic. Reese had arrived and now they stood looking down at the body.

'This is Albert Roper?' Reese grimaced at the slumped form, the brains smeared over the tarmac, the eyes mere red holes of gore.

'Right height and weight, same tread marks on his shoes to the ones found on Luke Croft's body and the door of his house.'

Reese glanced at her as the paramedics appeared through the gates with the unfortunate Keith Barnes on the stretcher, Susan Romney following closely behind. Seconds later they loaded him into the back of the ambulance, Susan climbed in with one of the paramedics while the other leapt behind the wheel. The siren wailed, they pulled away from the kerb and shot off down the road.

'What a total, bloody mess,' Reese sighed, looking back down at the body.

Marnie glanced at him, he seemed worn out, dark circles beneath his eyes, his skin sallow.

'Are you OK?' she asked.

Reese shook his head. 'Not really,' he replied with a sigh.

Marnie slipped her hands into her pockets but kept her mouth closed and her eyes locked on the body.

Reese cleared his throat as he moved to the right. 'I just don't get any of this, what the hell is Roper doing in the middle of the road minus his bloody eyes?'

'Not a clue.'

Reese flicked her a look. 'We know Roper killed Oldman but who did this to him and why?'

Marnie tried to think of a rational explanation but she had none to offer, it seemed utterly surreal, Roper had been chased, and then stabbed Keith Barnes, no doubt in an effort to buy time while he made good his escape, and yet here he was sprawled in the street his brains splattered all over the road.

'If it wasn't for the eyes then I'd say RTA,' she offered.

Reese nodded in understanding. 'And you saw no one else as you were running through the woods?'

'To be honest I didn't even see Roper but I spoke to Romney and she said as far as she could tell there was only Roper, they shouted and he made a break for it.'

Reese shook his head again in dismay. 'And how long was it from him escaping to finding him in the road?'

'Well, I stopped to help Keith and then set off after Roper so it couldn't have been more than two, three minutes at the most.'

'And in that time, someone killed the bugger and left him in the middle of the bloody road and then simply vanished?'

Marnie didn't reply, her mind was starting to fill up again with distress. She couldn't shake the feeling that her sister was still in the woods – nothing more than a scattering of bones waiting beneath the black earth to be found by a cadaver dog, no head, just bones, the tip of the little finger missing. She tried to steel herself against the inevitable but the years of trying to keep the small flickering of hope alive were taking their toll, she imagined the small internal flame slowly dying, waiting to be extinguished when she got the call to tell her Abby had been found.

'You OK?' Reese asked.

'I'm fine,' she lied.

'Do you think Luke Croft was in the woods?'

Marnie looked back at the bank of tall trees and shivered. 'If he was then he'll be long gone by now.'

'You don't think he could have been responsible for this?'

'Not a chance,' she replied instantly. 'Luke weighs about eight stone, he wouldn't have had the physical strength to take on Roper.'

More flashing lights as a blacked-out van pulled up closely followed by Doc Kelly's Mondeo.

'OK, I want you at the hospital for eight in the morning, I'll meet you there so you may as well get home and try to get some rest.'

Marnie opened her mouth to protest but Reese didn't give her the chance.

'Look, with Roper out of the way at least you don't have the worry of him catching up with Luke.'

Marnie knew her boss was right, it was a relief to know that Luke was no longer being hunted down by the thug Roper.

'Sooner or later he'll turn up and then we can try to find what happened to the lad but for now I need you to put him out of your mind, we have tough times ahead and we all need to be on the ball over this.'

Marnie dragged up a smile as he used the word "we", and then she nodded.

'OK, I'll see you in the morning,' she turned and walked away down the street.

Reese watched her vanish into the darkness before turning back to the body as Kelly approached.

'Messy,' the doc said, looking down at Alby Roper.

Reese raised an eyebrow, sighing heavily.

69

The black car came to a halt on the gravel drive, the headlights died, the man stayed behind the wheel, his eyes peering out into the darkness. The white barn owl flew back and forth over the garden, reaching the boundary of trees it looped and soared back, silent wings beating the night air.

The engine pinged as it cooled and yet the man remained unmoving, relishing the momentous moment. He had the girl, she was unchanged, frozen in time just for him and now the fates had delivered another prize to him in the most fantastical way. The man shook his head in disbelief, if he hadn't stopped in the lay-by, if he had driven straight back to the house then he would never have found the boy. The fates had made him wait and then there he was trapped in the glare of the headlights and now here they all were – together at last.

He smiled and sighed before glancing around the car, Mandy was still asleep, the boy sprawled across the back seats, his eyes open and filled with terror. The man sniffed and the smile on his face grew wider, the scent of fear filled the car, he could have stayed here forever drinking in the glorious emotion, tuning in to the torment. Though he knew that, eventually, the hateful sun would crest the horizon for another day and he still had plans to make. Clicking open the door, he stepped out into the darkness and opened the rear door.

Reaching in, he grabbed the boy's right leg and yanked him from the car, Luke yelped as he tried to break his fall but he crashed down onto the gravel path and groaned in pain. Then he felt the hand grab his sweatshirt and haul him to his feet.

'I'll teach you the error of your ways,' the man said and Luke felt his legs shake with the terror of the words.

Then he was being dragged around the car, when the man opened the passenger door Luke's eyes sprang wide as he saw the child held in place by the seat belt.

Keeping one hand locked on the back of Luke's neck the man reached in unclipped the belt and lifted the girl out with ease.

'Happy families,' the man rumbled as he carried the girl and hauled the boy to the house.

Luke tried to hold on to his sanity, after being tortured by Alby Roper he had thought nothing in life could have scared him more than the hulking viciousness of his roommate at Park View.

Though now he knew there were worse things in life than a sadistic bully, he closed his eyes picturing the man slamming Roper's head into the hard ground. The wet splat, the dark look in his eyes as the man turned his gaze towards him, the nothingness, the void that seemed to go on forever.

'In you go,' the man thrust Luke over the threshold.

He staggered forward trying to stay on his feet but then his knees hit the hard, wooden floor. Luke resisted the urge to cry out as if he somehow knew that any sound would infuriate the man who stepped into the long hallway and slammed the door.

It was then that the small, internal flame spluttered and died, and Luke Croft realised he would die in this house, this time there would be no escape, no rescue.

Somewhere in the cavernous space he heard a clock chime.

The witching hour.

70

Marnie lay in bed, despite the open window the room felt warm, the duvet pulled up to her chin, her eyes closed as she ran through the facts. She could feel all the anguish closing in on her mind but she blocked it out, concentrating on what she knew rather than what might happen. She thought of the arm in the woods, it seemed an age since she had brought Luke down in the mud and leaves. She pictured the daisy rings on the fingers of two of the remains they had found. One killer must be responsible for the murders and she had no doubt that links would be found to the other remains. Long-ago murders but were they linked to Jenny Bell?

Marnie felt the sweat break out on her forehead and wiped it away with the duvet, was it possible that the same man had been responsible for Jenny's death? Despite her best efforts, an image of Abby crashed through her defences. Over the years, Marnie had tried to picture the monster who had taken her sister but the truth was she had never seen his face or if she had, her subconscious had kept it hidden from her all these years.

In the weeks following Abby's abduction Marnie had been questioned by the police on a number of occasions and yet every time she had only been able to repeat what had happened, echoing the same thing over and over again, while all the time the hope inside died. She could remember her mum asking her the same questions and Marnie had tortured herself trying to remember something new, something that would lead to her sister being returned to them. Her father had called at the house demanding to know why Marnie hadn't been looking after his youngest daughter. He'd been drunk and ranting and her mother had called the police, by the time they arrived he had gone, leaving Marnie stunned and riddled with a guilt that she had carried with her for almost fifteen years. Her father had planted the poison seed that had grown, despite her mother's attempt to remove the growth of guilt from her daughter's young mind.

The years passed and Marnie had been determined to join the police, determined to spend her life trying to make sure that others never had to feel the way she felt over her sister. She sighed as she rolled onto her side, it had been ridiculous to think she could have helped anyone, the bones in the woods and the death of Jenny Bell were stark proof that no matter what you did, terrible things would still happen to good people.

Sleep came to claim her and she slipped into the familiar nightmare; within minutes she was crying in her sleep.

•

71

Hambling woke with a start, legs thrashing as light poured in through the grimy window, the rats darted left and right before vanishing through the holes in the floorboards.

'*Shit,*' he groaned as he squinted against the light.

Clambering to his feet, he hobbled over to the window before wiping a hand across his eyes. He must have slept the night away, curled under the filthy duvet, exhausted, his body and mind closed down through exhaustion. The problem was he had a day to fill, ensnared in these four, drab walls with the crumbling plaster and scurrying rats. His stomach muscles gripped tight, his dry mouth flooded with saliva, he was starving, the last thing he'd had to eat was the stale sausage roll countless hours ago. Hambling turned and slid down the wall, his knees drawn up in despair, the smell of his body wafted up, mingling with the stink of piss and shit coming from the far corner of the room. When the rat popped back up through the hole he sat and watched as it scuttled over to the pile of human waste in the corner to feed.

Hambling closed his eyes and wondered if his life could ever possibly get worse than this. Outside one of the ducks on the canal squawked, the ratchet noise sounding like bitter laughter.

72

Marnie and Reese arrived at the hospital at eight a.m. to find Doc Kelly still working on the body, the metal sluice tray ran red, the doctor's latex gloves speckled with droplets of blood.

'It's definitely Roper,' he said, pulling down the paper mask from his tired face.

They stood about four feet away from the body, both looking grim.

'You checked the fingerprints?' Reese asked.

'Still waiting to hear back from the lab,' Kelly replied.

'So, how do you know it's Roper?'

Kelly flickered a weary grin. 'Because he has his name tattooed on his arm.'

Marnie moved forward as the doctor pointed down at the right forearm.

'It's done in Indian ink,' Kelly explained.

Sure enough, the phrase Alby R Rules had been scratched onto the skin in a childlike hand.

Reese sighed and shook his head. 'You couldn't make it up,' he said, loosening his tie.

'What else can you tell us?'

Kelly looked at Marnie, the smile sliding from his face as he saw the brittle look in her eyes.

'Whoever did this had his thumbs in Roper's eyes...'

'*What?*' the DCI barked in disbelief.

Kelly ignored the outburst. 'He gripped the head, as soon as Roper felt the pressure on the eyes, he wouldn't have been interested in fighting back. Chances are he tried to grab the hands and the killer slammed his head into the ground.'

'Jesus,' Reese muttered.

Kelly pursed his lips. 'See the bruises along both shins?'

Marnie looked down at the body whilst Reese continued to glare at the doctor.

There were matching bruises on each leg about four inches in depth. 'These are new bruises?'

'Roper was found in the street, right?' the doctor asked.

'You know where he was found,' Reese grumbled.

'Well, I think Mr Roper was hit by a car, nothing major, but enough to leave the marks and probably knock him on his backside, in fact both buttocks are bruised.'

Reese rubbed his chin thoughtfully. 'Right, so Roper dashes out into the road and the car knocks him down. Are we saying the driver then jumped out and did that to the lad?' he asked, pointing down at the ruined head.

'Not quite,' Kelly replied. 'You see, before I started on the body I checked the knife, it contains the blood of what I assume to be PC Barnes, along with some soil traces.'

'That makes sense,' Marnie said, sliding her hands into her pockets.

'Yes, but the blade also showed traces of black paint, especially around the tip, the flakes had adhered to the blood.'

Reese's frown grew deeper still as he absorbed this latest snippet of information.

Marnie looked down at the remains of Roper, he'd died a violent death and yet when she thought of the senseless pain he had inflicted on Luke she found herself without a shred of sympathy for Albert Roper.

She imagined him clambering over the wall, blood dripping from the knife he had just used to stab Keith Barnes, landing sure-footed, before dashing into the road confident that he would make good his escape and yet somehow the car had come out of the darkness and knocked him down. According to Kelly, impact had been minimal, just enough to knock Roper to the ground.

Marnie closed her eyes picturing the scene, Roper slowly climbing to his feet, his fury rising and then...

'He stabbed at the car,' she whispered.

Reese looked at her in surprise, Kelly smiled and nodded in agreement.

'Stabbed the car?' The DCI asked in astonishment.

'Think about it, Roper killed Oldman and stabbed Keith Barnes, he has no qualms about attacking anyone. The car knocks him down, he jumps up and lashes out; if there are bumper marks on his legs then chances are the blade hit the bonnet of the car.'

Reese thought for a moment. 'Perhaps Roper tried the flag the car down with the intention of nicking it, he goes to the driver's door but this time it's no weakling behind the wheel, this time he's bitten off more than he could ever hope to chew.'

'I've had the flakes of paint sent for analysis,' Kelly said.

'Good man,' Reese said as Kelly flicked the sheet over the remains and slid the trolley into the fridge.

73

Mandy Farmer ignored the woman who stared at her damaged face from the opposite seat on the bus. The doctor at the hospital had decided to keep her in for observation just to be on the safe side and Mandy hadn't argued in fact, she'd been glad of the rest, making the most of the peace and quiet to evaluate her life. She had sat propped up in bed thinking about her relationship with Cal Wilson, the arguments, the beatings and in amongst it all there was Emma, cowering in the corner, her hands over her ears as she wailed and Cal bellowed while Mandy took the abuse. She thought of her sister and the tears welled in her eyes, the woman opposite looked away as if embarrassed by the show of emotion from the woman with the battered face.

If it wasn't for Dawn then Mandy knew her young daughter would have been taken from her, whisked away to foster parents and then eventually adopted. She thought back to giving birth and the true joy she had felt when the midwife had placed the child in her arms. The father was long gone, another wastrel of a man who had said he had no interest in becoming a father. In that moment, none of it had mattered, Dawn had been with her during the birth and she had been there for her every minute since. Mandy felt the shame wash over her, in the past when the sisters had argued Mandy had said some hurtful things, terrible things to Dawn, accusing her of thinking Emma was her own child, getting her digs in about Dawn's inability to have children of her own. The shame increased, how could she have said those things, how could she have been so cruel to the one person who had always been there for her.

The bus rumbled to a halt to let someone off before pulling away from the kerb again, and she watched as the shops sailed past, the people on the pavement weaving their way around one another.

Pulling out her phone, she checked for messages and frowned. She had tried to ring Dawn on several occasions, she'd even left voice messages on her phone but all to no avail. Mandy had no doubt that her sister would be furious with her, after all Dawn had told her repeatedly to leave Cal for Emma's sake if not her own.

Every time it happened Mandy had promised she would throw Calout but every time she relented, letting him back only to get another beating; but not this time, this time she had suffered enough. She knew that Cal would never change, men like him never did, they carried on secure in the knowledge that the woman would continue to put up with the abuse.

Mandy gritted her teeth and then winced at the pain in her lip; rising to her feet she rang the bell. Seconds later she climbed off the bus and watched as it pulled away, the heat of the day beating down on her head and shoulders as she set off walking. She would make Dawn believe that this time she meant what she said, it was over between her and Cal, there would be no having him back or falling for another bad boy. This time she would concentrate on making sure that Emma was happy and taken care of in the proper way, no more men, no more abuse.

Reaching the side street, she turned left heading towards her sister's house, her mind trying to work out the right way to thank Dawn for all her help and support. Mandy's hands were damp with sweat as she realised that Dawn might not be prepared to listen to her promises, she could very well slam the door in her face, wash her hands of her younger sister. Mandy felt the agitation build as she drew closer to the house. At the bottom of the drive she stopped and drew in a deep breath, if Dawn ranted then she was determined not to respond, she would remain calm and apologise until her sister knew she meant it.

Tapping on the door she waited, the tension mounting; after thirty seconds, she tried again knocking, a little louder this time. At her back, she heard a car drive past, the exhaust rattling before silence descended again and Mandy frowned before moving to the front window and peered into the empty room. In the corner, she could see the toy box that Dawn had bought and filled with toys for when Emma stayed over.

Mandy turned, frowning, her sister's car was on the drive so she must be in. Perhaps they were in the back garden, Emma on the slide while Dawn sat on the sun lounger watching her at play.

Mandy walked back past the front door and turned right, she was halfway alongside the house when she saw the body lying under the privet hedge. When her eyes fell on her sister's face Mandy Farmer started to scream.

She was still screaming when the neighbour came out to see what all the racket was about.

74

The man looked at the two figures huddled side by side in the corner of the cellar, the girl pressed tight to the boy's side; when he looped a protective arm around her shoulder, the man frowned.

'If you feel the need to scream then go ahead, no one will hear you,' he paused, 'no one except me and I *love* to hear people scream,' the smile leached onto his gaunt face. 'Believe me, lots of children have screamed in this house, screamed until their lungs burst and no one ever came to investigate.'

He scowled when he failed to get a reaction, the boy and girl remained locked together like a single, living entity.

This was the first time he had ever had two people down in the cellar. He pondered the ramifications and then the smile was back as he realised that he would be able to instil twice the amount of terror; twice the amount of fear to be absorbed and used.

He felt the air thrum with possibilities, days, weeks, months of torment and all seen with a clarity that he had thought was gone forever. Time itself had stood still, freezing the girl in the perfect moment, waiting to be claimed and now here she was with the hated boy by her side.

The fates had smiled down upon him, leading him from the mists of confusion to be reborn in his old image, a man who would defeat time and roll back the years to the glory days.

But first he had something to see to, something that would not wait.

Turning, he headed for the wooden steps, his heavy feet thudding as he climbed to the top.

Reaching the doorway, he stopped and turned, the smile still locked in place as he pulled the cord, the light vanished and the cellar was thrown into darkness.

When he heard the girl whimper, he sighed in ecstasy before stepping into the hallway and closing the door. Turning the heavy key, he left it in the lock before stalking back through the house. Slumping down on the sofa he closed his eyes, the heavy drapes at the window would keep the daylight at bay and when the darkness came again he would head out and see to the final task.

Then he would come back to the house and the real fun would begin.

Closing his eyes, he drifted off to sleep, the smile still in place.

75

Reese pulled up at the front of the house, the tyres squealing in the gutter, the street clogged with squad cars, a line of half a dozen officers keeping the growing crowd of neighbours back from the scene. He saw Marnie leap out of the car in front, by the time he'd yanked on the handbrake, she was hurrying up the drive to where Susan Romney was standing, her face ashen.

As soon as Marnie spotted Dawn Farmer, a hand shot to her mouth in shock and an image of Alby Roper steamrollered into her paralysed mind.

Doc Kelly was crouched by the side of the body, his normally calm face twisted in a grimace of disgust.

Reese appeared at Marnie's shoulder, his face taught with disbelief. 'Jesus Christ what the hell is happening here,' he hissed, as he saw the twin holes where Dawn Farmer's eyes use to sit.

'Where's Emma?' Marnie asked.

Romney looked at her before licking her lips. 'Emma?'

Marnie felt her stomach lurch.

'I was first on the scene and the woman who found her is called Mandy, I...'

'Emma is Mandy's daughter,' Marnie interrupted.

Romney shook her head rapidly. 'I am sorry, boss, but the woman was alone, there was no child with her.'

Reese looked at Romney, his eyes haunted. 'Where's Mandy now?' he asked.

'The next-door neighbour took her in, the local doctor's with her.'

Reese grunted, heading down the drive, Marnie watched as he approached the house next door, the front door opened and Reese glanced at her before vanishing into the house.

Kelly stood up and sighed.

'Is it the same cause of death as Roper?' Marnie asked.

The doctor nodded his eyes still locked on the body. 'What are the chances of two people being killed liked that? It has to be the same bastard,' he said with conviction.

'Has anyone been in the house?' she asked.

PC Romney shook her head. 'Not yet.'

'Right, I want that door open and I want it done now, get one of the lads to break it down.'

Romney nodded, looking relieved to be away from the horror as she strode down the drive.

Kelly scratched at his chin, his eyes sorrowful. 'Like Reese said, I don't understand any of this.'

Marnie tried to think but she couldn't get past the fact that first Alby Roper had turned up minus his eyes and a few short hours later Dawn Farmer had met the same fate. She thought of Dawn with Emma in her arms as she ranted about her sister and her refusal to leave her violent partner Cal Wilson.

Marnie turned away to find Paul Clark at the front door, battering ram held in his hands.

'Break it down,' she said, flicking her head towards the door.

Clark took a swing, once, twice and the door banged inwards.

Seconds later, Marnie entered the house, her face set in grim lines, the anger rising with every passing second.

76

Every time Luke tried to move he felt the girl tighten her arms around his waist, her body trembling in fear. They were both pressed tight to the wall, the darkness closing in around them.

'What's your name?' Luke whispered.

The girl didn't reply but he heard her sobs well enough, Luke felt the tears trickle from his own eyes. In the darkness, the death of Roper played out in all its gory horror.

He heard the splatter as Roper's head was smashed into the unforgiving concrete, thumbs had plunged into his eyes as his skull collapsed and the brains spewed out through crushed bones.

Luke swallowed the sense of revulsion and screwed his eyes closed.

'*Emma,*' the voice whispered.

Luke's eyes sprang wide in surprise. 'My name's Luke,' he replied, in the same hushed tones, as if afraid to wake some monster that slept in the darkened cellar.

'I want my mummy,' the girl said in a quivering voice.

Luke tried to find some words of comfort but the fear was rampaging through his mind. His body still ached from the beatings that Roper had subjected him to and then there was the terror of being chased through the trees ending with his tormentor's terrible death. He thought back to the car bumping Roper to the ground, he had stabbed out at the bonnet, the blade gouging into the metal and Luke had been convinced that the man who had climbed from the car was in for a beating, or worse, from the furious Roper.

'Is it a monster?' Emma asked.

Luke wanted to scream the word 'YES!' but he clamped his lips closed and pulled the girl closer still as the darkness swallowed all hope.

77

Marnie turned another page of the Cox family album. She had found it in a bedside cupboard and it reminded her of the one her mother kept; every page filled with images of her and Abby, and this was the same. There was the occasional single image of the sisters but most of them showed the girls side by side, Dawn with her arm draped protectively around Mandy's shoulder.

Marnie could hear the sounds of the house being searched by fellow officers, drawers pulled open, the clomp of booted feet on the stairs.

Turning a page, she felt the prickle of tears in her eyes, it showed Mandy on a swing being pushed by her sister. Mandy's hair was flying, her mouth wide open – no doubt hollering in glee – Dawn was smiling, the older-sister smile that Marnie knew so well.

With a sigh of sadness, she placed the album on the bed and picked up the cardboard box she had found in the bottom of the wardrobe. It contained a scattering of memories, things that would have been meaningless to anyone else but obviously, they had meant something to Dawn Farmer.

Marnie lifted out an old Barbie doll, the hair had been cut short, the right hand had been chewed leaving the plastic fingers elongated and flat. Placing it back in the box she pushed a bundle of ribbons to one side, at the bottom of the box were a few pin badges, one or two were antivivisection badges, another had a yellow, smiley face imprinted on the front, yet another showed a red rose in full bloom. Marnie picked up a single earring with a blue stone and a couple of necklaces that were wrapped together in a tangle.

More thudding on the stairs, a few seconds later Reese appeared in the doorway.

'Mandy was released from hospital and came straight here to get collect her daughter and found her sister dead.'

'So, Emma's been taken?' Marnie said, placing the box on the bed.

Reese nodded. 'I don't get any of this, I mean, was Emma targeted and if so then what has it got to do with finding Roper in the street?'

'Maybe we can get something off the town centre CCTV cameras. I mean, whoever killed Roper must have taken the girl, right?'

Reese thought for a moment before answering. 'Agreed.'

'So, to get from here to where we found Roper the killer would have had to drive through the town centre, we know the vehicle is black...'

'Because of the paint found on the knife?'

Marnie nodded.

'Check it out,' Reese growled, turning and stalking from the room.

Marnie took one last look at the box full of memories and then she was striding along the landing taking the stairs two at a time as if she could feel the pressure of time running out. Every second that passed, Emma Farmer was in the grip of some maniac, a monster who killed on impulse but also seemed to be working to some insane plan.

She stopped for a moment in the doorway, the frown on her face gelling into a look of fear. Roper had been killed on the road that ran parallel to the woods, the same woods Abby had vanished in, the same woods they had found Jenny Bell and the other remains of the missing or unknown girls.

Suddenly Marnie Hammond was running for the car, the fear spurring her on.

78

Hambling sat against the wall, listening to the birds singing to one another in the thick undergrowth outside.

He felt sick with hunger, his body shaking and bone weary. A rat stuck its head from a hole in the floorboards and Hambling threw a chunk of plaster towards it, grunting in satisfaction as the rodent vanished from sight. He kept his eyes on the shadow on the wall opposite, watching it slowly shrink in size, the tortuous hours passing at a crawl as he waited for the light to fade. The hunger pains pulling and twisting his stomach muscles until he gasped and drew his legs up tight. His skin crawled and he started to scratch, his hand darting around beneath his shirt scrabbling at the skin with long, dirty fingernails. The bottle of water had long since been drunk and he ran a dry tongue across his cracked lips, it was as if he could feel his insides shrinking as they dried out. He felt like crying again but his body refused to give up the valuable moisture on something as pointless as tears. He thought back to his last stretch inside and shivered at the memory. Once the other inmates had found out about the girl, they had made it their business to beat him at every available opportunity. Eventually, he had been placed in the special wing with all the real perverts and child molesters and the beatings had stopped, though having to spend time with the paedophiles had left Hambling feeling sick with disgust.

He thought back to the girl in the shopping mall, she had been wandering, lost, her eyes wide and tear filled, Hambling had picked her up and looked around for the mother. He remembered asking the girl where she had last seen her mummy and she had pointed left, so Hambling had set off walking and then the screaming had erupted from the crowd of shoppers as the mother appeared. He had tried to explain what had happened but the woman had clutched the child to her chest, her eyes burning with disgust as she took in the straggly hair and unwashed clothes. When he'd tried to walk away the woman had followed, screaming the terrible words at him, 'pervert', she'd yelled, 'animal', '*paedophile*'.

Christopher Hambling had quickened his pace and still she continued to follow, jabbing out her finger and screaming obscenities, the crying child still held in her arms. Hambling had seen the looks from the other shoppers as they backed away, their eyes full of loathing.

In desperation, he had started to run, the fear clambering through his mind as the woman gave chase. When the security guard had tackled him to the floor the crowds had gathered around, all staring down at him with repugnance, the woman had continued her tirade of abuse, her voice becoming more strident, her vitriol more acute. By the time the police arrived, Hambling was just glad to be loaded into the back of the van, away from the glaring eyes and hateful words.

That was the reason he had done a runner when he'd seen the police arrive at the flat. The idea that he could have walked over and tried to explain that he had been in his flat watching television the day Jenny Bell went missing had never even entered his head. He knew they wouldn't have listened to anything he had to say, after all, according to the records he had served time for the attempted abduction of the girl, he was a deviant, a weirdo, a pervert.

Now he sat in this filthy hole and tried to see a way out of the nightmare but the truth was there was no escape, no way to set the record straight.

The light on the wall began to fade slowly and Hambling struggled to his feet in anticipation, when his jeans started to slide down he grabbed them, his eyes widening in shock. Over the last few weeks the flesh had fallen off him and now he was beginning to realise that at this rate if the police didn't get him then the starvation would. He thought of waking one day and finding he was too fragile to move, to weary to even stand. Hambling closed his eyes and pictured the rats moving closer as he jittered beneath the duvet trying desperately to move but his body was too weak to obey the commands of his terrified brain. They would close in tight around him, burrowing under the duvet, and then his clothes, their claws scratching at his skin, yellow teeth nibbling until…

'*No!*' Hambling snapped open his eyes and staggered forward.

From the hole in the floorboards the rat watched him with its rapacious oil-drip eye.

79

By the time Marnie pulled up in front of the small office block the light was starting to fade. After parking up, she headed through a set of double doors into a small reception area.

The woman behind the desk smiled as Marnie explained what she was doing there. Thirty seconds later she was shown through to a room with one wall taken up with banks of monitors. A solitary man sat in a chair facing the screen, when he heard the door click he glanced over his shoulder.

'Ah, Sergeant Hammond, I take it?'

Marnie smiled as he spun around in his chair and thrust out his hand.

'My name's John Chambers, I hear you want to take a look at last night's town centre footage?'

Marnie slid the zip down on her jacket. 'That's right.'

'Well, I've just been getting things organised but I can tell you nothing momentous happened, we have the usual drunks cavorting in the street, one or two urinating in doorways. We did have a scuffle around nine o'clock, a couple of lads kicked off but it was over in seconds, handbags at dawn really,' he finished before tapping at the keyboard.

Marnie leaned forward as the screens sprang to life, her eyes roaming over each monitor in turn.

'We have a runner on screen four,' Chambers said matter of fact.

When Marnie saw Luke Croft sprinting down the street she felt her heart flutter, she could see his face clearly, the panic, the fear, evident as he ran. She felt the guilt wash over her as he drew closer before angling right and vanishing from view.

'I've had a look but I have no idea what he was running from, no one was chasing the lad,' Chambers explained, easing back in the chair.

Marnie knew exactly why Luke had been running, the girl called Sarah had offered him money and he had bolted, this simple act of kindness had crushed him and forced him to run as if the gates of hell were swinging open behind him.

Marnie's eyes refocused just as Alby Roper came into view, she watched him collide with a girl, his face twisted with malice, striding down the street, a hotdog held to his mouth as he took a bite.

She felt the anger build inside, seeing him strut along the pavement looking cocky, confident in his ability to take care of himself. Marnie pictured Luke's battered body, the bruises smothering his pale flesh, his eyes haunted by what he had been forced to endure at Roper's hands.

Chambers continued to tap at the keys, his eyes scanning the screens. 'It pretty much stays like this until about two in the morning and then the streets empty as people head home,' he said.

Marnie kept her eyes on Roper, knowing that when he reached the junction of Market Street he would turn right.

'Nice car,' Chambers said.

Marnie was still leaning forwards, her hands planted on the desk, her eyes fixed on the now-deceased Roper, the words flitted through her mind and she almost disregarded them and then she shook herself.

'I'm sorry what did you say?' she asked, turning towards Chambers.

He smiled and pointed at the screen. 'I was saying "nice car", you don't see many old Mercs like that nowadays.'

Marnie followed his pointing finger, when she saw the gleaming car parked at the traffic lights her eyes narrowed slightly, then the lights changed and the vehicle turned right.

Her brow furrowed in concentration, she was sure she'd seen the car before though she couldn't remember when or where.

Her mind seemed to fast forward through the last few day's events, images came and went, Luke curled on the bathroom floor, his body blooming yellow and brown. Jenny Bell, dark earth clogging her sightless eyes. Gareth Walls, looking at her with insolence as he realised she wasn't there to discuss his daughter. The images swept by, the Donalds looking broken, Alby Roper sprawled in the road, his body intact, his head a ghastly horror of splattered brains. The bones in the woods – white and broken – the yellow daisy ring on the finger, the...

Marnie's eyes sprang wide though she remained locked in her own mind, she could see Dawn Farmer placing Emma in the back seat of the estate car.

She remembered walking to the gate as Dawn drove away, Reese had been with her, hands in pockets, the street crowded with squad cars, lights spiralling into the night tinting everything with blue light.

Then she pictured the car opposite, gleaming black in colour and looking strangely out of place on a street lined with council houses and wheelie bins, the driver had pulled away from the parade of shops that had wire mesh over the windows, then stopped as if the occupant were having one last look at the commotion before driving away.

'You said it was a Mercedes?' Marnie asked.

Chambers looked at her in surprise. 'Don't know the model but it's definitely an old one.'

'What do you mean by old?'

Chambers shrugged. 'Well, at a guess I'd say late sixties early seventies but like I say I'm no...'

'I want you to get the best image you can of the car and have it sent over to the station,' she said, standing up and pushing the chair back to the wall.

'OK, no problem.'

'Thanks for your help,' she said, pulling open the door and leaving the room.

John Chambers frowned for a moment before turning back to the screens.

Outside Marnie climbed into the car and turned the engine on, trying to gather her thoughts as she peered through the windscreen at the blank brick wall.

When her phone began to trill, she blinked before retrieving it from her coat pocket.

'I've just had the lab on the phone, they've identified another set of remains,' Reese said, his voice worn and bristling with anguish.

Marnie held her breath, somehow convinced that he was going to utter the name of her sister.

'Pam Oaks is on her way to see Gareth and Sally Walls as we speak,' he finished.

Marnie felt as if she were playing Russian roulette, the cold, unforgiving metal pressed to her head as she pulled the trigger, knowing that eventually her luck would run out and it would be Abby's name she heard blasting through her mind as they unearthed her bones. She thought of Walls and a sense of guilt plucked at her mind. Perhaps she had been too harsh on the man, taking out her frustrations on the governor, seeing him as an authority figure, someone to blame for the damage done to Luke.

'You still there?' Reese asked.

'Yeah, yeah, I'm still here.'

'So, how have you fared with the CCTV?'

By the time she had finished explaining about the black car seen in the town centre and her conviction that she had seen the same car, or a similar one, pulling away from the shops opposite the Cox house, the light had vanished altogether.

Leaning forward, she flicked on the headlights before easing back in the seat.

'We need to find Emma Farmer,' Reese said with a sigh.

'I know,' Marnie replied, in a quiet voice.

'The question is, how the hell do we do it?'

Marnie closed her eyes in despair.

80

As the lights of the town centre approached, Hambling felt the fear grow.

The towpath came to an end and he cut left onto the pavement, the hood of his jacket covering his head as the stream of traffic sped by, the draft from the vehicles buffeting him as he walked.

Slipping his hands into pockets, he glanced up and winced when the car lights glared in his eyes. Groaning, he lowered his head, concentrating on controlling the fear and putting one foot in front of the other.

The road began to climb steadily upwards, his pace slowed, his breathing becoming ragged as his bones ached and his chest tightened. At the crossing, he paused and waited for a break in the traffic before heading to the other side. In the distance, he could see Market Street, people milling about as the pubs and clubs opened, the sight made him halt for a moment, the fear rampant now as he realised he would have to head amongst the revellers to reach the bins around the back of the shops. The thought that he could spend another night searching and find nothing substantial to eat was too dire to contemplate, he had to find food or the nightmare about the rats would come true, he was sure of it.

With the terrifying thought locked in his brain he set off walking again, hands still in his pockets, gripping the top of his jeans to stop them from sliding down. He felt like some shadow man held in a concentration camp, the flesh falling from his frame as starvation took hold.

Drawing nearer to the crowds, he started to hear the muffled shouts and calls of laughter mingling with the thump of drum and bass coming from the pubs.

Christopher Hambling tried to swallow the fear but his bone-dry mouth and throat seemed locked tight as he headed into town.

81

His eyes opened in the darkness, the smile creeping onto his face as he recalled instantly where and who he was. The feeling made the euphoria roar through his soul, he was back, *really* back in the moment, no longer living in a netherworld of doubt and confusion. Swinging his legs to the floor, he sat up and listened to the steady tick-tock of the clock in the corner of the room.

Easing to his feet he headed into the hallway, his steps thudding on the wooden floor. Reaching the cellar door, he looked at the key in the lock, cocking his head he listened and frowned. In the past, some of the victims had screamed and cried for endless hours and he had stood in the hallway relishing the sounds of their fear. He thought of the boy and the frown turned into a scowl. Perhaps leaving the two of them together had been a mistake. He pictured them clinging to one another in the darkness, drawing comfort and strength from each other. His face soured as he realised that his initial idea could prove to be the wrong one. Reaching out towards the key he paused, he had a busy night ahead and the man knew how quickly the dark hours passed, before you knew it the sun would be crawling over the horizon, spreading its filthy light onto the earth.

With a grunt, he strode towards the front door, his face set with a look of determination. The two of them could wait – after all they weren't going anywhere – he had one final problem to solve. His face locked in a savage snarl, he snatched open the front door and strode out into the night.

82

Hambling stretched down into the bin, the cloying stink drifting out around him as his hands pushed the rubbish left and right. He lifted out the soggy burger box and opened it, grabbing at the scraps. Closing his eyes, he shovelled the food into his mouth, despite the sour taste he chewed and swallowed before dropping the litter to the floor and delving back to search for more. Another box, this time it contained the plucked carcass of a chicken. Hambling sucked at the bones relishing the taste, his hands shaking and coated with grease. Licking his fingers clean, he sighed before moving to the next bin. This time he hit the jackpot, he found a box of chicken nuggets and a bottle of dandelion and burdock. Unscrewing the lid, he gulped at the flat, sugary drink, his Adam's apple bobbing, trying to quench his thirst. Then he stuffed two nuggets into his mouth, jaw working he wolfed them down and grabbed two more.

'Check this fucker out.'

Hambling spun around, the fear taking his breath away when he saw the two men standing in the shadows of the alleyway. He heard the splash as one of them started to take a piss against the stack of black bin bags.

'Fucking tramp,' the man said, shaking his member and stuffing it back into his jeans.

Hambling could taste the grease on his lips, mingling with the sudden taste of fear. Taking a step back he kept the box of nuggets clasped to his chest, his heart stalling as the two men walked towards him.

He could see them in the gloom, they looked to be in their early twenties, faces narrow, eyes mean. Suddenly the stink of their aftershave hit him, the pungent scent overpowering. Hambling gagged and then he hurled the package at the two men before turning and sprinting along the darkened alleyway.

'*Dirty fucker!*' one of the men shouted.

He didn't have to look over his shoulder to know that the two men had broken into a run, he could hear their feet thudding behind him. The fear mutated into terror and he grabbed a bin on his left and yanked it over, the rubbish spilling out across the flags as he sprinted forwards.

'*Grab the bastard!*' the voice at his back bellowed.

Bursting free from the alley, Hambling tried to dodge around the people crammed on the pavement, he slammed into one man who spun around, his eyes widening in surprise as Hambling's hood fell back from his head. For a fleeting moment, he saw recognition in the man's eyes and then he spun away and dashed left.

'*It's the fucking paedo off the telly!*' the voice bellowed out, loud and strident.

Hambling pushed and shoved his way into the road and then he was running, headlights flared yet he carried on, the terror of being discovered swept all other feelings away as he tried to make his escape.

'*It's the fucking kiddie fiddler!*' the voice screamed again and Hambling threw a terrified glance over his shoulder.

He could see the man, the one he had barged into, standing by the side of the road, the two men from the alley by his side. When they broke into a run, Hambling whimpered and turned, the adrenalin flowing as his legs ate up the ground, his worst nightmares all coming true at once.

83

Marnie stopped as the lights flicked to red; the pavements were crowded with people dressed for a night on the town. The girls shimmering in glitter tan and sparkly tops, the boys strutting in time-honoured fashion. She sighed and ran a hand across her eyes trying to remember the last time she had got dressed up for a night out on the town.

The light flicked to amber and she dropped the clutch just as a man sprinted past the front of the car, when three other men shot past she frowned and indicated before turning right, her eyes locked on the running men.

Reaching out, she flicked on the siren and flashing lights, the man at the rear of the three running men slowed his pace and looked over his shoulder then he was waving his arms as the car approached. Marnie frowned and pulled up, his face ballooned at the side window. As soon as the window started to slide down he threaded his fingers over the top, his face running with sweat, his eyes wide.

'It's him!' he gasped.

Marnie glanced forward, the two men were closing the gap on the running man.

'Calm down and…'

'*It's Hambling!*' the man shouted through the open window.

Marnie slammed the car into gear and planted her foot to the floor, the man leapt back, startled, as the vehicle roared forward.

Pedestrians watched the car power along the street, some shouted abuse whilst others simply watched with drink-infused eyes.

Up ahead the two men were within feet of the man she assumed to be Hambling.

Snatching at the handset she barked an order in for assistance, waiting impatiently for a reply.

'*Position?*' the voice asked.

'Market Street, heading north. And make it quick because this could turn ugly,' she said urgently, as one of the men reached out and grabbed the hood of the man's jacket.

Tossing the handset onto the passenger seat, Marnie slammed on the brakes as she drew level. By the time she had flung the door open, the two men were lashing out at the man who tried to cover his head with raised hands.

Dashing forward, she snatched the arm of one of the men as he tried to smash his fist into the cowering man's head.

'*That's enough!*' she bellowed, dragging him back.

His accomplice glanced over his shoulder and scowled at her before turning his attention back to Hambling.

Thrusting the man to one side, Marnie stormed over to the second and pulled him back.

'I said "*enough*"!'

The two men glared at her and then one of them jabbed out a finger.

'It's the fucking pervert who took that little girl,' he snarled.

Marnie glanced left as Christopher Hambling looked up at her, his eyes pleading, his gaunt face covered by a scruffy beard, his clothes grimy and stinking.

'Please, I never touched her,' he whispered, in a trembling voice.

Marnie reached out and grabbed the sleeve of his parka, pulling him back with her as the two men closed in, the crowds on the pavements watched with interest.

'Do you lot know who this fucker is?' one of them men shouted to the bystanders. 'He's the one who took Jenny Bell, the one who fucking abused and killed her!'

Heads turned and Marnie glanced at the faces, they had changed from curious to anger-filled in a matter of a few short seconds.

She continued to drag Hambling towards the car as the atmosphere suddenly became charged with fury.

'*Bastard!*' a woman, dressed in next to nothing, screamed from the pavement and then spat at them as they passed.

'*Keep moving,*' Marnie hissed, seeing some of the people move from the kerb and into the road.

She could hear Hambling breathing, his sour breath bloomed into her face as he drew close to her.

'Please don't let them hurt me, I've done nothing I…'

When the woman, who had shouted the abuse, dashed forward and lashed out with her bag, Marnie snatched Hambling out of the way.

'*Fucking bitch!*' The woman screamed at Marnie, her made-up face smothered with anger.

Marnie ignored her and glanced back over her shoulder only to find the path to the car was now blocked by a gang of men and women, all wearing matching looks of fury.

Christopher Hambling started to cry as the crowd closed in around them.

'*Everyone move back!*' Marnie shouted, though she knew that they wouldn't listen. She glanced at some of the faces, most looked to be in their late twenties or early thirties, no doubt some were fathers and mothers and having Hambling here was causing them to lose all focus.

One of them lunged forward and Marnie managed to slip in front of the attacker as he lashed out. She ducked before snapping up and driving her knee between the man's legs, he hit the ground hard and then suddenly others dashed forwards and she fell back under the onslaught. She felt her hair grabbed from behind and she spun around to find the woman sneering at her, the same one who had shouted the odds when she was trying to get Hambling to the car. The woman lashed out, her red nails flashing at Marnie's eyes but Marnie beat her to it, slamming her fist into the woman's face, her nose exploded in a spurt of red and then a fist slammed into the side of Marnie's head and she fell to her knees.

Through a blur of tears, she saw Hambling go down as a swarm of hands and booted feet lashed out.

Someone barged into her and she sprawled to the side, somewhere in the distance, she heard the wail of a siren but Marnie knew it was going to be way too late to save Christopher Hambling.

84

L uke gripped Emma's hand as he slowly climbed the wooden stairs, his right hand sweeping back and forth in the darkness, the sweat running down his forehead in rivulets of distress.

'I'm scared,' Emma whimpered.

Luke stopped and gripped her small hand tighter. 'It's OK, I won't let you go,' he said, in a soothing voice.

'But…'

'There's a light up here and we need the light so we can find a way out,' he explained, continuing to climb.

When his hand touched the door, he sighed in relief, reaching to the left his fingers grasped the cord and he said a silent prayer before tugging down. The cord clicked and the pale light bulb flickered to dull life.

Luke glanced down at the girl and managed to smile. 'Better?' he asked.

Emma looked up at him, wide eyed, and nodded.

Luke gave her hand another comforting squeeze and they carefully made their way back down the steps.

'I don't like it here,' Emma's bottom lip trembled and Luke threaded his arm around her shoulder.

He knew exactly what she meant, he looked around the large space properly for the first time. Cardboard boxes were crammed along three of the walls with not a window in sight. Luke felt the fear threatening to take hold again as he pulled the girl close to his side. When he saw the door set into the far wall he felt a flicker of hope rise and led Emma across the cellar, keen to see what was on the other side.

As they reached the door, he felt Emma pull back slightly and he stopped and looked down at her. 'You OK?'

'Want my mummy,' she replied.

Luke crouched down until he was on eye level with her. 'We'll find your mummy but we need to be clever, OK?'

'*Clever?* she repeated, a frown creasing her smooth brow.

'Yes, we…'

'The bad man hurt my auntie Dawn,' she whispered. 'He hurt her eyes and she was crying red tears.'

Luke felt the terror clutch at his guts as he absorbed the words, when the tears spilled onto her cheeks he stood back up and took her hand, the urge to find a way out of this place swamped him, he reached out a hand and opened the door.

Pale light from the main cellar bled into the second smaller room and Luke moved into the doorway, Emma at his side. Reaching a hand to the right he found the light switch, praying he would see a window as he flicked it on.

The light illuminated the room, the table and single chair, the paraffin heater…

Emma Farmer screamed and Luke pulled her back from the room, his terrified eyes locked on the white skulls lined up on the table.

Luke slammed the door closed without even bothering to look for a window.

85

Cal Wilson closed the front door with a bang before stalking down the path and onto the street. Pausing for a moment to light a cigarette, he blew out a plume of smoke before turning right. He still couldn't believe what had happened, Dawn was fucking dead and the brat had been snatched. He was just grateful that he'd been banged up when it had happened or no doubt the filth would have tried to pin the blame on him. He spat onto the pavement as he strode along, the smoke trailing over his shoulder. He was glad that Mandy hadn't been in when he'd got back to the house, he couldn't have been doing with listening to her scream and cry over the death of her sister and the disappearance of her daughter. Anyway, chances are Emma's real father had probably snatched the girl and killed Dawn. Wilson nodded to himself in agreement; as he reached the last of the houses the streetlights ended and fields opened up on the left and right. No doubt the coppers would hunt the prick down and find the girl. Cal scowled as he thought of Dawn, he had hated the bitch, she was always sticking her nose in and telling Mandy to fuck him off. If he'd had his way, he would have slapped her down but he knew that Dawn wasn't like her sister and she would have had him locked up in an instant. The smile crept back onto his face, at least that wouldn't be a problem anymore, she was dead and as far as Cal Wilson was concerned it was brilliant news.

When he saw the headlights approaching he winced at the light, they flicked to full beam and he raised a hand to shield his eyes. 'Twat,' he grimaced as the glare bore down on him.

The car came to a stop about ten yards away and Wilson heard the clunk of a door closing, though he could see no further than the twin lights.

'Wanker,' he spat, flicking the cigarette into the grass on the right.

The headlight continued to blast into his eyes, drawing alongside the vehicle he saw the boot lid standing open and he glanced into the car ready to give the driver a mouthful, but the vehicle was empty. Throwing back his shoulders, he strode towards the rear of the car to find a man bent over as if searching for something in the small space.

'Hey, dickhead, you nearly fucking blinded me there.'

The man straightened up and turned. 'Blinded?'

Wilson jabbed out a finger. 'Yeah, now...'

The man lashed out with frightening speed, the tyre iron slammed into the side of Cal's head, blood sprayed, his legs buckled and then the man grabbed him and rolled him into the boot of the car.

Cal Wilson's eyes flickered as the face loomed towards him. 'Oh, I'll take your eyes, my friend, don't you worry about that.'

Wilson opened his mouth to scream but the boot slammed shut.

86

Sally Walls watched as her husband stood in front of the television screen, she was scrunched onto the sofa gripping the cushion to her chest in fear.

'It's believed that the man is Christopher Hambling, who was wanted by the police over the disappearance and subsequent murder of Jenny Bell.' the reporter stated.

Walls shuddered and Sally squirmed, feeling the waves of anger coming from her husband.

'Do we know what happened to Hambling?' a voice from the studio asked.

The reporter on Market Street nodded slightly. 'Hambling was spotted in town and it seems that he was chased by a group of individuals who brought him to the ground and subsequently attacked the man, possibly fatally.'

'Do we have any idea where Christopher Hambling has been hiding?'

'I'm afraid not, but given the fact that he was here in the centre of Kirkhead, then we can assume it must have been somewhere close by.'

'*Bastard!*' Walls hissed.

'We do know that Hambling has been taken to a local hospital though we have no further details on his injuries at this time.'

In the background a police car flashed by, siren wailing, lights flashing.

Sally winced as the report ended and her husband turned slowly to face her.

'Your fault,' he whispered, his eyes alight with fury.

Sally felt the weight of his hatred slam into her.

'If you hadn't been driving like an idiot, then our daughter would still be alive.' He took a step towards her.

Sally lurched to the left, the cushion fell to the floor as she ran for the door, her hand scrabbled for the handle but then she lurched forward as Gareth thrust his hands into her back. She hit the door hard, the breath blasted from her body and then she felt his hand, curled in her hair, snatching her back.

'*Please, I…*'

His hand lashed across her face and she cried out in terror as he pushed in close.

'My *girl, my* Suzie would still be alive if you'd done your job, she would be here *safe and sound,* instead you lost her and that piece of filth took her and killed her and left her body *in the stinking woods!*'

Sally heard his words of accusation swirl around her mind, knowing that he was right, she had been responsible for their daughter vanishing, and yet she was helpless to change the past.

'And now he's in the fucking hospital being patched up!' Walls screamed into her face.

For a couple of seconds, confusion reigned as she tried to fathom the meaning of the words. When she looked into her husband's eyes she felt the terror grip her heart, she realised that he thought Hambling was responsible for the death of Suzie.

She could smell whisky on his breath as he snarled at her.

'He's been living his life while my girl was lying in a trough of filth!'

Sally opened her mouth, unsure what she was going to say and then the hand hit her again only now it was a closed fist that smashed into the side of her head. This time she didn't cry out, the years of anguish wouldn't allow it, after all Gareth was right, Suzie had been taken and she had failed as a mother to stop it happening. She closed her eyes and pictured her daughter in the passenger seat, she had been busy playing with her favourite doll, running the plastic brush through her hair when the car came careering around the corner and…

Walls slammed his fist full into her face and Sally crashed to the floor.

'*Useless bitch!*' he bellowed, before snatching the car keys from his pocket and storming from the room.

The television continued to flicker, thirty seconds later Sally heard the sound of wheels spinning on gravel. She listened as the engine faded into the distance before vanishing altogether, then she slumped to the floor and welcomed the darkness that claimed her.

87

Marnie sat at the small table sipping from the coffee cup and wincing at the pain in her lip. Reese sat opposite, his eyes fixed on her face.

'Are you sure you're OK?' he asked.

Placing the cup on the table, she kept her hands wrapped around the mug. 'I'm fine.'

Reese raised an eyebrow. 'You were lucky to get out of there with just cuts and bruises.'

'Yeah well, Hambling wasn't so lucky that's for sure.'

The canteen of the hospital was empty apart from a couple of nurses who sat across the room talking and drinking, one of them yawned and stretched her hands towards the ceiling.

'Look, he's alive and I'm sure that wouldn't have been the case if you hadn't stepped in.' Reese replied.

'I don't think he did it,' Marnie said, as she held the DCI's gaze.

Reese eased back in the chair and folded his arms. 'What makes you say that?'

Marnie sighed, trying to think how to put her feelings into words. 'When I saw him I hardly recognised him from the mugs hot...'

'Because he's been sleeping rough, he...'

'I understand that but Doc Kelly said Jenny Bell had been kept somewhere warm and dry. Wherever Hambling has been staying it must be filthy with no running water, his face was almost black with grime and he stank to high heaven.'

Reese didn't look convinced.

Marnie took a deep breath and continued. 'Look, he must have been staying somewhere close by, chances are he only ventured into town when he was hungry or thirsty. There's no way he could have kept Jenny for over two months without someone finding out about it. He would have had to leave her while he scavenged for food and she would have at least screamed...'

'He could have tied and gagged her.'

Marnie shook her head. 'If that were the case then Kelly would have told us about it. He said he found no damage to the body except for one fading bruise on her jaw, if he had tied her there would have been evidence and if he'd gagged her there would have been residue left on the skin.'

Reese ran a hand across the back of his neck.

'The only thing Hambling said to me was that he didn't do it.'

'Well, he was hardly going to admit it with the baying mob surrounding him, was he?'

Marnie lifted the cup and took another sip. 'I've looked into the case in Liverpool and, yes, he picked the child up but perhaps he was telling the truth, maybe the girl was upset and he was trying to help her find her mother...?'

'Then the man's an idiot,' Reese retorted with a scowl.

'I don't doubt it, and you're right he would have said anything with the crowd closing in. But we found nothing at his flat to tie him to Jenny, Kelly said there was no sign of any sexual abuse, so if Hambling did take her then why did he bother and he doesn't drive so how did he manage to take her without anyone seeing, keep her for two months and then dispose of the body?'

Reese drummed his fingers on the table, his gaze thoughtful. 'OK, so if he didn't take her then who did?'

Marnie swallowed as she thought of the remains found in the woods, Jenny Bell, Suzie Walls and Josie Roberts. 'I think the same man killed all the girls including Jenny,' she paused, 'and my sister,' she finished with a heavy sigh.

Reese leaned forward and planted his elbows on the table. 'Think about what you're saying, the gap between the remains we've found and Jenny Bell is almost two decades.'

'So?'

Reese glanced at the two nurses before leaning further forward. 'How can one man kill four children and then nothing for years until Jenny Bell?' he asked.

'But we don't know that he stopped the killings, there may be other bodies buried in the woods, more recent victims.'

Reese sighed, looking up at the ceiling in distress.

Marnie gripped the cup tight. 'The remains have all been found close to one another which points to a local man, someone who knows the area; and yet Josie Roberts came from North Wales. When we do identify the others, I'll guarantee that they'll be from other parts of the country.'

Reese lowered his head and nodded in understanding. 'That makes sense, so we're looking for someone who travelled a lot, someone who worked away from home and then brought the victims back to the town.'

Marnie nodded.

'But what about Roper and Dawn Farmer? What about Emma?' he asked, his eyes reigniting with turmoil.

Marnie pushed the cup away before sitting back and folding her arms. 'If you look at the victims then they fit the same profile as Emma, she falls into the right age bracket. Piper Donald, seven years old, fair haired, Suzie Walls, same age, same profile, Jenny Bell was a little older but not much, now it can't simply be coincidence, it all points to one killer who has taken and murdered these children over a long period of time. We see the gap between Jenny and the bones but who's to say he hasn't been living somewhere else and still taking the children, still killing them?'

Reese's eyes widened at the prospect. 'Jesus, don't even go there,' he muttered with a shake of the head.

'We need to try and find out if anyone has been living away from the area and recently moved back and...'

'Come on, Marnie, how are we meant to find out something like that?'

Marnie's gaze hardened as she looked across the table at her boss. 'Get it on the television and in the papers, we...'

'And how the hell will that help, you'll have people pointing the finger at every bugger who's been on a two-week holiday in Spain. You know what people are like, it could cause chaos and get us nowhere.'

'So, what do you suggest?'

Reese closed his eyes for a moment, his jaw clamped in impotent anger. 'Look, we have Hambling, he...'

'Hambling is on a life-support machine and besides he didn't take my sister, he was in the Liverpool Jail when Suzie Walls was taken,' she paused, 'Hambling is not responsible for any of this and we can't waste time thinking that he is. Someone killed Roper and Dawn Farmer, the same man now has Emma, Hambling didn't do any of that, we know that for a fact.'

Reeseslumped back in the chair under the weight of her words. 'OK, I'll try and sort something that we can put out to the media but there's no guarantee it will work.'

'I realise that but it has to be worth a try,' Marnie offered.

Reese grunted in acknowledgement, rubbing at his eyes. 'If what you say is true about Hambling then he could be completely innocent.'

Marnie thought for a moment before replying. 'The main thing is we know he's innocent of the crimes we're investigating. I mean, he *could* have been trying to help when he took the girl in Liverpool but somehow I don't think we'll ever know the truth about what really happened.'

Reese sniffed before unbuttoning his jacket. 'Right, come on I want a word with PC Romney before we go, she's on guard outside Hambling's room and I need to tell her that she'll be replaced in a couple of hours.'

Rising, they pushed their chairs back under the table before heading for the door, their shoes squeaking on the polished tiles.

88

L uke had no idea how long they had been locked together in the dusty cellar, their young minds shattered by what they had discovered beyond the peeling door. Emma had screamed as he yanked the door closed and it had taken all of his diminishing resolve not to follow her inventing the terror that soared through his mind.

Eventually, he had led Emma into a corner of the room and they had sat huddled together again, both lost in a maze of fear and dread.

Emma had her face turned away from the room, her fair hair covering her bowed head. Luke closed his eyes and tried to think but his mind was full of the horrors they had discovered in the small room. He had seen the skulls lined up on the table in a rough semi-circle, the chair pulled close to the table, the...

Luke's eyes opened as he pictured the paraffin lamp standing on the table, he sniffed the air as if he could detect the faint whiff of fuel.

Looking across the room, his gaze rose until he saw the door standing at the top of the flight of wooden steps.

Dipping a hand into his pocket, Luke pulled out his lighter and spun the wheel, sparks flew and the flame ignited.

He felt Emma pull closer to him and he gave her shoulder a squeeze, deep in thought he looked back at the door.

When the tiny part of his mind, not affected by the fear, started to formulate the crazy plan he shook his head in the negative.

The lighter started to heat up, removing his finger from the gas lever, the flame died but the idea continued to burn in his mind. It was their only way out, if he didn't try it then both he and Emma would die in this cellar, their skulls eventually joining the others on the table like gruesome decorations.

Luke tried to think if anyone would even bother to look for him. During his time in Park View his mother had never visited. He thought of her sitting at home neither caring nor concerned about his wellbeing, she would sit in the same chair, smoking her knock-off cigarettes without giving him a second thought. Luke tried to conjure someone from his life who would mourn his loss, an image of DS Hammond lurched into his head and his eyes filled with tears. He knew she had tried to help him, and the irony was that if he had let her this nightmare would never have taken place. Chances were that Roper would still be alive instead of his brains being smeared over the black tarmac and...

Suddenly, Luke stopped as the truth crashed through the self-pity, if he hadn't run from DS Hammond's house then he wouldn't be here now – but Emma would and she would have been alone. Luke glanced down at the girl's bowed head, apart from her name he had no idea who she was or why the man with the dark eyes and bloodied hands had taken her, what he did know was that he had to get them out of here.

'Emma, are you OK?' he asked in a soft voice.

The girl shook her head and sobbed.

'Do you trust me?'

This time she raised her head, her eyes swimming with tears, her cheeks wet. 'I don't know,' she whispered. 'My mummy has a boyfriend and he shouts a lot and my auntie Dawn told me that all boys are the same.'

Suddenly, Luke felt a swell of empathy for the girl, he knew only too well what she meant. After all, hadn't he spent countless years listening to the screaming and shouting as his mother battled with whichever man happened to be on the scene at the time?

He looked at Emma and saw a young female version of himself, wide eyes full of confusion as she found herself in a situation over which she had no control.

When the anger came, it hit hard and fast, Luke felt the fury boil up through his body, this wasn't fair on either of them. By some cruel twist of fate, they had found themselves in this place of horrors but he knew that if he was going to die here he wouldn't give up without a fight, he'd fight for both of them.

'Emma, I need to go into the other room, I...'

'*No!*' she gasped, clinging to him harder than ever.

Luke waited, counting the seconds until he felt her grip loosen slightly. 'I still need to check for any windows but I promise I won't be more than a minute and then I'll come straight back.'

Emma looked at him, her eyes brimming with tears as she seemed to sigh and sag back against the wall. 'Do you really promise?'

Luke nodded. 'Cross my heart,' he replied, whipping his finger twice across his chest.

'If I get scared can I shout you?' she asked.

'Of course you can,' he said, as he slowly pushed himself to his feet.

Emma looked up at him with uncertainty in her eyes, then Luke spun away and strode across the cellar, his shoulders thrown back, his head held high.

She watched as he vanished into the room, her feet shuffled back and forth on the dusty floor, her bottom lip quivering in fear.

The seconds stretched out and she opened her mouth, the scream building but then suddenly he appeared through the door and Emma gasped in relief.

When Luke smiled, Emma Farmer found herself smiling back. 'Whatcha got?' she asked.

Luke had a big glass bottle in one hand, the clear liquid sloshed back and forth as he walked towards her.

'We're going to get out of here, Emma, and then we're going to get you home,' he said.

Emma looked into his eyes and for the first time ever she found herself believing someone utterly and completely.

Luke continued to smile as he placed the bottle at his feet. When he looked up, his eyes burned with fierce determination.

'You trust me, right?' he asked again.

Emma wiped at her tearstained cheeks and nodded. 'I trust you,' she replied.

'Good,' Luke replied, as he went to work.

89

Gareth Walls turned down another empty, bland corridor, the fury rising as he strode along, glancing into wards as he passed. The only person he had seen since entering the hospital had been a porter pushing an elderly man along the corridor, the wheels on the chair squeaking and setting Walls's teeth on edge.

Summoning the lift, he waited, ten seconds later the doors slid open and he stepped inside. Pressing the button to the fourth floor he moved back, the image of his daughter branded and burning in his furious mind.

Over the years, he thought he had learned to cope with her disappearance, immersing himself in work and climbing the slippery slope to what others would consider a successful career. Yet he now knew it had all been a charade, a pathetic attempt to paper over the chasm of Suzie's disappearance. While he had been trying to forget the pain, his daughter had been in the hands of a child molester, a disgusting pervert.

The lift rose and he couldn't block the image or the sounds of his daughter crying out to him, all the time he had been helpless to save her.

The female DI who had visited the house to tell them that Suzie had been found had looked devastated as she broke the news, but Walls had known it was all an act. She hadn't meant a word of it, she had merely spouted the platitudes of empathy as if she had been reading from a script, when in reality she had no clue how it felt to have your child spirited away by some monster.

The lift doors opened and Walls suddenly found that he couldn't move. His fevered mind pictured the monster that had appeared on the television screen and in the papers, long straggly hair, eyes devoid of humanity and the name *Hambling* stencilled below the hateful image in bold, red italics.

The lift door started to slide closed and he shot out a hand before stepping into the corridor.

When he glanced to the left his heart almost stopped as he saw the female police officer sitting in a chair halfway down the corridor.

At his back the doors slid closed, the lift started the trip back down to ground level.

90

The car came to a halt outside the front door of the house, his hands resting on the wheel, his eyes peering out into the darkness. Flicking a wrist, he checked the time and smiled. Things had gone wonderfully well, the fates had smiled on him, he had been driving slowly down the street trying to formulate a plan and suddenly his prey had been there striding along, the cigarette smoke drifting into the night. The man had seized his opportunity and everything had fallen into place, he sat in the darkness of the car searching his mind and feeling the euphoria grow as he realised that the hated confusion was no longer clinging to his senses.

Clicking the door open he climbed out and looked up at the sky, stars shone, the moon hanging high, bathing the large garden in silver light.

Turning, he studied the house, his eyes roaming over the darkened windows, the smile widening as he felt the power surge through his body and mind. Closing the car door with a clunk, the smile slipped as he saw the gouge in the paintwork of the bonnet. For a few fleeting seconds, he felt the confusion as he tried to recall what had happened and then it all came to him in a series of crystal-clear images. The headlights glare, the two figures dashing in front of the car, the squeal of brakes, ending with the splatter of blood and brains, the warm sensation as his hands suddenly became coated with red.

Walking to the rear of the car he opened the boot, the one named Cal Wilson was curled tight, his legs drawn up, chin against his chest; blood seeped from the wound in the side of his head, soaking into the heavy mat.

Reaching in, he grabbed the man by the back of his jacket and hauled him out of the boot. Bending at the knees, he flipped him over his shoulder before heading for the house.

He stood on the threshold, the front door open, the long hallway stretched out in front of him, he could hear the silence, broken only by the chime of the grandfather clock. Part of his mind felt disappointed that he hadn't arrived to the sounds of pitiful screaming and the feeble slapping of hands on hard wood.

With a grunt of annoyance, he stepped into the hall, closing the door with an almighty bang and then smiling again, imagining the two of them in the dark, the terror flowing as they heard the sound of the crashing door heralding his return.

Heading for the wide staircase, the man started to whistle a tuneless dirge, his dark mind filled with ecstasy at what was to come.

91

'As soon as we're done here I want you to look at the old files again, go over everything we have about the victims, double-check and see if we missed anything, see if you can find anything that links them,' Reese said as the lift doors slid open and they stepped inside.

Marnie nodded in understanding, the doors closed and the lift headed upwards.

'If the killer worked around the country then I want suggestions on possible occupations, get a team together and start delving. Remember, Steven Cox had co-workers, assistants who would also be in the same towns at the same time, so check them out,' he finished as the lift droned.

'What about you?' Marnie asked.

Reese gave her a sidelong glance. 'I'll have a word with the chief, run the idea of getting the media on side again, as you said we need to cover more ground and we need to do it quickly for Emma Farmer's sake.'

Marnie blew out through inflated cheeks, the lift slid to a halt and the doors opened. Gareth Walls stood facing them. The three of them looked at one another, Marnie's eyes widening as she took in the crisp white shirt splattered red, his face speckled with blood. Then Walls exploded forward, raging obscenities, lips pulled back, teeth bared, eyes touched by madness his face twisted in fury, his right arm shot out blood drops flew from the knife in his hand and the blade sank into Reese's stomach.

The DCI staggered back, the blade sliding free he hit the wall of the lift with a bang and then Walls turned his vengeful gaze onto Marnie.

'*Bitch!*' he screamed, lunging into the confined space.

For the briefest of moments Marnie was stunned into immobility, but then she saw the red knife rise into the air, a sprinkling of blood patterning the Perspex roof light. She heard Reese grunt in pain, then she lurched back as the knife hissed through the air, Marnie felt the blade slice through the front of her jacket and then the fury that was always buried below the surface roared through her mind and body.

Lunging right, she pivoted and lashed out her elbow, slamming it into the side of Walls's twisted face.

The governor screeched in agony, his jaw cracked and he staggered left in a crouch before clattering into the metal wall. Marnie didn't hesitate, didn't give Walls the chance to recover. As he turned his hate-filled gaze towards her she leaned back, hands braced against cold metal, she lashed out her right leg. The sole of her shoe blasted into Gareth Walls's face, three of his teeth rocketed from the ruin of his mouth, his nose erupted in a gush of blood. The slick, red blade fell from his twitching fingers and he crashed onto his side, his mouth spewing blood onto the shining, steel floor.

Marnie looked towards Reese, he sat with his back to the wall, both hands gripping his stomach, the blood oozing out between his laced fingers, his eyes screwed tight closed, teeth clamped as he fought the pain. She turned and ran out into the corridor, when she saw Susan Romney sprawled on the floor she set off running. Seconds later she skidded to a halt, Romney had blood seeping from her scalp, her eyes fluttered and opened momentarily, Marnie glanced through the window into the small room, the horror rising. What remained of Christopher Hambling was sprawled half on and half off the bed.

Marnie walked forward and pushed the door open, her mind unable to take in the carnage. When she saw Hambling's head was only attached to his body by strands of sinew and muscle, she felt her stomach lurch. His face had been slashed bone deep, his right eye had been dislodged from the socket, part of his right ear had been sliced off and lay on the pillow in a stain of red.

Fighting the disgust, Marnie turned and hit the panic button on the wall, her legs unsteady as the buzzer drilled into her head.

92

A t the sound of the slamming door, Luke felt Emma jerk at his side. They stood in the middle of the cellar, frozen in terror as they heard the tuneless whistling grow closer and then fade into silence.

Luke could see Emma's eyes flood with fear. When she opened her mouth to scream, he crouched down quickly and put a finger to his lips.

'Emma, don't scream, you have to trust me now, OK?' he asked her gently.

The girl blinked and looked into his eyes. 'The bad man's back.'

'I know, but we have to stay quiet, OK?'

He saw the trust seep into her eyes and the weight of that faith almost broke him, he knew what it was like to put your trust in someone only to be let down. But this time the consequence for Emma wouldn't be bitter disappointment, it would be death at the hands of the monster with the dark eyes.

'I promise I won't scream,' she whispered.

Luke felt the smile quiver on his face and then he leaned down towards the girl. 'I need you to wait over there, OK?' he said, pointing to the left.

Emma nodded, she let go of his hand and backed away.

Luke watched until she bumped into the wall and then sat down, drawing her legs up to her chin.

Satisfied, he reached up to his shoulder, his fingers pulling at the wadding that poked out through the hole in his jacket. Crouching to his knees, he unscrewed the lid on the bottle and tilted it, letting the contents soak into the wadding. The tart chemical whiff of paraffin rose into the air.

He glanced left, Emma was watching him with interest and he gave her a reassuring smile before pushing the stuffing into the neck of the open bottle, carefully forcing it down, all the time trying to ignore the voice inside that told him to stop, that this was madness.

Luke dragged his sleeve across his sweating brow and twisted the material further down into the clear liquid. When there was a couple of inches poking through the opening he stopped, his teeth nibbling at his bottom lip, his ears straining to hear any sound of the monster's approach.

Lifting the bottle, he carried it carefully back to where Emma sat, she looked up at him, her brow creased in confusion.

Luke crouched down in front of her and drew in a thin breath. 'I need you to *really* listen to me, Emma, we can get out of here but you're going to have to be very brave.'

'Brave?' she asked, as her frown of confusion deepened.

Luke nodded before shuffling closer. 'I'm going to have to take out the light bulb and...'

'But I don't like the dark,' she replied, her eyes widening again in fear.

'I know, but when the bad man comes back he'll turn on the light and see us, so we have to stay hidden, Emma, we have to stay quiet and...'

'But how will we get away if it's all dark?'

Luke reached out his hands and she looked at him, puzzled, before taking hold, he pulled her to her feet and looked her in the eyes. 'This bottle will give us light when we need it but when that happens I want you to close your eyes and put your hands over your ears for me.'

Emma tilted her head slightly. 'But how will I see where we're going if I have my eyes closed?'

Luke smiled. 'You don't have to worry about that because I'll be carrying you.'

A look of relief swept over her face and she nodded and smiled. 'I like that,' she said.

'Good, now we need to find somewhere safe to hide, OK?'

'I like hide and seek,' she replied innocently.

Luke stood up and kept hold of her hand, looking around the cellar he could see three walls crammed with boxes, when he saw the small space beneath the stairs he nodded to himself. 'Come on, Emma,' he said, as he picked the bottle up and led her across the room. The gap behind the wooden steps was tight and he turned her around before placing the bottle at his feet.

'I'm going to get rid of the light now so it'll be dark but I need you to keep quiet for a few seconds until I get back to you.'

'I can do that,' Emma replied.

Luke let his hands slip from her shoulder as he backtracked into the centre of the room. Once he was beneath the bulb he turned, he could see Emma peeping at him between two of the wooden steps.

'You ready?'

She nodded, her eyes wide, her fingers laced over the step.

Luke glanced up at the bulb, then he closed his eyes and leapt into the air, his right fist lashing out, the bulb exploded in a pop, the tinkle of glass hitting the floor sounded loud in the silence.

Seconds later, he had fumbled his way across the cellar, when he felt Emma's hand on his sleeve he gripped it tight.

'What do we do now?' she whispered.

Luke crouched down by her side, his right hand grabbed the bottle and gripped it tight.

'Remember what I said, Emma, we need to be very quiet – even when the bad man comes back, then it's eyes closed and hands over ears time?'

'Thank you for not leaving me,' her voice wavered in the dark and Luke Croft said a silent prayer, hoping that he could keep his promise.

93

Marnie went through the gears, her eyes fixed on the road ahead, her mind still locked in the blood-splattered lift and the charnel hospital room, Hambling's body in ruins, his blood drenching the bed and coating the walls in splashes of red small lumps of flesh and gristle lay all around. After hitting the panic button, she had stepped back and watched as doctors and nurses seemed to appear en masse.

One doctor had eased Susan Romney into a sitting position, shining a light into her blinking eyes, Marnie had moved back towards the lifts on unsteady legs as Reese was loaded onto a stretcher, the two porters rushing him to theatre, a young doctor running alongside the trolley as they vanished down the corridor.

Soon after, an unconscious Walls was being carted away, leaving the blood-soaked knife in the lift. Marnie had stayed until DI Oaks had arrived, her narrow face set in haggard lines as Marnie explained the situation.

Five minutes later, she was left alone in the empty corridor trying to come to terms with what had happened. She pictured Walls behind his desk, face carved in fury as he realised that Marnie hadn't come to Park View to tell him about the latest on Hambling. She shook her head in dismay, suddenly realising that behind the hardened mask Walls must have been unravelling over the disappearance of his daughter. Marnie knew how easily desperation could turn into hatred, after all, she felt exactly the same over Abby. The years went by and yet the guilt and horror never lessened, it was always there, below the surface like the trunk of a tree that grows around a line of barbed wire. Smothering it and burying it deep, though the wire was still there slicing and gouging.

She thought of the governor, stalking down the corridor, looking for the man he believed was responsible for all his anguish.

Marnie had been standing in the corridor as the image of a faceless woman swam through her distress, she remembered Reese saying that Pam Oaks had been to see the Walls's to tell them that they had found their daughter's remains in the woods.

No doubt the finality of the situation had tipped Gareth Walls over the edge into a rage of insanity, but what of his wife?

Marnie had made her way through the hospital, by the time she made it to the car park she was running, the anxiety mounting.

Now, she sat hunched over the wheel, the lights lancing out into the darkness as she made her way out of the town and onto the narrow, country lanes.

En route, she had patched a call in to Bev Harvey to get an address for Walls.

The car rattled over a cattle grid and Marnie slowed down as she spotted the narrow entrance on the right. Turning into the opening she paused for a moment, the headlights illuminating the white stone cottage at the end of the long drive.

Dropping into first gear, she crawled forward through the darkness, twin lines of stunted hawthorn grew either side of the drive. After a hundred yards the drive opened up into a large well-kept garden, the house shining pale in the moonlight. Marnie glanced up, she could see light in one of the bedroom windows. Pulling up at the open front door, she felt the anxiety morph into a feeling of dread.

Turning off the engine, she climbed out in time to see a black cat flee from the house, its green eyes peering at Marnie. The animal spat, dashing off to the left and vanishing into a bank of bushes.

Marnie moved forwards and stepped into a narrow, wood-panelled hallway, a darkened room to her left, kitchen to the right, both doors standing open, both empty.

Moving to the bottom of the stairs she saw light pooling onto the landing.

'*POLICE! Anyone home?*' she shouted, her voice strident in the darkness.

Marnie hesitated, waiting for a response, then she set off up the stairs, one hand on the banister as she climbed. Reaching the top, she looked right, at the end of the landing a bedroom door stood open, she could see a woman sitting on the edge of the bed, a tangled mess of fair hair covered her face.

Marnie chewed at her lip and then winced at the pain. 'Mrs Walls?' she asked, taking a few hesitant steps along the landing.

When the woman looked up Marnie grimaced as she saw the bruises on her face, her right eye swollen almost shut, dried blood on her lips.

Sally Walls didn't look surprised to see the stranger moving towards the open bedroom door, her eyes were vacant and full of tears.

Reaching the threshold, Marnie hesitated as if waiting to be given permission to enter.

Sally held her gaze for a moment before looking back at the cardboard box held across her legs. Marnie watched her reach inside and lift out the doll before walking over to the side of the bed.

'This was Suzie's favourite doll,' Sally explained, smoothing down the doll's hair.

Marnie felt the emotion thrum in the air, waves of anguish filled the room. She watched as Sally placed the doll by her side on the bed and lifted out a crayon drawing, it showed three stick people, two adults, the small child between them holding onto the hands of the mother and father. It was the type of drawing you would find on any infant classroom wall.

'Suzie drew this the week before she was taken,' Sally explained, the tears broke free and slid down her bruised cheeks.

Before Marnie could reply, Sally reached back into the box and pulled out a strip of red ribbon. 'We'd had a day out in Chester,' she said, as she ran the ribbon through her fingers. 'It was late when we started for home, I decided to take the quiet route, thinking it would be nicer than the motorway.'

Marnie hesitated before sitting down by Sally's side.

'She was in the front seat, combing the doll's hair and I wasn't speeding – I swear to God I wasn't speeding.' More tears trickled free. 'It was dark, no streetlights and then this car came around the corner... I knew it was going too fast and then the lights filled the windscreen and I threw an arm across my daughter,' she paused, 'and then the car hit us.'

Marnie listened, no doubt Pam Oaks had heard the story but this was new to her, new and heart-breaking to listen to.

'When I came around, Suzie had gone,' she looked at Marnie in desperation, reliving the terrible events of that day. 'I couldn't understand it, she had been there in the passenger seat and then she simply vanished.'

'What did you do?' Marnie asked, in a whisper.

'I got out of the car and started shouting her name, the other car was on the opposite side of the road and...' she reached back into the box and pulled out a folded piece of newspaper.

Marnie watched as Sally carefully unfolded the paper, when she saw the image she felt her heart leap, the gasp caught in her throat.

The paper had a picture of a young kid on the front who looked no older than sixteen, though it was more than that, the image was a dead ringer for Luke Croft, the same narrow face, same colour hair.

The headline simple said. 'Joy rider killed in tragic accident.'

Suddenly Marnie pictured Gareth Walls meeting Luke for the first time. No doubt it would have been like a knife to the heart seeing Luke standing there looking like the kid who had smashed into his wife's car in a stolen vehicle.

'I ran down the road but there was no sign of Suzie,' Sally said, as she folded the paper neatly and placed it back in the box. 'There was no sign of my daughter, the police looked but we never found her. I tried to explain what had happened but it was as if no one believed me, as if I was lying about having her in the car.'

Marnie didn't know how to respond, so she kept quiet as Sally wiped a shaking hand across her eyes.

'Sometimes it's as if I never even had a child. I've been over that day so many times thinking how if one thing had been different then the accident wouldn't have happened and Suzie would still have been here. If I hadn't got stuck in traffic, if we hadn't taken so long at the dentist, if…'

'Dentist?' Marnie asked with a frown.

Sally dipped a hand back into the box, when she pulled out the smiley-face badge Marnie felt something in her mind warp and then snap forward into perfect clarity.

Suddenly, she was back at the Donalds' house, looking at the images on the mantel piece, Piper on the beach with a melting ice-cream cone in her hand, Piper in her school uniform smiling for the camera, the smiley-face sticker placed below the school emblem. She could hear John Donald talking about the day Piper vanished.

"Piper had an appointment at the dentist, when we got there the surgery was full, apparently one of the dentists had called in sick and they were behind."

Marnie gripped her hands onto her knees as the image shifted to the bedroom of Dawn Farmer's house, the photo album showing the smiling sisters and the cardboard box full of memories – including the small, smiley-face badge.

An image of the rusting pin badge they had discovered in the woods rushed into her mind, the metal perished but what if…

'Which dentist did you go to on the day Suzie vanished?' she asked, stomach muscle's clenched tight, her heart picking up speed.

Sally continued to look down at the badge, when Marnie touched her arm she felt the woman jump under her touch.

'Sally, which dentist did you visit?' she asked again.

Sally's eyes slowly refocused. 'Boland's, it's the one…'

'In town?' Marnie finished.

Sally nodded as Marnie rose from the bed, pulling out her phone as she walked out onto the landing. The phone droned in her ear, the tension flowing through her body.

'*Is everything OK?*' Bev Harvey asked and Marnie blew out a sigh of relief.

'I need an ambulance at Walls's place right now.'

'*Jesus, don't tell me...*'

'Sally Walls is battered and bruised but she's alive.'

'*I'll sort it now.*'

'And I need a contact number for the Donalds.'

'*The Donalds?*' Bev asked with a hint of confusion.

'As soon as you can, Bev, this could be urgent.'

'*I'm on it.*'

Marnie tapped at the screen before turning back to Sally, she had her head bowed again, the smiley badge resting in the palm of her hand.

Suddenly, Marnie felt a thrum of apprehension roll through her body, her skin crawling. In her mind, she heard the low, deep, rumble of thunder.

94

Cal Wilson coughed and the side of his head exploded in a blast of pain.

He blinked several times trying to focus his eyes but his brain slammed inside his skull, he could feel blood, warm and wet running from his scalp and trickling down the side of his bruised cheek.

He felt another cough building and screwed up his face in an effort to stop it, knowing that it would bring more agony punching through his brain.

Wilson tried to lift his arms and found that he couldn't, he felt the panic turn to fear as he realised his hands were tied behind his back; as soon as the realisation hit he felt the muscles in his shoulders lock and throb with a dull ache.

'As a child, I spent a lot of time in this room.'

Cal managed to raise his head, through a blur of tears, he could see a shadow – darker than the rest – standing over by the door.

'My father was a harsh man, a man of stark principles.'

Wilson felt the tension in his neck as he fought to keep his head up, his vision cleared a little but the shadow remained indistinct.

'He brought me here to show me the error of my ways,' the shadow stepped forward. 'Though I gradually came to realise that my father was nothing but an animal.'

'Who the fuck are you?' Wilson managed to croak.

'Fathers are meant to be strict, spare the rod spoil the child – and believe me he *never* spared the rod.'

Through the pain, Wilson heard the heavy footfalls as the shadow moved closer.

'You can get used to many things in life, eventually pain becomes bearable, you learn how to block it out, control it. Of course, once your tormentor realises that then they become more,' he paused, 'extreme in their approach.'

The words drifted out of the darkness bringing terror into the mind of Cal Wilson.

'But you know all about inflicting pain, don't you, Mr Wilson?'

Cal felt the breath hitch in his parch-dry throat. 'I...'

'I know all about you, about the way you treat the woman you live with, the way you treated little Mandy.'

Wilson blinked in confusion, he tried to make sense of the words but the pain and fear were locked inside his mind, competing against one another for supremacy.

'You are an abusive man, you shout and scream and lash out...'

'*Please, I...*'

The shadow loomed closer and Wilson's head was thrust back, slamming into the wooden strut. He felt the huge hand on his sweating brow, the fingers gripping tight, the pain cranked up and Cal Wilson felt his bladder let go as the black eyes swam into view.

'Dishing out pain is easy, Mr Wilson, but learning to take it is a completely different beast.'

Wilson opened his mouth to scream but before he could vent the terror his mouth was suddenly full of cold steel, he gasped as the pain ballooned, the pressure mounting. His two front teeth shattered with a crack.

Wilson thrashed against the bonds that held him tight to the chair, blood spewed from his mouth, running down his chin and coating his jacket.

The man stepped back and studied the teeth clamped between the prongs of the tooth extracting forceps. 'You know nothing of pain, Mr Wilson, but don't worry, I'll educate you.'

Wilson screamed as the monstrous figure loomed over him, forceps at the ready.

95

Marnie sat in the car watching as the paramedic led Sally Walls towards the ambulance, doll held to her breast as she stepped into the back of the van, her face blank with shock.

When her phone rang, she sighed and pulled it from her pocket.

'*I've got the number you asked for,*' Bev Harvey explained.

'Good, send it over,' Marnie replied.

'*Have you heard anything about DCI Reese?*' Bev asked.

Marnie trapped the bridge of her nose between thumb and finger and closed her eyes. 'Nothing yet.'

'*I still can't believe any of this, I mean, what the hell was Walls doing at the hospital and why did he kill Hambling?*'

'Bev?'

'*Yeah?*'

'Send me the number,' Marnie said in a low voice.

'*Sorry, boss, I'll send it over now.*'

Marnie ended the call, seconds later the phone beeped as the number came through.

The ambulance pulled away down the lane, blue light swirling out over the fields as Marnie's fingers flicked over the screen, when it started to ring she tapped at the loudspeaker icon and waited.

After ten seconds, she lifted the cigarettes from her pocket and lit one with a trembling hand.

The seconds stretched out and the tension mounted, she was just going to end the call when it was answered by John Donald, his voice thick with sleep.

'*Who is this?*' he asked.

'Mr Donald, this is Detective Sergeant Hammond...'

'*What's happened?*' suddenly he sounded wide awake.

'The day we came to question you about Piper, you said that you were late for the birthday in the park.'

'*Yes but...*'

'You'd been to the dentist in the morning?'

'*We've been over this hundreds of time and...*'

'Can you tell me the name of the dentist?'

A heavy sigh floated from the phone and Marnie pulled hard on the cigarette, her eyes narrowed as she waited for Donald to respond.

'*Look, I want to...*'

'Please, just tell me the name?' Marnie's voice came out as a harsh gasp.

More silence, she pictured John Donald sitting up in bed, his wife by his side, probably rubbing sleep from her eyes as she listened to her husband, the familiar fear crackling through her mind.

'*It was Boland's, the one in the town centre.*'

Marnie felt the rusted wheels in her mind start to move, as if the name was unlocking all the memories that had been buried for years.

'Thank you,' she mumbled.

'*But why did you want to know, I mean...?*'

'I'll be in touch,' Marnie said automatically, as she ended the call.

She looked out into the darkness, the cat she had seen earlier appeared from beneath the tall bank of laurel bushes, green eyes shining in the headlights.

Sliding the window down she flicked the cigarette through the gap before retrieving Bev Harvey's number, she answered after the second ring.

'Bev, I need an address and I need it now,' Marnie said.

'*Fire away,*' Bev replied, without missing a beat.

Marnie did as she asked.

96

The man stepped back and tilted his head, studying his handiwork.

Cal Wilson's head was slumped forward, his mouth a ragged maw, bubbling red, the blood coated his chin, the front of his coat stained crimson.

'Weakling,' he mumbled.

Wilson gurgled like a new born, his mind unable to cope with the agony that detonated through his misfiring brain.

'It's easy to abuse the weak, Mr Wilson. My father was an expert but I didn't stay weak for long and then...' his voice drifted to a halt.

He stood in the darkness, feeling the thrill seep through his mind, a small aperitif before the main course. He thought of the hatred he had for his sister, hated all the devious tricks she played, hated her sly smile when she sent the plate clattering to the floor he thought of her naked in the shower, her mouth springing open, the scream blasting out as she stood looking towards the keyhole. When the door along the corridor had banged open she had smiled as if she knew she had summoned the monster and her brother would suffer.

The man opened the forceps and two more of Cal Wilson's teeth dropped to the floor. He pictured his sister, standing naked on the landing, her eyes alight with dark joy as their father dragged him up to the attic. Then the image shifted to the garden, he had been nineteen and the young frightened boy had vanished, the dark hair swept back from his forehead, his dark, brooding eyes full of fury. Closing his eyes, he listened to the memory of hands banging on the glass and smiled, when he turned he saw her face at the upstairs window. Her mouth was open, her muffled screams bringing a smile to his face as her hands slammed on the windowpane. He remembered standing there, looking up; at last the tables had been turned, the hunted was now the hunter. He could see the distress in her eyes, hear the torment in her screams. Turning away, his gaze had been drawn to the old oak, his father was sat at the base, bound to the thick trunk by the same length of rope that had once held the boy, the whippersnapper.

Despite the fact that the man who had abused him for years had no eyes, he *knew* he was still alive, after all monsters were never killed that easily. The girl continued to scream as he walked towards the tree, axe in hand.

In the attic, he blinked and the images floated away into the mists of time.

Suddenly, he thought of the two of them down in the cellar; Mandy, his Mandy, and the boy clinging together. No doubt the fear would be building as the realisation seeped into their young souls that they would never see the outside world again. In the grand scheme of things, the boy was unimportant, though the man knew he could be used as a tool to instil true terror into the girl. It was a new concept to the man and one that sent a thrill through the core of his dark heart.

His eyes refocused and he dropped the blood-slick forceps into his pocket.

'I'm a busy man, Mr Wilson, you could say I'm up to my eyes, but don't worry I'll be back at some stage, and won't that be an eye-opener!'

Through the agony, Cal Wilson heard the words and for the briefest of moments the pain subsided, but he knew, in reality the pain had only just begun.

Bitter tears of agony leaked from his screwed-shut eyes.

The man sighed in satisfaction. 'I'll leave you now to think on the error of your ways,' he said, turning and heading for the door.

Cal caught a brief glimpse of light as he cracked open his eyes, the shadow hesitated in the doorway and then laughed, a deep rumbling sound, before slamming the door closed.

The light was cut off and the darkness absorbed Wilson's fear and hurled it back at him until his mind cracked and insanity swept in to claim him.

97

Within minutes, Marnie had caught up with the ambulance on the country lane. Flicking on the siren and flashing lights she sat hunched over the wheel, heart thudding, eyes narrowed. Seconds later the ambulance moved left and Marnie pulled out and flew past, her foot planted to the mat as she jammed into another gear.

Her mind was a whirl with a kaleidoscope of images, smiley badges mingled with bleached bones devoid of flesh. The road straightened out and she risked more speed, the bushes flashed by, in the darkness the spectres loomed. Jenny Bell, a starved husk in her party dress, skin stretched over sharp bone, her milk-white eyes clogged with fresh, dark earth. A bend appeared at speed and Marnie feathered the brakes, the car slewed to the left then she was off again, the speedometer touched sixty. She pictured Luke sprinting from the house, then Alby Roper sprawled like road kill, his eyes gone; Dawn Farmer suffering the same fate and her niece taken, then she thought of Abby, her sister, lying amongst the ferns, so vibrant and shimmering green, only this time there were red holes where her brown eyes should have been.

Above it all she saw the hulking shadow, a killer who had plied his trade for the best part of two decades, travelling the country, searching out new victims, watching and stalking before taking them and bringing them back to the town, only to kill them and dispose of their dismembered bodies in the woods.

Marnie's lips drew back in an animalistic snarl, her speed continued to increase. After all these years, after all the heartache and despair, she had a name.

'*Boland,*' she hissed, as the car touched seventy.

98

The man made his way down the staircase, his tread heavy, his soul singing with joy. Reaching the bottom, he turned and walked down the long hallway and through the room with the ticking clock, the darkness pressing at the windows.

When he reached the cellar door he stopped and listened, the joy stuttered and the scowl crawled over his gaunt face. By now they should have been crying and screaming, the sound of their distress should have been floating up from below.

He took a step closer to the door, this wasn't right, this wasn't acceptable, he would kill the boy and do it in front of the terrified girl, then he would leave her with the body for a few hours. The smile slipped back onto his face, imagining the girl sitting in the dark – with the corpse of her new-found friend growing cold by her side.

'That should do the trick,' he whispered, reaching out for the handle.

The hinges creaked as he pulled the door open, the cellar was in darkness, he stepped through the door and reached out to the right, his fingers found the cord and he tugged down, the smile faltered as the light failed to illuminate the cellar floor.

Letting the cord spring back into place he pulled again, his expression sliding from cheerfulness to aggravation.

Leaning forward, he peered down into the darkness then he sniffed the air as if searching for the scent of fear. Grunting, he reached out his large hand, grasping the handrail he took a tentative step down and then halted.

Suddenly, he felt the anxiety seep into his mind, a precursor to the feeling of confusion. He stood in the darkness, chest tightening as the hated feeling began to reassert itself. How could it be happening again, everything had gone to plan, he had Mandy, he had the boy and yet…

His foot thudded on the next step as he tried to hold onto the facts, once the boy was dead and the girl was screaming then the confusion would vanish and he would feel in control again.

Another step down, the darkness was absolute and yet the sense of unease continued to clamber up through his guts, the feeling of calm that the dark usually provided was absent. In fact, for the first time ever the lack of light made the unease grow. The man snarled, his heavy hand gripping the rail tight, his mind starting to solidify with fear.

'*Where are you?*' He hissed, as he clomped down another step. 'You can't hide from ME, I won't allow it!' his voice rose but the roar died in an instant and the silence crowded back in as if taunting him.

His left hand closed into a shaking fist, they were hiding in the darkness, clinging to one another for support, waiting to be found and dragged from their hiding place.

When his foot came into contact with the floor, the man grunted in surprise, his hand slipped from the rail and suddenly he felt his body sway, his heart thumping, he felt as if he had been cut adrift on a black sea never to find the shore.

'No, no, not now,' he gasped, staggering forward into the abyss.

His arms swept back and forth and then his foot crunched on something brittle, he stopped in confusion and moved his foot left and right the cracking sound flared and then died.

'*The light, you fool!*' the voice boomed in his brain, making him jerk in shock.

Reaching up, his hand fumbled in the dark until it touched the light fixing, his fingers grasped the shattered remains of the bulb.

'*The whippersnapper did it,*' the voice informed him in a hiss. '*Find him, kill him.*'

The voice brooked no argument, the man knew he was right, he should never have brought the boy back to the house, he should have killed him on the road along with the other one, the one who stabbed at the car before stalking towards him, his young face ripped with anger.

'*Your mess, you clean it up,*' the internal voice demanded.

'*I will,*' he replied with determination, as he strode forward into the darkness.

Four steps and he saw the door to the skull room, the sight made him stop in his tracks.

Suddenly, he felt the fear twist into anger, they were hiding in the room, in his special place. The thought turned his stomach to ice, the urge to kill thrummed through his body as he headed towards the door.

Beneath the wooden steps, Luke held Emma tight, he could feel her shaking in terror and he tightened his grip. When the man had passed overhead Luke had been convinced that Emma would have screamed out her horror, Luke had prayed for silence, his lips moving in the dark, his own fear thrashing inside as the heavy thuds drew closer.

Now, they peered between the steps, eyes wide and filled with fear.

When the light clicked on in the small inner room Luke hoisted Emma up with one arm, her hands snaked around his neck, he picked up the bottle and moved out from their hiding place. He could feel the tension stretching in an agony of apprehension. Reaching the bottom of the steps he started to climb, his ears straining for the sound he dreaded, his eyes fixed on the open door at the top of the stairs.

Emma whimpered as she clung on tight, her arms squeezing his neck making it difficult to breathe her legs wrapped around his waist.

The door grew nearer and hope flared as he tried to increase his speed.

'*Bad man!*' Emma suddenly squealed in fear.

Luke felt the hope die as she trembled in his arms.

'*No!*' the voice bellowed across the cellar.

Emma screamed again and Luke tried to block out the fear as he dashed up the remaining steps. Reaching the top, he staggered through the open door into the hallway.

'You have to let go now, Emma,' he gasped and spun around.

The man was standing at the foot of the steps, his face hidden in shadow though Luke knew his dark eyes would be shining with hatred.

'Emma, please, you...'

'*No!*' she wailed, clinging ever tighter to his neck.

The figure below placed a foot on the first step, Luke saw his hand emerge from the darkness and grab the rail.

'*Trust me!*' Luke said, in a shaking voice.

Emma drew back and they locked eyes, below, the man climbed another step, his footfall heavy, his hand made a dry squealing sound on the wooden rail.

Then miraculously Emma's arms sprang open and Luke grunted, taking her weight and easing her to her feet. He felt her hand grab the bottom of his sweatshirt as if she needed to keep some form of physical contact with her saviour.

Luke Croft stared down, the man started to emerge through the darkness. His huge bulk seemed to fill the space, his face gradually appearing, his mouth twisted in a snarl, his eyes locked on Luke.

'*How dare you!*' he roared, his foot fell with another thud. Luke tried to move but the eyes held him in their hypnotic gaze.

Then Emma tugged down on his arm in fear and the spell was broken.

Lifting the bottle, Luke watched a look of confusion flit over the man's face.

'Time to close your eyes, Emma,' Luke said.

Immediately Emma did as he asked, eyes screwed shut, hands over her ears, exactly as Luke had asked her to do.

Another step closer and Luke raised the lighter and spun the wheel, the small flame sprang to life.

The man stopped ten steps down, his eyes widening as they moved from the lighter to the bottle.

'*No..!*' he screamed, bolting upwards.

Luke touched the flame to the fuel-soaked wadding then he drew his arm back, his eyes locked on the man who raged towards them, then he hurled the bottle down into the darkness.

Glass shattered a sheet of flame erupted and suddenly the monster was engulfed and roaring in agony.

Luke took one last look at the burning man before slamming the door and turning the key. At his side, Emma shivered in terror, Luke took hold of her hand and her eyes sprang open in alarm.

'Come on, Emma, time to go.'

They turned as one and then the door shuddered in the frame as the man threw himself against it.

'*Whippersnapper!*' he screamed.

Luke staggered back, taking Emma with him. There was pain behind the screamed word but there was anger too, a fury so black and never-ending that Luke almost collapsed to his knees at the sound of it.

'*Take your eyes!*' the voice bellowed.

Another blow hit the door and Luke stood agog as the lock started to splinter.

'*Please, Luke, the bad man...*'

Luke swooped down and picked her up, then he was running, the sounds of agony and anger increasing as the door shook under the weight of the man's madness.

99

Marnie hit the roundabout, brakes squealing, smoke pouring from the tortured tyres; as she shot across the junction she caught a fleeting glimpse of a taxi driver on the other side, his eyes wide in surprise as the car shot past.

The car snapped left and she hit the gas hard, the rear end twitched back into line again. Wiping the sweat from her brow, she blew out between pursed lips, the anger and fear tearing through her mind, spurring her on.

The streetlights ended again and she flicked on the main beam, the car screaming down the road, engine whining.

Hitting top gear, she risked even more speed, if this man, this monster, had taken Emma Farmer, if he followed the same pattern as Jenny Bell then the girl could very well still be alive. Yet the fear echoed through her mind as she pictured the other victims dumped in the black earth.

The road began to narrow, forcing Marnie to slow down, the frustration mounting as the speedometer dropped, she almost missed the left turn that appeared out of the darkness. Her right foot came off the gas and slammed on the brake, her hands spinning the wheels. The car sped down the lane, the road twisting and turning, slowing her down even further.

Rounding another tight left-hand bend, the road went into a bottleneck before ending in a set of tall, wooden gates, both standing open. Marnie didn't hesitate but raced through them, huge trees and stunted bushes crowding in on either side, the lights illuminating the vivid greens and browns.

The car started to bump down potholes in the ground and Marnie held on tight to the wheel as she kept the car moving over the troughs of hard-baked earth.

Suddenly, she emerged from the trees and her heart lurched as she saw the house appear out of the darkness, a large, three-storey affair, the multitude of windows glowing orange, smoke pouring from below the shingles. As she approached she caught a whiff of smoke drift through the heater vents.

The car sped over the rough ground, the siren screeching, Marnie bouncing in her seat; she slammed on the brakes as she arrived at the front of the property.

Snapping her seatbelt off, she thrust the door open and leapt out.

Marnie looked up at the house, her eyes narrowed as the wind changed direction and the smoke drifted towards her. When she saw the black car parked to the right, the anger flared, seeing the gouge in the paint of the bonnet. The sight of it made her gasp and she suddenly realised all the guesswork, all the possibilities were now fact.

Roper had been knocked to the ground by the black car and then he had been attacked and left for dead in the middle of the road. Marnie felt a shiver of disgust ripple through her mind, goose bumps rose on her arms as she looked back at the house. She could see flames flickering in the downstairs rooms reflected through the glass, the shifting orange light spilling out into the darkness.

She had taken two faltering steps towards the front door when she heard a dull thud from above. Marnie stopped and looked up, her face blanching in a gamut of confusion.

Luke Croft looked down at her from the second-floor window, his hands splayed on the glass, his face stark and full of terror.

Marnie took a step back and shook her head as if her brain were playing tricks on her. She looked back to the window, Luke was still there peering down in fear then he started to slam his hands against the glass, his mouth open, his voice muffled by the barrier and the wail of the siren.

Marnie ran forward, she hit the front door hard, yanking on the handle slamming her shoulder against the wood.

Somewhere close by she heard the sound of shattering glass as the heat built inside the house.

Marnie looked left and right in indecision and then she sprinted right, running along the front of the house before turning left and dashing into the darkness, the blue lights spiralling off into the void.

100

He stood in the burning house, the skin on his face red raw, his clothes smoking and charred, an agony of pain swamped him and yet the fury still rose through his body in dark shuddering waves.

'*Spared the rod and spoiled the child*,' he barked, the curtains in the room ignited in a flare of orange.

The man shook his head as if unaware that the house was burning around him.

'*Fool!*' the inner voice roared.

'*Shut up!*' he screamed in reply and for once the voice fell silent.

More flames rose, hitting the ceiling and spreading out, the dry, oak beams crackled as the flames took hold.

The bastard boy had tricked him, and then the pain had ripped through him as the fuel ignited, the whippersnapper watching him burn before slamming and locking the door.

He closed his hands into fists, in his madness he relished the pain as the burned skin tightened over his bulging knuckles.

All the doors in the house were locked and bolted which meant they were still in here somewhere, no doubt hiding and...

He blinked in confusion as he looked towards the window, when he saw the flicker of blue light the fear sliced through the anger and pain. He stormed left, peering through the small pane of glass, his eyes cracking with disbelief as he saw the car parked at the front of the house, door open, lights glaring, siren wailing over the sound of the fire roaring through the house.

'No, no, no,' he screeched, watching the blue lights turning.

Suddenly, he felt the weakness hit him, his legs shook with the effort of staying on his feet, the burned skin on his face seemed to shrink, pulling tight to the bone beneath. He felt it tear and split. He touched his face and looked at his fingers, puzzled by the blood and yellow pus. Another rip and more blood oozed out and down the wreckage of his face.

When he heard the sound of shattering glass he turned, the heat blasting into him as the grandfather clock in the corner caught fire.

He looked around the burning room, astonished as the fire raged.

'*Find them!*' the voice demanded, and suddenly clarity filled his mind.

Nothing mattered now except finding the whippersnappers and killing them, he would no longer be able to take his time but he wanted the thrill of seeing them die, his hands locked on their faces as his thumbs sank into their terror-filled eyes.

Turning, he stalked from the room, ignoring the smoke and flames, determined to finish what he had started.

101

Marnie scrambled through the broken, kitchen window, clambering over the sink she leapt down to the tiled floor. The room felt cavernous, the walls covered with stark white tiles, in the centre of the room stood a huge, wooden table, she could see gouges in the surface, long deep scars as if someone had attacked the wood with a meat cleaver.

Marnie hesitated, her frantic mind conjuring an image of a heavy blade cracking through muscle and bone, human bone, children's bones, Abby's bones.

The anger raged, and then she thought of Luke at the window, the sight of seeing him there was beyond believable and then she thought of Roper leaping over the wall, bloodstained knife in hand, only this time she pictured Luke staggering out into the road with the thug close on his heels.

Suddenly, it made sense, Luke had been spotted heading towards the park, and then the police had arrived and Roper had bolted but what if Luke had been there as well and somehow Roper had spotted him. Luke was in this house, his pale face at the window upstairs and…

Thick smoke drifted under the closed, kitchen door, the sight of it broke the stupor and Marnie ran across the room and snatched the door open. The narrow corridor had thick smoke drifting at ground level, and she felt the heat rush down the passage, making her gasp. Then she was running, her feet pounding, the smoke rising as she dashed forwards. The end of the passageway was glowing orange, the heat intensifying, the passage ended and she sprinted into the hallway just as the man appeared from the right.

Marnie skidded to a halt, her skin crawling at the sight of him, he was dressed in a black suit, the kind an undertaker would wear, though the cloth was scorched and smoking. The white shirt beneath was black and burned, his face like raw liver, the skin blistered but the obsidian eyes that shone from the destruction were wide and full of madness and malice.

The door in Marnie's mind swung open on rusted hinges and the memory she had for so long denied careered into her brain. She saw the man walking away with Abby over his shoulder, she had lifted her head from the wet gravel, her left cheek lacerated and bleeding, and the man had turned and looked at her with his dark eyes, the same eyes that now stared at her over a distance of fifteen feet.

'*You!*' he suddenly roared, his voice thundering out, laced with a hatred so intense that it made her step back.

He took a step towards her and Marnie felt her own rage ignite, all the anger of countless years rising in one savage blast of fury.

Then through it all she heard a child screaming, and an image of Luke and Emma lanced through the hatred.

'*Whippersnapper!*' he hissed as he took another step.

Marnie fought the urge to fly at the monster, instead she spun right and started to dash up the stairs, her feet flying, hair streaming out behind her.

'*Teach you!*' he screamed, setting off after her.

Marnie blocked out the words, flames suddenly erupted left and right, the hungry fire probing, searching for dry timber.

When she felt the hand close over her ankle, Marnie grunted as he snatched her back, she squirmed onto her back but the scarred face ballooned towards her through the smoke. Bracing her hands on the stairs she lifted her right leg and slammed it into his shoulder, the snarl erupting on his face, his hand tightening on her ankle.

'*Kill you!*' he sneered, trying to pull her towards him.

Marnie kicked out again, the sole of her shoe cracked into his forehead, this time the man bellowed as more scorched skin split, leaving a bloody smear across his brow. The hand loosened and she snatched her leg free, turning and scurrying up to the top of the stairs. She hesitated for a moment to get her bearings before dashing left along the landing, the flames rearing by her side.

Doors stood left and right but she ignored them, slamming into the one at the end of the corridor.

'*Luke!*' she screamed, her fists hitting the timber, her mind spinning in horror. '*Luke let me in!*' she turned to see the man appear at the top of the stairs, his face bloody, arms hanging at his side, the smoke billowed down the landing and the figure vanished in a shroud of grey.

Marnie felt the dread envelop her, she turned back to the door, her hand raised to slam against the wood just as it shot open.

Luke stood in front of her, his eyes saucer like and she saw them widen even further in fear as he glanced over her shoulder.

Marnie knew the killer would be emerging through the swirling smoke, dark eyes shining with abhorrence. Without looking back, she shouldered Luke into the room and slammed the door closed, her hand turning the key a fraction of a second before the handle was yanked up and down.

'The door won't hold him,' Luke said, as if the fact that Marnie was here was no big surprise.

She nodded in understanding, the handle continued to snap up and down.

'We need to get Emma out of here,' Luke said, flicking a glance towards the corner of the room.

Marnie turned to find Emma Farmer standing by the window, her face smeared with soot, her cheeks wet with tears.

'*Kill you all!*' the man on the other side of the door screamed, his voice blasting out, forcing more tears from Emma's terror-stricken eyes.

Marnie felt the anger flare and then she shook her head, Luke was right, this was about getting them out of here before the madman broke through the door. She strode across the room and Emma cringed at the sight of her.

Even when she crouched down, the child looked be wildered.

Marnie wiped a hand across her eyes then she looked down as the smoke started to drift up from the cracks in the floorboards bringing the heat with it.

'Emma, my name is Marnie and I've come to take you home.'

Emma opened her mouth to respond but Marnie suddenly stood up and grabbed the stout-backed chair from the side of the bed.

The door shuddered again and she heard Luke gasp at the sound.

'*Take your eyes!*'

Lifting the chair, Marnie swung it at the window, the panes shattered sending shards of glass flying out into the night.

Emma screamed, her hands over her ears watching as Marnie attacked the glass.

'*No!*' the voice beyond the door screamed in fury.

Marnie continued to slam the chair up and down, opening the gap, then she threw the chair through the window and leaned out.

The ground below was hidden in darkness and swirling smoke, Marnies wallowed the fear as the door was hit again with terrifying force.

'Luke, come here,' Marnie urged, glancing over her shoulder.

Luke was facing the door, his shoulders pulled in, hands clasped over his ears.

'*Luke!*' she shouted.

The boy spun around and she could see the stress coating his face, yet despite the terror, there was strength in his eyes. Marnie had no idea how they had survived but the fact that they were hiding in a locked room was proof that Luke must have brought Emma here, escaping the maniac who continued to hammer on the door.

With one last glance over his shoulder, Luke hurried to her side.

Marnie turned away from Emma, her voice no more than a frantic hiss. 'We have to go through the window.'

'*But…*'

'It's the only way. You go first, I'll hold your arms and lower you down as far as I can, 'she paused to lick her dry lips,' it isn't too far down and then you'll have to catch Emma.'

Luke ran a shaking hand across his mouth, then the door banged and they all heard the wood splinter, straightaway Luke swung a leg over the windowsill.

Another heavy crash, Emma continued to scream as she watched Marnie grab Luke's wrists. Just before he vanished from sight he locked eyes with the girl and managed to drag up a smile.

'Not long now, Em, I'll be waiting for you,' he said, and then he was gone.

Marnie leaned out, taking the strain, her feet planted on the burning floor.

'*Now!*' Luke shouted and Marnie let him go, her heart in her mouth as he fell through the darkness; she winced as she saw him hit the ground and roll to the left.

Time stretched out, when she saw Luke clamber slowly to his feet, Marnie heaved out a massive sigh of relief before turning to the girl.

Emma screamed as she realised what was going to happen but Marnie knew time was running out, the first of the flames had found their way through the floorboards; the room filling with smoke, she swung the girl out into the void, ignoring her cries of terror.

Luke stood below, feet braced in the gravel, his arms stretched upwards.

'*Let her go!*'

Marnie looked into Emma's face, then she closed her eyes and her hands sprung open, she heard the shrill cry as the little girl fell, when she opened her eyes it was to see Luke in a heap with Emma on top.

She could see him looking into Emma's face, his teeth flashed and Marnie felt another wave of relief blast through her senses.

Then she heard an almighty crack from behind, she spun around to see the man standing in the door way wreathed in the smoke that poured into the room.

'*Jump!*' Luke screamed up at the now, empty, window.

Marnie never heard the shout, her eyes were locked on the man in the doorway, she saw his eyes flick to the window in disbelief and then he looked at Marnie properly for the first time. She saw his face writhe with anger and confusion, he stepped forward as if he could not believe who was standing in front of him.

'*The one that got away*,' he whispered, as the flames from below spurted into the room, rising upwards, looking for fresh fuel to latch on to.

Marnie narrowed her eyes, and then she took a step forward into the room.

'You killed my sister, you *bastard!*' she snarled.

The man's scarred face twitched, the light from the flames reflected in his dark eyes.

He seemed to expand with hatred and then he lumbered forward, arms outstretched, his blistered lips drawn back in a snarl of hatred.

Marnie didn't hesitate, the room, the flames, the smoke, all seemed to vanish, all she saw was the monster in the black suit, the one responsible for the death of so many innocents, the one who had bequeathed her a life of pain and anguish.

His heavy feet thudded on the burning, wooden floor. '*Whippersnapper!*' he yelled, his hands shot out with a speed belying his age.

At the last second Marnie ducked low, dashing beneath his outstretched arms, and spinning behind him. Then without hesitation she leapt onto his back, her left arm snaked around his throat, her right reached out, her nails slashed across his ruined face.

He bellowed in pain, twisting around but Marnie kept hold, managing to lock her legs around his waist, her right hand scrabbled over his face, her mind shivering in disgust as she felt the charred flesh sliding beneath her fingers, then she felt the soft gelatinous eye and her index finger plunged forward.

His scream pierced the air as Marnie felt a savage roar of satisfaction blast through her soul.

'*That's for Piper!*' she screamed, her hand clamped on his face, her finger plunging deeper. '*Jenny!*' she started to twist the finger back and forth. '*Suzie!*'

Her finger gouged deeper, she could feel the blood spurting over her hand, the flames blasted upwards, the heat intense at her back.

Time seemed to stop, all that existed was the burning room and this abhorrent killer of the children.

'*Teach you!*' he screamed through the agony, his madness seemed to enrage the flames even further, as if they were feeding off his insanity.

Marnie felt the man spin around and lunge backward, she braced herself as he slammed her into the wall. She felt the full weight of her disgust as his loathsome body pressed tight to her own, then he slammed his head back, his hard skull cracked against her own and she felt her finger slip from the gore-filled socket. Taking two strides forwards, he lunged back again, crashing her into the wall. The air slammed from her body, when she drew in a shuddering breath she coughed as the thick smoke was pulled down into her lungs.

Another lunge forward and this time Marnie knew that she wouldn't be able to keep her grip as he prepared to slam her back against the wall for a final time.

At the last second, she released her grip, her feet landed on the burning floor and she planted her hands on his back and thrust him forward.

The killer staggered, trying to stay on his feet but the momentum was too much and he crashed do his knees in the centre of the room.

Marnie staggered back against the wall, trying to breathe through the smoke, she watched as the man turned slowly, the sight of his face made her want to gag.

The skin across his brow was nothing but a blackened smear, the flesh beneath raw and bloody, his right eye had vanished leaving a trail of slime on his soot-coated cheek. His left eye continued to glare through the wreckage, full of hate and madness.

Marnie glanced towards the window, smoke poured out into the night, she could hear screams coming from the darkness and she knew she was going to die in this house of death.

Her gaze flicked back to the man as he climbed slowly to his feet, he stood swaying back and forth, his large hands opening and closing.

'You got away and then you came back, how did you do that?' he demanded and then he coughed and dragged a hand across his mouth, opening up another smear of red flesh.

Marnie tried to fathom the words but her brain was too full of hate and anguish.

'Let me teach you the error of your ways,' he said, and then smiled showing a flash of white teeth amongst the gore.

Marnie pushed herself away from the wall, the tidal wave of fury rising again, her eyes narrowed against the smoke. The smile stayed on his face as his foot thudded on the floor and Marnie jabbed out a shaking hand, the bloody index finger extended.

'My time to take your other eye!' she screamed. 'My time to *teach you!*'

She watched as his good eye sprang wide and then he lunged forward and Marnie tensed; suddenly, the floor beneath his feet opened up, the flames that had been eating away beneath exploded into the room and he screamed – a sound of pure agony – as he fell through the opening. His clawed hand scrabbled at the floorboards, his face began to burn, the air redolent with the stench of cooking flesh.

The man's head thrashed in agony, his shriek rising with the flames, Marnie couldn't take her eyes off the monstrosity, deep inside she wanted his pain to last forever. Wanted to stay here for eternity and watch him suffer and burn for all the things he had done, the lives ruined, the children taken and butchered.

The floor groaned and Marnie felt the boards under her feet sag. The monster screamed one last time, the word '*Whippersnapper*' echoed from his flame-filled mouth as he vanished into the inferno below.

Marnie leapt back as the furnace heat filled the room, the floor moved again, sinking downwards, and then she was dashing towards the window, sticking close to the wall, her right arm held up in an effort to deflect the roaring heat.

Reaching the window, she scrambled onto the sill, down below she could see Luke with Emma in his arms, they were standing on the overgrown lawn about twenty feet away.

'*Jump!*' Luke screamed.

Marnie stood framed in the broken window, her hands gripping the frame, then she heard a huge explosion and glanced over her shoulder, a white-hot fireball roared along the landing.

The heat hit her and thrust her into the void, flames raged out into the night.

She hit the ground hard, the last of the air was wrenched from her body. When she tried to push herself upright the last of her strength deserted her and she lumped back down to the ground as another explosion boomed out into the hot trembling air. Then miraculously she felt hands on the shoulders of her jacket and Luke dragged her over the gravel and into the tall grass.

Marnie grunted as he continued to pull her along, then he let go and staggered back, sitting down with a thump.

Rolling onto her back Marnie twisted her head, her eyes wide as the house spewed flames and rolling clouds of black smoke into the starlit sky.

Sitting up she planted her hands in the long grass and turned her head, Luke sat beneath the huge, twisted oak, Emma Farmer held in his arms, the girl turned her head, burying her face into Luke's shoulder.

Marnie saw the boy glance at her and smile, the shadow of the flames flickering over his face.

Marnie mouthed the words, 'thank you' as the house began to collapse in on itself.

By the time they heard the faint screech of sirens, the building had all but vanished, consumed by the flames.

•

102
Two weeks later

Marnie placed the grapes on the cabinet before pulling up a chair and sitting down by the side of the hospital bed.

'So, how are you?' she asked.

Reese grimaced and slowly heaved himself up in the bed. 'Getting there,' he said with a sigh. 'What about you?' he asked, sagging back into the pillows.

Marnie shrugged. 'I'm OK.'

Reese didn't look convinced. 'So, come on, what do we know about what happened?'

'I'm sure Pam Oaks will have kept you up to speed.'

'Pam's been busy, I haven't seen her in three days, besides you were there so I want to hear what you have to say.'

Marnie took a shuddering breath before folding her hands in her lap.

'We now know that Boland worked for several councils over a twenty-five-year period. He moved around the country, it was his job to visit local schools to check on the children's teeth.'

'That's how he targeted the victims?' Reese asked.

Marnie looked at him closely. 'You must know all this, I…'

'Marnie, I've been out cold for the best part of a week, the powers that be have kept the visitors away, so I want to know what the bloody hell happened?'

Marnie held his gaze for a moment longer before nodding. 'That's why we found it hard to get a handle on the killings, he'd simply go wherever the job took him, chose a victim and then take them. It would have been easy for Boland to find out about the victim, he had access to their records, where they lived, family members, the whole works.'

Reese lifted a hand and rubbed at his haunted eyes. 'What about the local girls?'

'By the time Josie Roberts was taken in Wales, the contract had ended, most councils saw it as a waste of money to pay a dentist to visit the schools, so Boland opened a practice in town and started to target children closer to home.'

Reese looked at Marnie and nodded in understanding. 'Bastard,' he snarled.

'We think he must have targeted Suzie Walls and followed her the day she vanished. We know Sally had taken her daughter to see Boland that morning.

She was heading home, taking what she thought would be the quieter route, then she was involved in the RTA, and while she was out cold Boland took the girl and drove away.'

'Jesus,' Reese said, as his hands fell to the bed.

'He had the ideal job to watch and wait, he never seemed to have been in a rush to take the girls, after all we have no idea how long he kept them before killing the children.'

'Madness,' Reese shook his head.

'For the past ten years Boland hasn't been practicing, he had three dentists who carried on working and Boland simply took a slice of the profits.'

'Do we know why he stopped practising?'

Marnie shifted in her seat, the air felt hot and still, her brow coated with sweat.

'All three of the dentists have been interviewed and they all said the same thing, Boland was suffering from the early stages of dementia so he took a back seat. They said he would occasionally come into the practice but over the last three years they had seen less of him, and...'

'They never thought to check on the man?'

Marnie shook her head. 'The senior partner called at the house a couple of times but Boland never came to the door. In fact, he said that he was in the process of contacting the solicitor to see if they had heard from Boland but he never quite got around to it.'

'Typical,' Reese said, with a heavy sigh.

'It took a full twenty-four hours for them to put out the fire, they found the remains of Boland and Wilson...'

'Wilson?' Reese's eyes widened in shock.

Marnie started to explain about how Wilson had been found in the burned-out ruins, they had only discovered his identification through the use of dental records, although he had very few teeth left to use for identification.

'Believe it or not we got the records from Boland's practice, Wilson was on their books.'

Reese rubbed at his eyes. 'I don't know whether to laugh or bloody cry.'

'The day we were at the Cox house, I saw the black car driving away from the scene, we now think Boland went back and snatched Wilson.'

'But why for God's sake, what motive could he possibly have for doing something like that?'

Marnie tried to formulate an answer but she felt too worn out, too fragile to try to guess the workings of Boland's twisted mind.

'I have no idea but he snatched Wilson and took most of his teeth in the process, they were found in the ashes of the fire, we also believe that Wilson had been tied to a chair and there were a pair of bloodied forceps found close to Boland's remains.'

Reese grunted in discomfort as he leaned forward in the bed. 'Listen to me, Marnie, you did a first-rate job, linking the badges to Boland, if you hadn't been on the ball then we would never have found Emma Farmer and...'

'It was Luke that saved Emma not me,' she responded in an instant.

The DCI reached over and took a sip from the glass of water. 'Do we know how Croft ended up at the house?'

Marnie explained about Roper chasing Luke through the trees, the car appearing out of the darkness and then Luke had been thrust into the back and taken.

'A brave lad,' Reese said, before placing the glass back on the table.

'Luke kept them both alive, he was the one who started the fire but they couldn't find a way out so they tried to find somewhere to hide.'

'What about the cellar with the skulls in?' he asked.

Marnie scowled at the question. 'I thought you knew nothing about what had happened at the house?'

Reese flapped a hand. 'I might not have had many visitors but it hasn't stopped me reading the papers.'

Marnie sighed and nodded in understanding. 'All the victims have been identified and the parents informed.'

The room fell silent as Reese cleared his throat, his face suddenly flushed with colour.

'There was no sign of my sister.' Marnie said, before he had to ask the question.

Reese blew out through pursed lips.

Then she stood up and smiled at her boss. 'Make sure you eat your grapes, they'll do you good,' she said, heading for the door.

Reese watched her leave before sinking back into the pillows and closing his eyes, the fatigue carved on his anxious features.

103

Twenty minutes later Marnie walked into the park, heaving with families enjoying the sun.

A group of teenagers were playing a game of football, the shouts went up as someone scored a goal, over to the left a Boxer dog chased after a Frisbee. She watched for a moment before sitting down on the bench; unscrewing the lid from a bottle of juice she took a sip and sighed.

Easing back, Marnie tilted her head and closed her eyes, the sun warm on her face; her thoughts though, were a million miles away, she pictured the house burning against the night sky, the moon blocked out by the swirling smoke.

She pictured Boland, burning, trapped between the floors, mouth yawning in agony, though as far as she was concerned the pain he had felt would never have been enough.

Marnie thought of Gareth Walls locked in a cell awaiting trial for the murder of Christopher Hambling. She pictured Hambling on Market Street, his eyes pleading from a grimy face, hours later he had been slaughtered, an innocent man killed and it could all be traced back to Boland's poisonous acts.

In an effort to break the cycle, Marnie reached into her pocket and pulled out the picture of her sister, it showed Abby walking against a backdrop of woodland trees.

The picture had been found by a member of the SOCO team amongst the ruins of the burned-out building, along with shots of Piper Donald and Suzie Walls and other victims of the horror that was Boland.

The torment of thoughts flew around her head, picking up speed, twisting and turning with images of the dead. She felt the familiar sense of despair colliding with the glimmer of hope that her sister was still out there somewhere, still alive and living a normal life.

When the shadow fell across her face, she cracked open her eyes. Luke smiled nervously and Marnie slid across the seat as he sat down by her side.

'How are you?' she asked, dabbing at her moist eyes with the back of her hand.

Luke watched her closely, his face etched with concern. 'I'm good, how about you?'

Marnie smiled sadly as she pulled out the pack of cigarettes, lighting two before handing one over, a woman frowned as she walked past, her nose in the air.

'Snob,' Luke whispered.

'Have you settled in the new flat?' Marnie asked, watching as a father sprinted past before tossing a bright blue kite into the air. His young son ran in the opposite direction as the kite rode upwards into the blue sky.

Taking a long pull on the cigarette Luke nodded. 'Yeah, it's cool,' he paused, 'I painted the walls the other day, and I start the new job on Monday.'

Marnie looked at him in surprise. 'What job is this?'

Luke's face flushed red as he smiled at her. 'After what happened, someone saw my picture in the paper, they work for the council – doing the parks and gardens – and they offered me a job,' he replied, tapping ash onto the floor.

'Do you like gardening?'

Luke shrugged. 'I don't know, I've never done any but the money's good and I like being outside so it should be fine.'

'Well, I think you'll love it,' she smiled, before easing back. 'Have you spoken to your mother?'

This time Luke sighed heavily. 'I tried, but she blames me for what happened to Oldman. I mean, most of the time all they ever did was scream at one another, but now she's acting as if he was the perfect man and if it wasn't for me he'd still be alive.'

Marnie opened her mouth, her anger flaring at the injustice, and then Luke shrugged and she closed her mouth with a snap.

'I'm OK honest, I mean, I wish we could get along but I'm not taking the blame for any of this.'

'Good.'

A ball flew through the air, the teenage boys chasing after it.

'*Luke!*' the voice that shouted out was full of excitement and joy and Marnie watched as Emma Farmer dashed across the grass, her mother following, her face still bearing the scars that Wilson had inflicted.

Dropping the cigarette to the floor Luke jumped to his feet just as Emma arrived at full speed.

Marnie watched as he swept her up into the air and suddenly his face was split by a huge grin as Emma planted a kiss on his cheek. It was then and there that Marnie knew that eventually Luke would recover from the scars both mental and physical.

Easing back on the bench she closed her eyes as the sound of summer carried on around them, the shouts and screams of kids having fun.

In the wildflower borders, the insects buzzed.

Marnie sighed, knowing that the roll of thunder would be back and one day she would find out what had really happened to her sister.

A bitter smile turned up the corners of her mouth, her brown eyes smouldered with fury.

Marnie felt the tears stinging her eyes as she turned the picture over and read the scrawled writing on the back.

'*The one that got away.*'

END

Acknowledgments

I would like to thank Betsy and Fred for taking a chance on Marnie and making the whole experience a pleasurable one. Also my fellow Bloodhound authors for keeping the kennel clean.

To Emma for her insightful suggestions during the editing process.

Finally my heartfelt thanks to Val for her eagle eyes and never ending dedication to getting it right.

Lightning Source UK Ltd.
Milton Keynes UK
UKOW03f0625180417
299337UK00002B/54/P